FOR THE L

Jack Black 12

"Now, for the love of Love, and her soft hours,
Let's not confound the time with conference harsh;
There's not a minute of our lives should stretch
Without some pleasure now."

Antony & Cleopatra

THE JACK BLACK SERIES

1. Dangerous Conceits
2. Night's Black Agents
3. The Thoughts of Love
4. When Madmen Lead the Blind
5. Bottled Spider
6. The Whirligig of Time
7. This Fearful Slumber
8. The Chameleon
9. The Man in the Moon
10. Killing Swine
11. False Face
12. For the Love of Love

This novel is dedicated to Joan O'Donnell, with affectionate gratitude for her contributions to the plot.

Many thanks to my brother, Raymond, and his wife, Caroline for invaluable specialist advice.

1

Douglas Mortimer was rich. Filthy rich. That's the main thing most folk knew about him. In fact, it was the *only* thing most folk knew about him. He had more lollipops than half the African nations put together. He was richer than a mile down in Saudi Arabia. He was the kind of guy Croesus came up to in the pub on a Tuesday night and tapped for a lemon till he got paid on Friday. As the Swan says, 'rich as is the ooze and bottom of the sea, with sunken wrack and sumless treasures.' The man had bank, all right, and then some.

Mind you, he'd earned it. He left school at sixteen, with no qualifications other than a bronze medallion for life-saving. Nobody could ever claim he was a clever laddie. Where most humans have 85 or 86 billion neurons in the brain, Douglas had about 302, the same as a nematode worm. But he knew how to work. Oh aye; he was a grafter all right. He got a job on the Co-op delivery van the day he left school and didn't stop working till he was the head of Mortimer Logistics plenty years later. Not one day off, in all that time. When he had to take holidays, he hung about his workplace on them. Had no idea what to do other than graft. Had no interests, no hobbies, no desire to visit faraway places with strange sounding names. Or even neighbouring places whose names he'd heard all his life. So I didn't begrudge him his sumless treasure. Not one doubloon of it.

It was my father who told me about him. He'd been in Mortimer's year at school. Not his *class*, his year. This was back in the days of streaming, of course. Mad Jack was as clever as a fox with a Masters degree, where Douglas was as thick as shit in the neck of a bottle. But, Dad said, he was a decent lad and most folk liked him. He worked with the Co and saved every penny he could. He took his driving test and became the delivery driver instead of just the laddie, and saved all his pennies from that, too, till he bought his first van and set up his own delivery service. It all started from there. He worked like a Hebrew slave in the land of bondage. All day and most of the night. He slept as little as a walrus. Within two years, he'd got rid of the old van, had bought two new ones, and taken on another driver besides himself. After ten years, he had a fleet of lorries, a depot on the industrial estate, and was the head of Mortimer Logistics.

You couldn't miss one of his trucks. They were decorated in the bright, predominantly red, Royal Stewart tartan, with 'Mortimer Logistics' and 'Scotland' in huge white letters on the side. They were huge, 40-foot, 30-tonne shortbread tins battering down the motorway. Yeah, you saw them coming, all right.

Mind you, I'm guessing the firm's name was thought up by some Man at Law. Mortimer could never have come up with it. He wasn't a man for the polysyllables. 'Logistics' probably sounded to him like a series of exercises that lassies did to keep fit. It's a grandiose term in this context anyway, like calling a waiter a 'Field Nourishment Consultant.' It's a crock. For 'logistics' read 'driving things from A to B'. He was in the road haulage business; he was a carrier. But, whatever he was called, by the time he was in his mid fifties, he was sickeningly rich and had built himself a big house in the Bathgate hills, in a whack of ground railed off from the rag, tag and shagbag, and with a big set of electronic gates at the entrance to the driveway.

Before I met him, the only other thing I knew about Douglas Mortimer was that he was hung like a donkey. Big deal. Me personally? That's an attribute that never impressed me much. Mules and fools have got big tools. And donkeys tend not to be thought of as sensitive or skilful lovers. But my old man said the guys at school were embarrassed to go in the showers with him after P.E., because of the size of his unit. Mad Jack said he never actually saw it himself, but he heard the other boys talking about it and sniggering, so he reckoned there was some truth in it. But, he said, what was the point of having a leather team-ba' if nobody but yourself ever played with it? For my father was sure, king-size and all as it might be, Mortimer's todger still had the silver paper on it. He was unknown to woman.

For a while, at least. And certainly while he was at school. But I'm guessing that, by the time he got into his twenties, he'd got the foil off it and started passing it around. Because, by the time he was sixty, he was married to a Slovakian girl who had long, jet black hair and more curves than Jessica Rabbit. Oh, and who was twenty-five. Strange, isn't it, how these strikingly attractive young foreign women can fall for old Bathgate dudes with no brains, very few social skills and precious little to recommend them. Other than several million smackers in the bank. The bars in the town are full of guys like that. Without the millions, though. Or the glam young wives.

Ruzena Dolezal was a model. Surprise, surprise. She came to Scotland to sign up with the Brio Agency in Edinburgh, having been … 'spotted' is the term, I believe … by one of their snappers while on a shoot in the Slovakian city of Kosice. She was never going to topple Giselle Bündchen or Cara Delevingne, but she did okay, strutting catwalks in silly bloody togs and pouting like a huffy porn star from the fashion pages. She met Douglas Mortimer at an event in Auld Reekie, organised by the Hootsmon, round about the Festive Season, to celebrate their 'people of the year', or some such drivel. It was a piece for the Features section. She was there, no doubt, as Eye Candy of the Year and he was Scottish Businessman of the Decade, or People's Lorry Driver of the Lustrum, or something like that. Their eyes met over the sweet potato and quinoa salad. A riot of love hearts popped around Mortimer's head to the accompaniment of violins playing the theme to *Limelight.* A riot of pound signs popped around Ruzena's, to the accompaniment of the *ka-ching* sound of a cash register. And they were married three months later.

Wait the now; I've got something in my eye. Sorry, I'm just a sentimental old booby. Stuff like that just breaks me up.

Anyway, that's about as much as I knew about Douglas Mortimer of this parish. He'd done okay, for a dunderheid from Windyknowe. By the time I met him, he had depots on the southern outskirts of Edinburgh, in Birmingham and in Kent. And he had even more lorries - which now not only plied the motorways of the UK and Ireland; they were all over the *autobahns* and *routes nationales* of Europe. Oh, and he was married to a model. Yeah, some would say he was doing okay.

He called on me one Saturday evening last June. Like I say, I'd never met the man. All I knew of him was what my father had told me and what I'd read in the press. I'd seen his photograph in the papers too, so I knew who he was before he introduced himself.

It was almost two bells in the First Watch and I was just putting the finishing touches to my paper chase for the previous week. Someone came a-knocking at my wee, small door. I could see his shadow cast by the landing light on the frosted glass. Looked like he was wearing a hat.

I called, "Knock, knock, knock! Who's there, i'th' name o' Beelzebub?"

And that's when he came in. He *was* wearing a hat – a trilby in fact, and a dark woollen coat. He was quite a good looking dude for his age. Think a silver-haired version of Leonard Cohen, maybe.

"Jack Black?" he said.

"True. What can I do for you?" said I.

"Well," he said, "I'm hopin' you can do me a turn. But it's an awfu' private business. Delicate, like."

"Then you are in luck, Mr. Mortimer. I'm as delicate as rose leaves when I have to be," I said. "Pull up a tuffet, while you eat your curds and whey, and tell me what gives."

He ignored my lame jokes. Perhaps he didn't understand them. Maybe the 'tuffet' gag would have been more appropriate if his surname had been Moffat. I think I'm losing it as I get older. Or maybe he was only interested in the first part of my utterance. The self-centred type. "Aye," he said, "you ken me, I see."

"Well, I know who you are," I said. "Seen your likeness in the dailies and such. And my father was at school at the same time as you."

"He was, aye. I remember him. He was Jack Black tae, was he no?"

"He was. I'm gratified you remember him."

"It's the reason I picked you for this job," he said. "I coulda went ti Edinburgh or Glasgow. There's tons a private investigators in the cities."

"Undoubtedly," I said. "But I'm glad you picked me. I'm local – which might be useful. And my old man always said you were a decent stick, so I'll do what I can for you, whatever this delicate business is."

"Mind if I smoke?" he said. Then looked around the room. "Ah, I dinnae see any ashtrays. Sorry. Just leave it."

I opened the bottom drawer of my desk and took out an old pub ashtray in hefty ceramic, passed it across to him. "Feel free," I said. "I used to smoke like a fish myself."

"What made you give it up?" said Mortimer.

"I became a father and I didn't want my wee lassie breathing my smoke."

"Good for you. Does the smell of it no make you gag, these days?"

"Nope," I said, breathing in deeply as he lit up, "I could lift that stogie out of your fingers and demolish it in three draws. You smoke away, Mr. Mortimer."

He took a hit, inhaled, held it and blew it out in my direction. "Well, I don't know how much you actually *know* about me, Black," he said, "but I'm sixty four years old and married ti a wife less than half my age. We've been married two and a half years, nearly."

"Ruzena Dolezal," I said. "Slovakian model. I read about it."

"Aye, it was in the papers. The usual stuff: sexy young looker marries ancient millionaire – wonder what the attraction was? You know the kinda attitude."

I nodded. Indeed I did. I shared it.

"Well, you see, Black, it wasnae like that. I met Roozh at a do in Edinburgh and I liked her a lot right away. Some guy from the *Scotsman* introduced us and we spoke for a wee while. An' what I liked aboot her, apart from the fact she was a stunnin' looker, was she was bright. As clever as anythin', really. I wis right impressed. She speaks English wi nae accent, or nane to talk aboot. An' she speaks Italian, French an' German tae. Brainy lassie. But the maist important thing for me was – she's funny. I don't mean she tells jokes. She's no like Ken Dodd or that. I mean she's got the banter, you know? She's sharp an' sarky an' just… funny. So, at the end a the night I looked for her again an' I asked her if she wanted ti go for a meal. I told her I could afford ti take her anywhere she wanted to eat – if she wanted a Chinese in Singapore, I could a done that for her."

"Quite an offer."

"And you know what she said? She said she didnae doubt it. But, what she would really like was for me ti walk her hame ti her flat in Montague Street and buy her a poke a chips on the way. That was the only way she would go oot wi me that night."

"And did you?"

"Aye. Naturally. Like that!" He snapped his fingers. "I bought a fish supper and she et it – well, we baith et it - on the walk up the road ti the flat. She shared digs wi two other lassies.

I didnae go in that night. I left her at the door an' I asked if I could phone her, and she sais aye. So I phoned her the next day but she was at a shoot or somethin'; you know, what models dae. The work they dae. Photo shoot, no shootin' guns or that. She must a been gettin' her photo took that day, because I didnae get ti talk ti her. Nor the next day, neether. Photo shoots, that's what they ca' them. So I didnae get ti speak ti her for a few days, like. They photo shoots. Well, stands ti reason. She's a busy lassie. Modellin', and that."

It was like listening to Paw Broon talk but I'll spare you the rest of the verbatim account. He was a decent guy but had no idea how to pace a narrative. Ruzena – 'Roozh' – didn't answer his calls for three days and, when she eventually did, she said she liked him but didn't want to go on dates with him. She said she didn't want him to think that his money was what she was interested in. (Clever... big, subtle hook.) She didn't want a Sugar Daddy. Mortimer said that was just fine by him, because he had no intention of ever being anybody's Sugar Daddy. Primarily because he was diabetic. He might, at a push, be somebody's Canderel Daddy, or even their Hermesetas Daddy, but that was as far as he was prepared to go.

This is hardly the acme of wit – the divine Oscar would have scribbled it down, looked at it for a second and then screwed it up and horsed it into the waste paper basket – but it apparently amused the fuck out of Ruzena. (No accounting, is there?) She thought he was an amusing man as well as a nice one and so she agreed to go out with him.

And she insisted that he shouldn't spend too much money on her – that wasn't why she liked him. (All together now; one, two, three ... *Aye, right!*) So she wouldn't accept fancy gifts – oh, I don't know: mink, pearls, rocks – in fact, any of what he called 'joolery'. She wouldn't let him take her to ludicrously expensive restaurants or swanky levees. She refused to let him splash the cash on her.

And it worked. He fell heels over head for her. He was most horribly in love. And then, one time, she agreed to come and see his pad in the Bathgate Hills and she ended up staying the night, and they ended up shagging. Job done.

They got married, like I say, three months after they met. Spent their honeymoon in Jamaica and then came back to live in

Casa Mortimera up by the Three Dubs. At least once a year, Ruzena's parents came over to stay with them, flights paid for by the millionaire. The Dolezals lived in Mestre, the mainland part of the city of Venice, and had done for a few years. Although Roozh was born in Slovakia – in Kosice, actually - her old man had moved to Italy for work when she was still in pigtails. He got a job in the refinery at Porto Marghera and they stayed in the residential area there for a while until they moved to Mestre. The fact that Ruzena had been 'spotted' while working in Slovakia was just a coincidence. Slovakia could just as easily have been Sligo. Or Slamannan. She spoke Italian better than anything else, including Slovak.

And so the idyll rolled out. She still did modelling work – he had no desire to clip her wings. So she sashayed her ass on catwalks or smouldered her eyes in fashion spreads in the major towns of the world. And got talked about, like models do. New York, London, Paris, Munich, everybody talk about … pop music. You know the score. But now, when she went home, she went home to the Bathgate Hills. Unlikely as it sounds. Mortimer continued to be the 'heid bummer', as he called it, of Mortimer Logistics and ran the company with as much graft and dedication as he always had. It was just that, now, he had a twenty-five year old wife as well. So that, when he got home of an evening, slipped off his shoes and slid his feet into his zip-up red tartan slippers, he had a glamour puss to look at across the hearth if he couldn't be arsed with Coronation Street. Where he'd never bothered with holidays before, he went on three a year now, with Ruzena – one to Mestre and Venice; one to another European location, and a third always somewhere more exotic. Japan was one he mentioned; Sri Lanka another. And they were as happy as pigs in shit. (See opening remarks re the filthy rich.)

By the time he'd finished this lengthy preamble (and his version was much lengthier than mine), he'd smoked another two fags and my little cell was beginning to smell like it used to. He stopped and ground out his third dout.

I said, "So where does the delicate aspect come in?"

He stared at the fag-end as he was grinding and pursed his lips. Then he dropped the cigarette and looked at me. "What you're thinkin'. What everybody has always been thinkin' since the day an' 'oor we got married. I think she's havin' an affair."

"With whom?"

"I don't know. That's what I want you ti find out. That's why I came ti *you*. Ti ask you ti do a job for me."

"But you don't know who she might be seeing. All right - what makes you think she is seeing *anybody*, then?"

"Just a feelin' I've got. She's no the woman she wis. I cannae really tell you anythin' that'll help you, and that's a fuckin' nuisance. But it's somethin' that's been botherin' me for a few weeks now and I need ti know if it's true. Maybe you can help me. Ask me anythin' you like. I mean, what would ye ask me if you were a polisman the now? Or a judge or somethin'?"

"Well, the obvious question is – *how* is she not the woman she was? What is it that's different? What's making you think that?"

"Och, a hunner and one things but they're aw *wee* things. You know? Nothin' I can put my finger on and say, 'that's the difference.' An' I suppose that's what a jealous mind's like, intit? They get somethin' in their heids and then everythin' else just *seems* ti prove what they thought, even if it doesnae actually. That make any sense?"

I sat back in my chair and said, "Makes a whole lot of sense. In fact, it's just about the dictionary definition of 'jealousy', as far as I remember. You familiar with the play, *Othello*, Mr. Mortimer?"

"Take a wild fuckin' guess."

I laughed at the dry sarcasm. "Well, in that play, the title character, Othello, a general in the Venetian army, is convinced that his young wife has been unfaithful to him. His junior officer, Iago, tells him that she has been having an affair with another officer, Othello's lieutenant, a young, handsome guy. But the thing is, it's a tissue of lies; there isn't a degree of truth in it. Iago is lying to get his own back on Othello. Anyway, in the play, one of the female characters describes jealousy perfectly. The young wife, Desdemona, tells her maid that she never gave her husband cause to suspect her. And the maid says, "But jealous souls will not be answered so; they are not jealous *for the cause*, but jealous *for they are jealous*; 'tis a monster begot upon itself, born on itself."

Mortimer screwed up his face. "That's just gobbledygook ti me. But I never sais anybody had told me that Roozh was havin' an affair."

"No, no. I just was making the point, agreeing with what you said earlier. If you're jealous, then everything seems to confirm the guilt of the one you suspect."

"Right. I heard you were a clever bastard, right enough."

"So. Anyway. Nobody's been telling you stories."

"Naw. Ah don't listen ti stories. I've nae time for gossip."

"Has Ruzena been different in bed, say? Is she losing interest?"

"Naw. Just the same as ever there. She's keen on the old hochmagandy, likes."

"All right - so is she keener than she used to be? Is that what's making you think?"

"Naw. No really."

"Is she more distant than she used to be? I mean, less animated in her talk, say. Like, you said you thought she was funny and smart with the old bants, right?"

"Aye."

"So, is she more distant than she used to be? Less funny? Less likely to come out with the one-liners?"

He thought for a second or ten. Then he said, slowly, "I don't know. Maybe that's it. I hadnae thought about that. It might be."

"Well, *is* she less funny than she was?"

"No sure. Maybe a wee bit. But then, mibby she's got a lot on her mind. She's a busy lassie. Up an' doon aw the time. Here, there an' everywhere. Gettin' a lot a work the now, you see. But, noo that you say it, maybe that's what it is. You know, like she's got somethin' on her mind? That must be it. Maybe what's she's got on her mind is another man."

"Has she talked about anybody else? Any other men? Younger men? Talked about what they say, what they do, just to make conversation even, and maybe that's got you jealous? Somebody she's worked with on the photo shoots?"

He chewed his lip. "No that I can think a. But maist a theym are shirtlifters, anyway." Then he sniffed and said, "It's maybe just that I'm gittin' the impression she disnae feel the same way as she did aboot me. Maybe just that. I don't know."

"Has she ever said she's unhappy? That she feels she made a mistake marrying you?"

"Naw. Never. I just feel… well, I told you. Will you find out for me if she's shaggin' anybody else?"

"I could try," I said. "The thing is, Mr. Mortimer, your wife is a globetrotting woman. Berlin. Melbourne. L.A. She might be seeing somebody in one of these places – *any* of these places. I can't fly all over the world just like that."

"Ah well, you see, that's no the worry. Because, when she's away on these jaunts, she's always got Jennifer with her. Her P.A., like. And Jennifer's an auld battle-axe. Well, no that auld, actually, but the battle-axe part's right enough. An' there's always a team a folk around her at these things. So that's no the worry."

"Well, what's the worry?"

"If she's at it, she's at it eether here or in Mestre. Venice, like. They're the two places where Jennifer's naewhere near her."

"Where is Jennifer usually?"

"Edinburgh. Lives in the toun."

"And Jennifer's full name is?" I said.

"Jennifer Kemp."

I wrote it down. "And her address?"

Mortimer took out his phone, thumbed up a Contact and passed me Jennifer's details. As I wrote, he said, "Jennifer sais ti me when me and Roozh got married, 'Dinnae worry about her when she's away, Mr. Mortimer. Ah'll be keepin' a close eye oan her.' An' I believe her. It's when she's here an' I'm at the work. Or when she's in Mestre. She goes over ti see her folks regular. I go with her once a year, but she goes mair often. Could be up ti anythin' over there tae."

"I can try and keep an eye on her here," I said. "But I don't know Mestre at all. Or Venice, more than just the touristy bits."

"She's aff ti Mestre in a month's time ti see the faimly. For a week. I want you ti go tae, an' check her oot. I'll pey, of course. But will you see what you can find oot here, tae?"

"Aye. I can try at least. Does Ruzena pal about with any lassies here in West Lothian?"

"No really. She's civil ti folk, but she hasnae any pals local. Maist a her pals are models she meets in her work."

"Sure. Where is Ruzena just now?"

"Brighton. Due back the morra. Do ye need ti see her rooms or anythin'?"

Rooms, no less. Room-*s*.

"I don't need to, but it might be useful if I did. You never know what I might pick up."

"Well, come on then. I'll take ye the now."

He drove a pale blue Rolls Royce Dawn, with 'DM' monogrammed on the headrests - a quarter of a million's worth of sleek lines, not to mention its leather and wood interior. Told you this guy had many leaves of cabbage. You ever know me to lie?

2

The house wasn't quite Pemberley or Thornfield Hall. But it was surprisingly classic in its appearance and surpassingly splendid for an edifice in the Bathgate Hills. Or maybe I should say for a *modern* edifice there. For, in the past, the Bathgate Hills could boast of places like Avontoun House and Kipps; and it can still crow of Cathlaw, Williamscraigs, and Belsyde House – all impressive dwellings built by folk with candy. The Mortimer place was just the most recent of them. It was built in the style of an earlier era, as I say, in the warm honey colour associated with Bath stone. Whether Mortimer's house was actually built in it is debatable. But also decidedly beside the point. Suffice it to say that the place was vaguely neoclassical and very impressive as you motored down the driveway from the closing electronic gates. Even just in headlights – or maybe more so. The façade was high and wide with bay windows and a stone porch.

"Like it?" Mortimer said, slowing down the wagon so I could have a good dekko.

"Very much so," I said. "Has it got a name?"

He accelerated slightly again and said, looking at the house as he drove, "Manderley. Manderley Hoose. Ken where that's fi?"

I smiled at him. "Indeed I do. From the novel *Rebecca* by Daphne du Maurier. I wouldn't have thought that was your kind of thing, to be honest."

"It isnae," he smiled back. "I never read it. In fact, I never read a book since I left school. And no many when I was there. But I seen the picture. It was one a my old lady's favourites, and I mindit the name a the hoose was Manderley. So I called this one Manderley in memory a my mother."

"Good for you," I said. "I take it you've got a staff."

"Oh aye. No quite Upstairs Doonstairs, but I've got Jean Gilmour that comes in and cooks, Jana and Radka that comes in and does the cleanin' and the washin' and that. You know, hoosework. And Jean's man, Alex Gilmour, that does the gardenin' and a' the handyman shit. Four folk."

"But they don't live in?"

"Naw, naw. Alex and Jean live in Torphichen. Just a couple a mile away. They're here Monday ti Friday, Alex aw day, Jean for meals. The weekends I manage for mysel'. Roozh cooks at weekends when she's here, but I'm no the worst in a kitchen, mysel'. The other two lassies is Poles that comes in fi Bathgate Tuesdays, Thursdays and Sundays. They're nice folk."

So. None of them around today.

"They ever said anything about your wife to you?"

He shook his head. "Naw. No like that. They're hard workin' folk and they keep theirsels ti theirsels. Nice folk, but no nosey that way. No telltales."

We got out of the wagon and he unlocked the hefty wooden front door, flicked on a light. A thought struck me as we went into the house. "Okay, Mr. Mortimer. You've got a doofer in the car that opens the gates at the drive. What happens when you're in the house and somebody wants to get in?"

"Strangers, you mean? I dinnae bother wi theym. There's a wee intercom thing at the side a the gates. Anybody visitin' can call fi the gates. Maist folk, I just say 'No interested.' If anybody important wants ti see me, they make an appointment. An' there a remote control in the livin' room tae. And there's two CCTV cameras at the gates. One covers the area a the gates theirsels, an' the other yin's facin' the hoose doon the drive. So the front a the hoose is covered. The monitor's in ma wee livin' room."

"All right. So none of Dougie's pals drop by unannounced?"

"Naw. I don't really have any pals. And naebody ca's me Dougie. My name's Douglas. My old lady never let anybody call me 'Dougie' or 'Doug'. She used ti say that 'Douglas' is a guid Scots name wi a lot a history behind it and 'Dougie' isnae."

"Sorry. I meant no offence."

"Oh, none ta'en, son; none ta'en. It's just I've never answered ti it."

"So is that it, for security? Any cameras inside the house?"

He hissed in a breath. "Naw, naw. There such a thing as privacy, you know. The cameras are enough, I think; theym an' the steel fence. I thought aboot a big dug but there's times when naebody's here. Wouldnae be fair. We've got an alarm system, right enough. Controlled fi ma office upstairs. Seems ti work well enough. Noo. This is the lounge..."

The house was sumptuously appointed. What Mortimer called the 'lounge' was actually an old fashioned drawing room with an open fire, a vast mantelpiece, an antique grandfather clock, Welsh dressers, plush sofas and armchairs, pot plants and a carpet that smelt and felt of money. There were, in addition on the ground floor: a dining room: what he called 'the living room' - which was a smaller room than the lounge, with a TV and a hi-fi system, as well as the monitor for the CCTV cameras; the home cinema room; his smoking room; what he called the 'library' but which was really just a billiard room – I have more books in the toilet - and the kitchen.

"We've got open fires in a couple a the rooms," he said, "But they're only used in the winter. It's underflair heatin' everywhere."

Upstairs were many more rooms, including Ruzena's suite of them. This consisted of a bedroom with a canopy bed, heavy drapes and flouncy lace curtains on the window, and the most elaborate dressing table I'd ever seen; a bathroom, and a sitting room with comfortable looking chairs, a table heaped with magazines, a window that would spill light into the room in the daytime, and books. Real books. There was a tall ancient bookcase on the back wall full of them. Granted, some of them were ordure – what arseholes call 'chicklit'; celebrity autobiogs ghosted by the desperate; Dan Brown and things like that. But I could see at a glance that there were one or two novels by writers I respected: William Boyd, Kate Atkinson, Chimamanda Ngozi Adichie, folk like that. And there were a dozen old Penguin Poetry Library paperbacks. Keats, Tennyson, Burns. I nodded in approval at the shelves.

"Some good stuff here."

"Aye, Roozh is the reader in the hoose," Mortimer said.

"Poetry, I see. She like poetry, I take it?" I said, moving closer to the bookcase.

"Aye, *she* does. I cannae make that stuff go at aw."

There were, besides, a dozen or so old black paperbacks of the Thames & Hudson 'World of Art' series. Sixties and seventies vintage. I recognised them because I had them too, inherited from my mother, something of a buff in her day. There was 'A Concise History of Painting from Giotto to Cezanne', and 'A History of Western Art'. There were volumes on movements like 'Baroque & Rococo', 'Impressionism' and 'Surrealist Art'. One or two on individual artists.

I said, "Ruzena into art as well?"

"Oh that? Aye. I could see aw that far enough. Look around. See if there's anythin' that gives you clues."

"Well, I don't know about actual clues. Just hints, maybe, wrinkles, suggestions."

The mantelpiece was lined with wedding photographs.

"Aye, she's a beautiful bride," I said. "And you're not too bad either. As the groom, I mean."

"Aye, I brush up no too bad."

"I see there's a phone in every room."

"They're internal phones. It's a big hoose and if we want each other, we jist ring. There's nae landline. We work aff mobiles."

"How many has Ruzena got?"

"Mobiles? Just the one. An iPhone 7. You want her number?"

"No, no. Does she upgrade every time a new one comes out?"

"Natch. She's young and these things are must-haves, a they no? For the young."

I turned from the bookcase and looked around again. On a table in the far corner was a Bose Lifestyle 650 in black – a cool three Large worth of stereo system – and a stack of discs. A wireless headset was lying on one of the chairs.

"Mind?" I said, indicating the music centre.

"Be ma guest."

I sifted through some of the discs. Mainly modern stuff that I would frisbee out the window rather than actually attach to any sound system – Justin Bieber, Little Mix, Taylor Swift, Rihanna, etc. Effluent, all. Some retro acts that I approved – Bowie, The Beatles, the Stones and, gloriously, an act that I dug because my father obviously had done and had bought their entire catalogue – Sparks. Some classical. I mean, serious classics, not just classical pops. Wagner. Mussorgsky. Saint-Saëns. I turned the gizmo on and clicked play. The Flower Duet from *Lakmé*. I nodded and smiled at Mortimer. "Lovely," I said.

He shook his head again. "No for me," he said.

"Not a Delibes man?"

"I don't even know what that means. I'm no really inti all that fiddle music and opera. But Roozh likes it. So long as she plays it in her ain rooms, fine by me. I just don't want ti be bothered wi that stuff. I like a pipe band."

I clicked the music off again. Walked to the window and looked out. Outside, it was as dark as the heart of time. But, in daylight, I knew there would be a special view of the countryside spread out there. I could see why any young woman would like these rooms.

"Okay," I said, turning back from the window. "Seen all I need here. You got a suite of rooms like this?"

He chuckled. "Hardly like this. 'Mon I'll show you."

He showed me his bedroom, his 'office' and his bathroom. Apart from the internal phones in every room, there was nothing of any great interest. His office consisted of a desk, a pricey leather chair, a state of the art PC, a metal cupboard, a low but large table, and not much else. He said he didn't do any real work there. He went into his offices in the Bathgate or Edinburgh depots for that. There was a kitchen chalkboard on the wall by the door with the names of three places on it in chalk: London, Canterbury and, over a smudged earlier effort that had obviously been rubbed out with his cuff or his fist, Birmingham.

"What's that?" I said.

"Oh, that's aboot the only thing I keep a note ae, here. Places I need ti go when I'm away on business. Last time was they three. Bar Birmingham. That's this time. I rubbed oot … what was it? Derby." (He pronounced it, 'Derr-by'.) "That's where I wis before."

"Right." I asked him what he did in his spare time.

"Ah," he said and smiled sheepishly. "I'm no hard ti please. I'm inti gamin'. You know – Grand Theft Auto? Angry Birds, Resident Evil, Call of Duty – most a these things over the years. Donkey Kong – even Tetris."

"Now it's my turn," I said. "I have no idea what these things are, apart from the fact they're video games. No interest. Anything else?"

"Oh, I'm a man a simple tastes. You know what I like ti dae best ae aw? Have done since I was a kid. Jigsaws. I can sit with a jigsaw for 'oors. I've got tons a them in that big cupboard in my office. Clear them oot once a year and gie them ti charity shops. Good yins, mind; up ti twenty thoosant pieces. Best yin I ever did was jist white. Jist that. A thoosant pieces. Ta'en me three month."

"Jigsaws?"

"Love them."

What the low table was for.

"Do anything physical? Running? Gym work? Tennis? Anything like that?"

"Me? Naw. But Roozh does. She likes ti run four or five mile every mornin'. Well, maist mornin's. She cannae always dae it, if she's workin', you know?"

"Right. What does she drive?"

"'Mon, I'll show you."

He took me out a back door to a low, long building and pressed six digits into a keypad by one of three roller doors, saying, "The gizmos in the cars have a button for this tae." The door rolled up vertically and a light came on, revealing a lipstick pink sports car. (I don't do cars, really. No petrolhead, me. If it goes when I turn the key, that's all I need from a bogey.) Mortimer mentioned several letters and digits, which I presumed constituted its name. Meant nothing. To me, it looked like Lady Penelope's yoke, FAB 1, from the old 60s show, *Thunderbirds*. I nodded and said, "Flash."

"Should be at the price."

"Surprised I haven't seen that around the county."

"Ah, well. She disnae always drive it." He pressed the zero on the keypad and the roller slid down as the light went out. "When she wants ti be a wee bit less … famous … she drives the Mazda." He pressed the numbers into the second keypad, the next roller rippled up and a second light revealed an altogether more mundane motor. A silver grey Mazda.

"Okay," I said, "I got both reg. numbers"

"You didnae write anythin' doon."

"I don't always need to."

"So, Black," he said, closing the door and turning back towards the house, "Think you can take the job on for me?"

"I'll give it a bash," I said. "I'll need to know where she goes, her plans for the next week or so, anything like that."

"Well, she's due back hame the morra. No much on the calendar for a week or two. She'll probably just chill oot the morra. I could take ye back in and check her diary. She keeps one in her sittin' room. In a drawer in the table."

"No. I'll leave you in peace, Mr. Mortimer. I've seen enough. What I want you to do for me, though, is text me the details of her next week from her diary. Could you do that?"

"Aye, aye, easy enough."

"And are you away at all in the next … when did you say she was going back to Mestre? A month?"

"Aye, about four weeks."

"All right. Are you away from home any time in those four weeks?"

"Aye. I'll be in Birmingham from Tuesday ti Thursday, next week."

"So. Check your own diary too and let me know the times you won't be around the county. Okay?"

"Easy as winkie."

And, on that pearl of dialect wisdom, we left Manderley and he ran me back to the office.

3

I got in, shut the door, bubbled up some jamoke, and sat down behind my desk to think that all through. The richest man in the county by some way had just hired me to find out if his little coo ca choo was turning into sweet cheatin' Rita. Hey - see? And folk think I can only do Shakespeare. Oh ye of little faith. I can do your popular culture too. Mind you, I don't know if I'd use the word 'culture' in reference to Alvin Stardust. Still. Digression. Maybe it was an indication of how much all this Mortimer stuff had me bamboozled.

I mean, here we had a sixty plus guy who was a multi-millionaire and who had married a twenty five year old model – who wasn't interested in his means. She'd married him because he was a nice, funny man. Yeah – don't they all? Now he was telling me he thought she might be getting extra lessons from the tennis coach. But he couldn't exactly say why. In fact, he couldn't even vaguely say why. And then, at one point, he'd shown some insight into the jealous mind. The green-eyed monster. If you suspect somebody of being unfaithful, every little thing they say or do will contribute to that corrosive emotion, no matter how stupid it seems. He'd said. Or words to that effect. Poorer words to that effect. But he couldn't identify one thing she'd said or one thing she'd done that might make him jealous.

I took a swig at the java. I mean, why would he think his wife was fuckin' around? It just seemed so unlikely. They were such a perfect match. She was young and fit; ran several miles a day; liked poetry, art and classical music. And he wasn't and didn't. He did jigsaws and liked pipe bands. As Mistress Ford says, 'Would you desire better sympathy?' He was convinced, too, that any shenanigans would be happening here in West Lothian or in her parental town of Mestre in Italy but not, ludicrously enough, when she was farther away, with her work. On extended wings. Because some bint called Jennifer Kemp was *in loco parentis* there.

I'd already made a note to check out Jennifer Kemp.

And… *here*? Where every idiot and his wife knew who she was, because she was a model, because she was in the papers and on TV, because she was that most meretricious of modern achievements, a celebrity? How easy would it be for her to put the horns on Mortimer right here in West Lothian? Who kept her company? As Emilia says, 'What place, what time, what form, what likelihood?'

I noticed I was quoting from the Swan's female characters. Was that an indication that, initially at least, I was on Ruzena's side? Mmm. Wasn't sure. Interesting that Emilia and Mistress Ford are from plays where sexual jealousy is a big theme. One treated tragically, one comically, of course, but nevertheless …

Maybe Mortimer's domestic staff would be worth checking out too. The Gilmours ought to be easy enough to trace. I pulled the Phone Book over the desk, skiffed through it. Alex Gilmour lived in Greenside, Torphichen. I jotted down the address and the digits. The Polish girls would be trickier to trace. I had no surnames. Still, that could be remedied easily enough.

Of course, Ruzena Mortimer might *well* be playing beds on a different path. As the local wisdom has it, stranger things have happened. None stranger, some might say, than her marrying Mortimer in the first place. And I was hired to find out the truth of it all.

I've done mountains of that shit before. It's a staple of a PI's existence, mince and tatties work, sniffing out where, when, who and how often. Mind you, usually, in an infidelity case, there are tangibles; things to go on, irrespective of whether the mark is XX or XY. Like a noticeable change of affect or habits. You know … *She's* more broody than she was. *He's* brighter than a beam of light. She's changed her hairstyle. He has a faint trace of perfume about him when he comes home. She goes out with her female friends more than she used to. He hums to himself in quieter moments. She says she's too tired for sex with her husband at night. He says he's got a lot on his mind – not tonight, honey. You get the picture – there's usually something to go on. In this case there was nothing. Nothing bar a vague sense of unease, and even that might be trapped wind. Well, Mortimer was an old guy.

I thought, what the hell. It was a job. I'd be well paid. It looked like I might even get a break in Italy. That had to be a good thing. It would give me a chance to practise my Italiano. You know what I hoped? That I could convince Mortimer that his young missus was as faithful as a mutt. 'Heavenly true'. True like ice, like fire. That's the old romantic in me. So what that I'd been sceptical about her motives in the first place? I hoped now I could gild her image afresh, prove her to be the woman he'd fallen in love with.

My phone hummed. Text alert. It was Douglas Mortimer getting back to me re Ruzena's and his own diary commitments. He was in Birmingham for three days the following week, and in Canterbury for two days the week after that. She had only one commitment between her return from Brighton and her departure for Italy: 'Edinburgh Castle, Shaun Mallon, No.1', for the Wednesday Mortimer was in Brum. Right. The following Wednesday. I guessed Mallon was a photographer. I knew 'No. 1' was a mag. Indeed, it was the self-styled 'Scotland's Glamorous Glossy.' Edinburgh Castle, eh? I reckoned that visiting the old fortress on its boss of rock was an easy way to see Mrs. Mortimer in her natural environment. There was no reason I shouldn't be one of the sightseers that day. Who knew what unco sights I might see?

Well, now I had time on my hands and a lot to learn. Strangely enough, I knew diddly squat about modelling. Yeah, surprising, isn't it? I guess I must have missed the Catwalk option; I did Latin. So I took to the old Internet breakers and did me some surfing. I reckoned some knowledge of what Mrs. Mortimer did for a living might be useful. Her *raison d'être*, if you like; what defined her in many people's eyes. I read about a dozen posts dealing with the day-to-day life of a fashion model. Gleaned some nuggets. Like, did you know that 'Fashion Week' happens twice a year in each of the four main fashion capitals of the world? Oh yeah. 'And which are they, Jackie boy?' I hear you say. 'Why,' I replies, 'New York, London, Milan and Paris, of course.' File that information away; you never know when you'll need it.

I found out that a 'lookbook' is a compilation of photographs showcasing an individual designer's output. That 'runway' is the hip word for 'catwalk'. That kids with talent are 'scouted', not 'spotted' as I said earlier – oh God, I'm so twentieth century, me.

There was, of course, much emphasis on the plus points of modelling, why so many kids go for it; why they assume all models are successful and fulfilled, with a glamorous lifestyle;

why they assume nothing is better in life than appearing on the cover of a magazine or slinking down a runway in Milan. The reasons are, of course: the new and glamorous places; the celebrities and royalty; the VIP clubs; the cameras and attention; the creativity; the hair and makeup transformations; the new friends from around the world. Just so much to take in.

But there was a mountain of stuff to balance that. To overbalance it. Most of the stories dealt with models who were unhappy for a variety of reasons, who hid it all behind tin smiles, three packs of snout a day, innumerable cans of fizz, or lines of jazz talc. There were tales of abuse and degradation, people saying vicious things about girls' appearances that made them cry and feel repelled by their own bodies; of eating disorders. Because shows take place at any hour of the day or night, and girls often travel from one to the other, many of them are working from before the sun comes up till long after it goes down. Some girls mentioned the fact that they hadn't had a period in months, or they pretended to ignore the clumps of hair that fell out in the shower. At work, they had someone yanking and tugging at their hair for hours every day, or trying to force their feet into shoes several sizes too small, or they were asked repeatedly to shoot topless when they'd made it clear they did not want to.

In one week, one model worked beside a fifteen year old high school drop-out, a twenty two year old who was telling clients she was eighteen, in order to get more work, and a coked up thirteen year old with a boyfriend fifteen years her senior. The *fausse* eighteen year old was suffering from extreme anaemia. She ate just 300 calories a day and that consisted mainly of peanut butter on rice crackers.

Girls who do modelling have little job security, they work freelance in an industry that makes billions, and yet their daily pay may still only be a free lunch. All the rice crackers you can eat. They experience constant criticism and rejection, some wind up in debt to their employers, and they're often too old at twenty four. For every star who earns gazillions, dozens of girls and young women get paid in clothes or in a free lunch or a hundred quid for a day-long shoot.

One woman who got wise after a while said she began to see herself as perpetuating 'an international epidemic of negative body image and self-esteem.' Sounds like her brain was still functioning okay. She looked at herself, and saw an emaciated body, a controlled life, negative thoughts. And realised she was working in an industry where she stood silently in front of photographers and designers to make other women desire what they couldn't have. Commercial work (e.g., catalogues and such) pays best, but nobody ever became a star wearing big knickers and duffel coats for the Grattan catalogue. The glamorous stuff is what they call the 'editorial' stuff – being a clothes horse who struts the runways and ramps. But, often, editorial models work for no pay but a gift of clothes and, hopefully, prestige that will eventually accumulate enough to land them a perfume commercial or something in that league. That's where the big bucks are.

Besides, agents and designers can treat models, to all effects and purposes, just how they like, and the reason for that is that modelling is an almost completely unregulated industry.
Models have no union, no health insurance or other benefits enjoyed by employees. Why? Because they're considered independent contractors. But models can only get work through an agency. This gives agencies absolute power, and models absolutely none. You're a freelancer who can't actually freelance, as the sharp one said.

It's an uncertain and unpredictable life, all told, except for the sexual assault, financial manipulation, loneliness, superficial interactions, minimal sleep and punishing working hours. You can see why a lassie would rather do that than work in Lidl or go into a profession. It must drive some of them mad. Mad enough to marry a Bathgate sexagenarian.

I shut down the PC and drove home.

4

It struck me later, as I sat with Phyllis and pretended to be watching some excrement on the box, that a good 'in' for this case, a case that otherwise would be 'in-less', would be to see the Mortimers together, see if I could assess their dynamic as a couple. (Did I just say that?) I had so little to go on that having some idea of how they behaved together might provide a base against which to judge Ruzena on her own. The more I thought of it, the more that seemed the way to go. So I picked my moby up from the table by the side of my chair and texted Mortimer.

Wd like to see you and Mrs. M. together. Can you arrange to take her somewhere, anywhere, for a meal or shopping or whatever, in West Lothian or Edinburgh. Tomorrow for pref, any time soon if not. JB.

Phyllis looked down at my flashing thumbs.

"Who you texting, babes?" she said.

"Mortimer. Trying to get him to take the trophy ball and chain out somewhere so I can see them together; see how they work."

"Strange one, isn't it?"

"Rum, for sure."

"You think he really does suspect her of being unfaithful? Or do you think there's something else going on?" she said.

I pressed 'Send', and looked at her. "Interesting question. What else *might* be going on?"

"Oh, I don't know, honey - you're the private eye, not me – but I was just thinking that, if this guy says he thinks his wife is playing around, then can't come up with any real reason why he thinks so, well maybe he isn't hiring you to find out if it's true. Or maybe not just that. Maybe there's something else. But I don't know what that would be."

"M-hm?"

"What's her name?"

"Ruzena Dolezal."

"Dolezal? That's familiar."

"She's well enough known. Keeps her own name for modelling work."

Phyllis was thinking. "Aye!" she said. "That woman in America, the one that was a black civil rights activist and taught an African Studies course - remember? And she wasn't black, which is what she was claiming. She was white."

"I do remember that," I said. "But they're no relation."

"No, I know. I just remembered the name. Maybe Ruzena's doing something like that."

"Like what?"

"Pretending to be something she isn't. Oh, I don't know what. Maybe she's really trans, or something."

"Oh, let's no go there, honey. Have you read some of the stuff that's out there between some trans women and feminists?"

"Aye. True. There's some funny folk out there."

"There are, indeed. I've met most of them."

"Maybe it's more that *he* is up to something else?"

"Darlin'," I said, "I've dealt with too many weirdoes over the years to rule anything out. It's entirely possible. In fact, I've been wondering all night since he came to the office what the hell this is all about. It does have an unusual bouquet off it; there's no doubt. But he might *still* just be an old guy who's insecure about his young wife's fidelity. And he has the feathers to hire a shmoe like me to indulge his insecurity. Until I find otherwise, that's what I have to work on."

"Aye, that's true."

"Food for thought, though, Phyl honey. As always."

My phone buzzed. Incoming text.

Wear wd you like to meet us

I smirked and passed the phone to Phyllis. She read it, smiled and handed it back. "The illiterate millionaire," she said.

I laughed and said, "That was Vanbrugh, wasn't it? Some Restoration dramatist, anyway. Actually, I doubt it's his literacy that Ruzena's interested in."

I texted back.

No meet. Don't tell her I'm going to be around. Just be somewhere and I'll be there to see you. But I guarantee you won't see me. It's part of the job.

I sent it and said to Phyllis, "The TV's boring the arse off me. Do you fancy a coffee?"

"I'll make it," she said.

I stood up and said, "No. You're watching this; I'm not. I'm on the java detail."

"There's perkins in the barrel."

"That sounds like spy code," I said and we laughed.

My phone buzzed.

Wear abouts

I texted back.

Anywhere – up to you. Have a think tonight, talk to R tomorrow and go out with her. A couple of places, if you like. Places she likes to go. Just let me know where before you set off. I'll see you; you won't see me. It's important for the job.

I went into the kitchen, rattled up the coffee and biscuits and brought them in on a tray, set it on the occasional table.

"Ta, love."

"Mon plaisir."

I lifted my phone as I sat down.

Okay Mondy best get back l8r

Olé. Success at last. You have to use a drill to get ideas into some folk's skulls, don't you?

5

Monday morning, I was in the office about half ten, when Mortimer texted that he and his wife would be in Edinburgh that day: in Stewart Christie's, the tailor's in Queen Street, at twelve - he was looking for a new overcoat – and after that they would take afternoon tea at the Balmoral. Well, well. I thought I'd give the interior of the tailor's a swerve. Too small. I could always scope them from the outside. But afternoon tea seemed just the ticket. I hadn't done that since the time I was in the Palm Court with the Hagan woman, to do with the Thornton case up at Lanark. Time to get whiskered up, I thought. So I got out the false beard from the drawer and the spirit gum and turned myself into Hipster Jack in ten minutes.

I locked up and drove into town via the Western Approach Road, swung a left down Lothian Road and on to Princes Street, then up Frederick and along George, a wee whizz round Charlotte Square and on to Queen Street. I was lucky. I found a meter only a few yards away from the Stewart Christie place. I fed it and then sat back and waited. I like waiting. I wait like Jeeves. I wait like a waiter. I like silence and solitude. And thinking.

I looked at the shop front of Stewart Christie. Distinctive green paint, pleasingly old-fashioned shop window. "Stewart Christie & Co. Ltd. Bespoke Tailors/ Country Outfitters/ Ladies Wear/ Highland Dress/ Est. 1720." That's a long time to be ested. Nearly three hundred years. The Wee, Wee German Lairdie was on the throne. It was the year of the South Sea Bubble. The year Swift started writing *Gulliver's Travels*. That's a long time for unctuous blokes with tape measures round their necks to be asking customers which side they dressed on and telling them the trousers would ride up with wear. I got my phone out and Googled them. There was a paragraph or two of blah concerning their origins, some discreet bragging that their books included invoices from Sir Walter Scott and various royals, and then a screed about working in the complete range of sporting and country clothes, including breeks and Plus Fours, waistcoats, gilets, jackets, shooting coats, capes and deerstalker caps. I could see why it was the sort of place Mortimer would buy his togs in. Not me, though. I don't go stalking deer or 'taking' game birds.

I put the phone away and looked over the road. Douglas and Ruzena Mortimer were walking along the built-up side of Queen Street, hand in hand. Split me, but the woman was easy on the eye. Her hair was black and shoulder length. She wore a tight black leather jacket with a fur collar, skinny blue jeans and ankle cracker boots. She was extremely pretty. Well, I guess she would be, being a model. She had her left hand in Mortimer's right, and was holding on to his right arm and smiling into his face. He'd probably made another diabetes joke. It sure didn't look to me like she had any trouble showing affection for him. He looked very elegant in a brown hat and camelhair coat. He was wearing his left glove and carrying his right in his left hand. He was doing the talking. They separated as they arrived at the shop and Mortimer went in first.

I bumshuffled myself comfortable in the seat and waited for them to re-emerge. Thought about what I'd seen. They looked like a well-heeled couple – a little misgraffèd in respect of years, certainly – but they looked in love to me. If your missus is fucking around, she doesn't carry on in public with you like a teenager. Not unless she's a consummate actress, that is. I wondered if Ruzena Mortimer was. But she looked like a woman who loved her man.

They came out three quarters of an hour later, Mortimer toting a large carrier bag. They were still smiling. Mortimer hailed a cab and they got in. Afternoon tea time. I pulled away, drove to Castle Terrace car park, berthed the boat, and got a cab myself back along Princes Street to the Balmoral. I asked for a table for one at the far end of the Palm Court. The Mortimers were at a table halfway down the side wall. They sat close together, ate their sandwiches and dainties, drank their tea, and conversed easily. They talked a lot. They laughed often. They looked at perfect ease with each other. When the old duck in the green dress started playing the harp, Ruzena cooed with pleasure. They were still absorbed in each other when I got the bill, settled and left. I'd be back in the office before they were anywhere near the city limits.

At eight o'clock, I got a text.

Sorry you cdnt make it tday we had a grate time

Sometimes a drill isn't enough. I texted back.

No probs. I'll just get on with the job and text you in a week or so's time.

What I had in mind was to keep an eye on Manderley from a distance. The road past the driveway had nowhere for a PI to skulk without looking like the fishiest man since Caliban. And there was nowhere along the road I could park that would afford me any sight of the house. But, if I drove along Ballencrieff Toll way, and up past that Vu place by the trout fishery, there was a quiet parking spot, I remembered. You could see little from the car park itself but a little stroll off-road farther up the hill and I'd be able to see Manderley and the grounds from on high. The very dab. A pair of bins round my neck and a copy of the *Collins Guide to British Birds* in my pocket, and I should pass as a twitcher to all but the most sniffy of observers.

So that's what I did. Tuesday morning, about nine, I parked the jalopy and went walkabout through the trees and shrubs to the top of the hill. This was the first of the three days Mortimer would be away, so I intended to keep as close an eye on Ruzena as I could. Nothing would be going on at Manderley: the Gilmours were there all week and the cleaning girls were due on Tuesday. If Roozh was up to anything, it would be played away from home. I had the bins, the book, and a couple of sandwiches wrapped in greaseproof paper. I was Bathgate's answer to Bill Oddie. I stood with my back to a tree and watched the house through the binoculars.

It was even more impressive in daylight and from that angle. The perimeter of the property was marked off by security fencing – palisade fencing, to be precise. Galvanised steel, 'W' section pales, eight feet high, with triple pointed and splayed heads; top and bottom rails, the top rails containing sharp barbs. That would have kept the hoi polloi out, I thought. The pales being 'W' in section made them difficult to grip and the height, together with the viciousness of the barbs, made them nigh impossible to climb. I'd only noticed the fence at the gates, the night I was shown over the place. Mortimer valued his privacy. The house itself was beautiful, of course.

I saw Alex Gilmour– at least, I assumed it was him - a couple of times, dressed in dungarees, going back and forward from the house to the garages. Then, at a bawhair after eleven, I saw Ruzena stroll into the garage and the rose coloured sports car back out of it and smooth its way up the drive. I waited till I saw it turn left towards Bathgate. Then I jogged and scuttered my way down the slope and back to my own machine. I gunned it out of the car park and down the hill. Anything coming up that hill, and we were both gone. Thankfully, nothing was.

I drove as fast as I could along the Torphichen road, on to Torphichen Street, turned down Drumcross Road and Hopetoun Street then North Bridge Street. I saw her at the traffic lights outside the Regal, three cars before me. Result! I'd thought the motorway might be on the cards. Edinburgh or Glasgow. She hadn't taken the sports job to check out the charity shops up the street, or go down to Aldi's for cat food; that was a sure five.

She took South Bridge Street and then the left turn into Menzies Road. By the time we were heading up the Whitburn Road towards the motorway at Junction 4, there were four vehicles between us. At the East Whitburn Interchange, she took the cut for Edinburgh. Now there was only one car between us but that was enough. I sat back and relaxed. Didn't matter what speed she went, I wasn't going to miss that lipstick-pink shaggin' wagon at any distance. Jack on the job, givin' it my A game.

When she got into central Edinburgh and turned right up Lothian Road, I knew where she was going. Jennifer Kemp lived in Spottiswoode Street, the other side of Bruntsfield Links. When we got there, there was one parking spot in the whole street and Ruzena got it. I cruised past her, hung a right into Spottiswoode Road and a left into Arden Street, found a parker there. Better name anyway. Well, this is the Forest of Arden. It was the easiest thing to walk down Arden on to Warrender Park Road and cut back up Spotty. All quiet.

I hung about the corner of Street and Road for half an hour until a black cab pulled up outside the tenement block where Kemp lived. Ruzena came out of the main door with a woman maybe in her forties that I guessed was, indeed, Jennifer Kemp. She was as tall as Ruzena, slim, with shoulder-length fair hair. Definitely older than Roozh. Like I say, she looked late thirties, forty-ish to me. But a battle-axe? Mmm; the word must have had a nuance for Mortimer that was lost on me. They were in animated conversation. Another taxi was heading my way along Spottiswoode Road. I flagged it down as the two women got into theirs and I said to the driver, "Follow that cab." I slammed the door shut and sat down. "I've always wanted to say that," I smiled at his stern eyes in the mirror.

"What you up to, pal? Followin' two women? I'm no wantin' to be an accessory to nae mental stalker, you know?" he said.

"Just follow them," I said. "It's my wife and her sister. The wife said this mornin' I'd never guess where they were goin'. I'm just gonnae prove her wrong. It's a joke. You're no gonnae be on the news."

"Better no," he said and set the meter.

You never hear that in old noir movies, do you? It's all, 'Follow that cab.' 'You got it, mister.' Kinda spoiled the moment for me. But maybe Edinburgh's too genteel for noir dialogue. We followed them along Melville Drive to Clerk Street and north on to the Bridges. Left on to Princes Street and right into St. Andrew Square. Round the square and they stopped outside Harvey Nic's. I got my cabbie to drive on past them and stop on the incline of South Saint Andrew Street.

I walked back up the brae and into Harvey Nic's. They were checking out clothes. Dresses, tops, jackets, accessories. They took an age and left not a garment unturned. Come to that, they left not a garment unheld up or uncommented on. I skulked as best I could until I heard Jennifer suggest they take lunch in the Forth Floor restaurant, then I lammed it. I snaffled a burger and a coffee to go and hung about the square till they came out, each carrying a Harvey Nichols white carrier bag.

They went to Jenners. I tailed them through Jenners. They came out of there with another carrier bag each. Then they did the George Street safari. Hobbs. Anthropologie. Sweaty Betty. Gant. French Connection. I dodged them all the way along George Street. There wasn't a paving stone, a lamp-post or a parking meter on that historic ole boulevarde that I didn't know intimately. I had to keep walking along one side of the street and then the opposite way along the other, to make myself less conspicuous as I waited and watched. I had no intention of being inside those places any more than I had to. For one thing was sure – Harvey Nics and Jenners had been more than enough spying on women buying clothes to do me for a lifetime. I don't even go with Phyllis when *she's* buying togs, for God's sake. I'd have thought a fashion model would have enough of clothes. But then, what do I know?

Somewhere in the neighbourhood of four, they came out of French Connection, laden with carriers and hailed a taxi. I walked along the street till I found another and went back to Arden Street for my car. When I drove down Spottiswoode, Ruzena's car was gone.

A day's girly shopping. Excellent. You ever get a feeling about a job? Her man was away but Ruzena spent the time shopping, rather than shagging.

6

Next morning, I was at Edinburgh Castle at half nine for Ruzena Mortimer's shoot. There was a trailer on the esplanade and Ruzena's pinkmobile was parked beside it.

Roozh was on the esplanade too, with a retinue of attendants including people I gathered were fashion stylists, hairdressers and make-up artists. There was one guy with a camera and another, younger, dude carrying all the photographic graith in a bag. The cameraman I took to be Shaun Mallon. He wasn't arch or limp or freakily dressed or braying, but he was the only one. He was just a six foot guy in a leather jacket with a few grand's worth of Box Brownie around his neck. His assistant was dressed in togs as bright and colourful as a bird of paradise. He had spiky hair and was a little on the camp side. Ruzena herself was standing stock still while another young woman, with palm tree hair and talons for fingernails, attended to her eyes. This dame was either applying eyeliner with the sharpest tipped eye pencil I'd ever seen or she was performing a cornea graft. The two of them stood in that position for a long time before the girl moved round to Ruzena's other eye.

Meanwhile, there was a rack of clothes behind them. But there was nothing outré that I could see, nothing obviously catwalky or calculated to make the ordinary joe in the street snort, "Who the fuck is ever going to wear that?" Roozh was dressed in blue jeans so tight they must have been sprayed on with a gun, and a black waistcoat over a white shirt with the sleeves rolled halfway up her arm. Heels. Obviously stylish but not, as I say, outrageous, But then I considered the magazine the shoot was for. Read by young Scots who, I guessed, wanted to be chic without being manic fashionistas. Maybe. Possibly; I hadn't studied the demographic. Another girl came and flicked a long, trowel-shaped comb at Ruzena's hair.

All of this had drawn quite a ring of onlookers, mostly female but one or two male, so I hung around the periphery of the gathering and observed, unobserved. After maybe twenty minutes, another guy, the one I jaloused was the fashion stylist in charge of the shoot, struck an attitude and said he wanted Ruzena shot against the esplanade wall that looks out over

Johnston Terrace to the south of the city. I assumed he meant shot with a camera.

There followed two or three hours of shit like this. Ruzena posed in many ways: a coat draped casually over her shoulder from a hooked forefinger; with a wide black fedora; wearing both coat and fedora; posing side-on. Posing face-on. Posing like a gunslinger in a modern Western, wide-legged, the brim of the hat low and her eyes smouldering out from under it. Mallon took a range of close-ups of her too.

She changed behind the rack of duds into a blue shirt with sleeve garters, a grey waistcoat, a grey tie with a blue tie-pin and grey trousers. They moved on. Under the Portcullis Gate, she was snapped in various poses, from the esplanade and from within the castle proper. Back to the blue jeans and heels and a variety of blouses, for each change of which she appeared to need her hair combed and her make-up checked. She was photographed on the Mills Mount Battery, by the one o'clock gun. Sitting on battlements. Leaning against the gun. A few taken where Mallon had his back to the battlements and she was outlined against the castle.

Crown Square, the citadel at the top of the castle. This was obviously where the fashion stylist had decided the summer tops and dresses were to be shot. Ruzena wore a wheen of them one after the other and was photographed in front of the turreted building of the Royal Palace, and posing against the lion sculpture at the right of the circular steps up to the doorway of the Scottish National War Museum.

And there was more; oh God, there was more. More clothes, more poses, more locations. St. Margaret's Chapel. Mons Meg. The Lang Stair. At every location, the crowd of onlookers changed, some having seen enough of a pretty young woman wearing clothes and standing in different postures, some drawn to it and burbling the same sounds of delight as the ones who had recently left. And, at every location, the fashion stylist would shout that they were happy for people to watch but could they please not take photos on their mobile phones. And, every time, one or two – always young women, I was interested to note – ignored his request.

Me? I was pret-a-porter'd out. My mind was more occupied with the Stuarts, with Mary Queen of Scots and with Queen

Margaret, the 'Pearl of Scotland'. Every time Mad Jack and Pious Peggy had brought me to the Castle in my childhood, they'd instructed me in its history. That interested me more than the shoot. There's no doubt that Ruzena Mortimer was a head-turner in terms of looks, but there's no shortage of good looking women. And I had no interest in fashion. Style is forever, whereas fashion is for this week only.

What I was interested in, the reason for Mortimer hiring me in the first place, was whether there was anyone hanging around the outfit that might have been a squeeze of Ruzena's. There wasn't. Mallon, the photographer, took no more interest in her than he would in a seascape, a wedding or a family portrait. It was another job. He took photos; he told the model how to stand. The other two guys – Mallon's assistant and the fashion stylist – would have been more interested in each other than in Ruzena. Nobody sniffing.

The fashion stylist called a wrap about quarter past one when they'd finished at Mons Meg. I turned from the crowd and legged it out of the Portcullis Gate and back on to the esplanade before anyone else. I headed to the north wall and made like a tourist, pretending to take pictures on my phone.

In minutes, the entourage was down too, babbling and laughing, one of the women rattling the rack of clothes with them. Jennifer Kemp walked towards Ruzena smiling. Ruzena looked up and smiled back. "Jennifer! How are you?"

"I'm good, Ruzena. Good morning's work?"

"Yeah, very good. Give me ten minutes and I'll be with you."

"Sure thing."

I wandered a little way up the esplanade while Ruzena went into a trailer and changed into her own togs. She emerged, said goodbye to several people and headed down the esplanade towards Castlehill and the Lawnmarket with Jennifer. I followed at a safe remove and saw them go into Deacon Brodie's. I guessed they were after a bar lunch rather than headed for a session. FAB 1 was still on the esplanade, so it was unlikely Ruzena was on the batter. I sauntered down Bank Street to give them time to find a table and get settled. When I got back, they were seated in a corner, at a table for two. I went to the bar and called a pint, stood where I could hear them, with my phone and my grog, while they ordered and ate some kind of brown rice, romaine lettuce & lemon salad. Then Jennifer had some thick chocolate looking dessert. Ruzena sipped at a glass of white.

Their conversation was, on the whole, dull – what I could hear of it. Ruzena said that she would enjoy the following few weeks' holiday, especially her time back home in Mestre. Jennifer asked what if a job came in? Ruzena said she wouldn't take it, and Jennifer was to make sure at her end that nothing was accepted till after Italy. Douglas, she said, was extremely busy and looking increasingly tired these days. She would try to get him away for a break after she came back. They talked about the news, about the morning's shoot, about some folk called Dorothy and Craig.

Then Jennifer said she had to get going. Ruzena said she intended to pop in on Geraldine, her old flatmate. They stood up, got their jackets on and moved to the door. I rinsed my suds down my throat, put the pint pot on the bar and left immediately behind them. They were on the street, giving each other a sisterly kiss and saying adieus. I passed them and walked over to George IV Bridge, where I hired a cab and got him to drive me to Montague Street. I hung about a hundred yards or so from the address, saw Ruzena step out of another cab and enter the building. She was in there two and a half hours. A taxi pulled up and she came out of the building and got in it. It pulled away and I walked on to Clerk Street, hailed another and went back to the car park in Castle Terrace. I sat in the bogey – which I had intelligently left on the surface level – till I saw the pink job drive past. Got into the traffic and followed her home to Bathgate, till I saw her stop at the gates of Manderley. Then I drove back to Edinburgh.

I got a parker in Montague Street. Good. Ruzena's old address. Bottom flat, right hand side. Rang the bell. A young woman, maybe Ruzena's age, answered.

"Hi," I said, sticking on a plastic smile. "Could I speak to the gentleman of the house?"

She looked at me like I was something she'd just picked up on her shoe. "There's no 'gentleman of the house' here," she said with heavy sarcasm. "We are strictly hen. Good evening."

And she shut the door. All right. Thirty seconds of being a klutz and I'd found out what I needed to know. I drove home.

Two dull days, following a woman around Edinburgh. Seeing nothing that might suggest an amorous intrigue. Unless Jennifer Kemp was her new squeeze, but I didn't get any whiff of that from what I'd seen of the women together. Nor was there any evidence of a male lover around. Certainly, I'd seen no stereotypical young buck hanging around with a bunch of flowers and a hard-on. I'd had to check the flat wasn't a love nest. It *had* seemed a little unlikely that the flat she had stayed in with two other girls, should now be where her lover lived, but I had to mak' siccar. The case still wasn't looking any more interesting.

The next day, the last that Mortimer was away in Birmingham, I stood in the pissing rain under a tree all day and watched Manderley for any sign of movement. The girls arrived to clean the place, then left in the afternoon. Later in the afternoon, a car pulled up at the gate and Gilmour walked up to talk to the driver, who had stood out of his car. Guy in a hoodie. The conversation lasted ten seconds, then the driver got back in and drove away and Gilmour walked back to the house. No question of the driver being allowed in the gate. An example of what Mortimer had described – no access to strangers. The guy could have been a door to door salesman or a Hallelujah. Wasnae getting in. Other than that, zip. SFA. I drove home and had a hot bath. I was more than a little hacked off. When I'd seen Ruzena with Mortimer, she looked like she was a woman in love. Strange but true. Over the previous two days, I'd seen no evidence, no *suggestion*, of an amorous intrigue. What the hell was Mortimer talking about? I wished the case could have a little more zing about it. I'd obviously forgotten the advice my mother gave me on innumerable occasions through my unsettled teenage years.

Careful what you wish for.

7

At ten to midnight, I was jarred out of sleep by my phone. I reached over, heart thumping, and looked at the caller I.D. Emma Wood. I.D. = D.I. Fuck, I hadn't heard or seen Emma for many months. I pressed the green button.

"Emma?"

"Jack, sorry to disturb you this time of night but I need you at Manderley House. You know where I am? Douglas Mortimer says he hired you to do a job for him?"

"That's right, he did. What's happened?"

"Can't say at the moment. Can you get over here, please? It's important."

"Sure," I said. "Be there in fifteen."

I shut the phone and put it back on the bedside table. Phyllis said, sleepily, out of the dark, "Emma Wood? What's wrong?"

"Don't know, love," I said. "She wants me at the Mortimer place yesterday."

"Jesus," said Phyllis and turned over. "Them again."

I lifted my togs and padded downstairs, got dressed in the cold living-room, and let myself quietly out of the house. I yawned a couple of times on the way over, said once to myself, 'Last night I dreamed I went to Manderley again,' and wondered why I'd never thought of it before. It took me just under ten minutes to get there. Two cops were at the opened gates. They stopped me, asked what I wanted and waved me through when I showed ID and told them I was there at the invitation of DI Wood.

The turning circle before the house was brightly lit from spots all along the roofline. There were several cars there, all to do with the police and the forensics guys, and an ambulance. I suppose one of the cops on the gate had phoned ahead because DS Jim Bryce came out of the front door to greet me, as I pulled up. I got out.

"Jim. What's the story?"

"Jack. Dead man on the kitchen floor. The husband came home tonight from England, about half past eleven, found this guy – Gilmour? – with a skewer through his heart. The gardener or something, this guy? You met him?"

"No, never met him. But aye, he's the gardener cum handyman. Or he was."

"Oh aye, past tense now, Jack. The other thing is – the wife's missing. Mortimer drove home tonight to surprise her – apparently, she wasn't expecting him till tomorrow - and he comes back to this. Guy's freaked, as you can imagine. He told the Gaffer that he'd hired you and we should talk to you. Didn't know we sometimes work with you, obviously."

"No way he would. No reason he should." We walked into the house. I think every light in the place was on. Back in the day, my mother would have chastised me for that. 'What do you think this is? Blackpool illuminations?' I turned to Jim. "Where are we?"

"Ma'am said she would talk to you in the lounge. Just go in and have a seat the now, Jack. I'll fetch her."

I sat in an armchair as soft as a cloud and looked around the quiet room. Here was the squeeze or two of zing I'd been looking for to add to the case. Alex Gilmour murdered and Ruzena unaccountably absent. Two obvious questions. Who killed Gilmour? And why would they? And where was Mrs. Mortimer? *Three* obvious questions. Nobody expects the Spanish Inquisition. Had Ruzena killed him? If she had, why had she? Was Alex Gilmour her paramour? A wee guy from Torphichen? Well, why not? Her husband was a wee guy from Bathgate, an *older* wee guy. But he had bankroll. Loads of scratch.

"Jack! Long time." Emma came in and closed the door behind her.

"Emma." I stood up and we kissed each other on the cheek before I sat down again. Emma sat opposite me and put her PDA on the table between us.

"What's happened here?" I said. "Well, Jim told me the basics."

"Can I ask you first why Douglas Mortimer hired you?"

"Sure. He hired me to find out if his wife was having an affair."

"Right. That's confirmed. He told us that. And is she?"

"Not that I've found. I've only been on the case five days, five and a bit days."

"What do you know about the gardener?"

"Gilmour? Next to nothing. I know his name, know that his wife is called Jean and works here as a cook – Mortimer told me that – and I know that they live in Greenside, Torphichen. And I've seen him from a distance a couple of times. That's the tank."

"So you wouldn't recognise him?"

I shook my head and drew in a sharp breath. "Nope. No way."

Emma made a face. "Pity. Do you think it's possible that Gilmour and Mrs. Mortimer were lovers?"

"I was just wondering that when you came in. I've never met any of the staff, so I know nothing about them or their relationship with Ruzena. This happening made me wonder if it could have been him. Gilmour. You see, Mortimer told me that he was convinced that, if she was having an affair, then it was either here in Scotland, or back home in Italy. Wasn't going to happen when she was on the road with the modelling stuff."

"Oh? Interesting. Why not?"

"Because, he said, she has a PA who looks after her. One Jennifer Kemp. Mortimer described her as a battle-axe. I've seen her. Her appearance doesn't chime with the word, as far as I'm concerned. But her nature might."

"Right. You've seen her. What have you done in the last five days or so?"

"Followed Ruzena Mortimer. First on Monday, with the hubby, so I could see them together. She didn't look like she was playing away from home when I saw them. She was all over him, like a bad suit. That might have been an act, of course. Tuesday she went clothes shopping in Edinburgh with Jennifer Kemp. First day Mortimer was away. Yesterday, well Wednesday, she had a photo shoot at Edinburgh Castle. Met Kemp again after that and had a bar lunch in Deacon Brodie's. They parted and Ruzena went to Montague Street, to an old flat she used to share, said she was going to see the girl who used to be her flatmate. Thursday, she never moved from the house."

"She told *you* she was going to see this girl?"

"No, no. She told Kemp. I overheard as I passed them on the pavement as they were splitting up."

Emma nodded her head. "So. Maybe Jennifer Kemp is the third party? Or the Montague Street flat is no longer shared by the girls but by somebody she's seeing on the side?"

I said, "Nope. Those thoughts crossed my mind. I've seen Ruzena with Jennifer Kemp twice. Nothing said 'lovers' to me about them. The flat thing struck me too. I checked it out. Young woman answered the door, told me the gaff was 'strictly hen' – her words. Of course, she wasn't on oath. You might want to double check. I just wonder if you were right the first time – that it was Alex Gilmour. Only time I was in the house, none of the staff were here and Ruzena was in Brighton, so I didn't see them, as I say. And there was no way I could get in the house these last three days without blowing the gaff."

"Do you think it's been Gilmour?" said Emma.

"I never thought of that till what's happened tonight. So he's been killed with a skewer, Jim says?"

Emma sucked a tooth. "Not a skewer. They're thinner than this thing. It looks like a sharpening steel. You know, for sharpening knives? It's an old-fashioned thing, much more solid. Looks like it's over six inches long. Hard to say at the moment; it's still in his heart."

"Can I see him?"

She shook her head. "Not just now. Paul Hodge is still with him. But I can show you these." She took out her phone and thumbed up a photograph, handed it to me. "There are six shots in all."

He was lying on his face on the kitchen floor, with a solidifying pond of dark blood beneath him. I swiped to the next. This was taken at floor level. I could see the ivory coloured handle of the steel and maybe an inch or so of the blade.

"Jeez, somebody had the power to punch that right into him," I said.

"Might have been driven farther in when he fell."

"Ah. True."

The others showed the kitchen from wider angles. It was a cowp. There were pots, broken dishes, a vase, a portable TV and various foodstuffs strewn over the floor. I handed the phone back.

"Some struggle."

"Yep. You think the wife could do this?" asked Emma.

"Christ, it's hard to say, Em. I've only seen her on a few occasions. She's slim. But she keeps fit. Gilmour looks a solid guy. I don't know what she'd be capable of if her dander was up, though. But why would she?"

Emma shrugged. "No idea. Yet. But she's absent without explanation. Mortimer's tried to call her phone and gets no answer."

"How long has this guy been dead?"

"Hodge hasn't said yet. But it's not that long. Just looking at the corpse tells us that, without being pathologists. From what you've seen in the last few days, is there somewhere obvious Mrs. Mortimer would flee to, if she was in trouble, or worried?"

"Obvious one is Jennifer Kemp's. Spottiswoode Street, Edinburgh. Maybe the girls in the Montague flat. Her family live in Italy. Mestre – mainland part of Venice. May be worth checking the airport to see if she's booked on a flight. Did she take her passport when she left?"

"Yep. Shirley checked the wife's rooms with Mortimer. Phone gone. Passport gone. She's done a bunk. Okay, Jack, thanks for that," said Emma, putting a finishing touch to her PDA entry. "Been a help, as always. You want to see Mortimer? I think he's keen to talk to you."

"Sure."

8

Mortimer was in his smoking room. Smoking. The ashtray on the table by his side was piled with ash and douts – twenty, at least. He looked like he'd seen a ghost. He planted his fag end in the heap of ash and stood up.

"Black," he said, "this is a fuckin' nightmare."

I shook his hand and patted his shoulder. "Hard one, Douglas, certainly. Twice over. Alex Gilmour dead and Ruzena missing."

"Do *you* think Roozh killed Alex?" he asked me. "Cos I'm sure these fuckin' polis dae."

"We're keeping an open mind, Mr. Mortimer," said Emma. "At the moment we're only asking questions to establish what happened here. Sit down, sit down and have a chat with Jack. I need to go and check on the kitchen. I'll be back directly."

He sat down and sparked another lung-dart. "I cannae believe it," he said. "I just cannae believe it."

I sat down on another chair and said to him, "When was the last time you spoke to Ruzena?"

"The polis asked me that."

"Well, they would. They need to know. So do I."

"Did you see her this week?"

I ran through my exciting week on the trail of Ruzena Dolezal.

"So you didnae actually see her the day? Yesterday. Thursday, whenever. Hell, ye ken what I mean."

"No. I kept an eye on the place and she never moved out of it. When did you speak to her last?"

"Thursday mornin'. I phoned her aboot eleven and said I had another day a that shite ti go through but I would be hame Friday mornin'. *This* mornin'. Aw the time intendin' ti su'prise her an' motor hame that night. Gie her a wee su'prise. Fuck, an' see what I come hame ti. I cannae believe it. Why *Alex*?"

"Since we're on the subject of Alex," I said, "here's a question. Why would Alex be in Manderley at this time of night?"

"You mean because he was shaggin' Roozh? Is that what you're tryin' ti say? Cos I'm sure that's what the polis think tae."

"Actually, Douglas, no. That's not what I mean. I don't think he was. I'm just wondering why Alex would be here after … what – five? Would Ruzena ask him to come up and help out if there was a handyman thing that needed done?"

He shook his head. "Naw. She'd wait till the morra. No unless it was a pipe burst or somethin' like that. But there's been nothin' like that."

"So why would he be here?" A thought struck me. "Does he have a key?"

"Aye. The Gilmours have a key in case of emergencies. An' an alarm in case there's a breck-in when we're no here."

"Right," I said. "Good. So he could have let himself in."

"Aye, I suppose so."

"Okay. Now. Back to Ruzena."

"Where the fuck *is* she, Black? What's happened ti her? I'm aboot aff ma heid here."

"Well, I'm trying to establish that – where she is. I need to know…"

"Why would she fuck off? Unless it *wis* her that plunged Alex? Here – dae ye 'hink Alex might a tried it on wi' Roozh? Know what I mean? No that she was shaggin' him, just that he tried it on, the night? "

"One of the possibilities I'm trying to examine here. Now. Detail. Think hard. When and how often have you phoned her this week?"

"Er … Tuesday. Phoned her aboot lunchtime. She was wi' Jennifer. Shoppin', like you say. Said she was gettin' lunch in the restaurant at that shop. Harvey Nichols."

"She was. Good. Next?"

"Wednesday. Phoned real early because I knew she had that job at the Castle. And phoned her again aboot eight that night."

"How'd she sound?"

"Aye, good. She was chirpin' on about havin' a good day. She met Jennifer efter the shoot, then she went back ti see what's her name … Geraldine, one a the lassies she shared wi' in that flat. Geraldine Hunter. Still lives there. New flatmates, right enough. But aye, she said she'd had a good day."

"And Thursday morning. She sound okay then?"

"Aye. She said she was lookin' forward ti me gettin' back. Aw sounded good, you know?"

"Think back. Anything different about Thursday's call? Or Wednesday night's, even? What I mean is, at her end, did anything sound different? Like she was somewhere else, I mean?"

"Somewhere *else*? Where the hell else would she be?"

"That I don't know. But I haven't seen her since Wednesday. No sign of her Thursday. I'm just examining every possibility here. Did it sound different in any way? Traffic, for example? Aircraft noise? Water lapping? Gondoliers singing?"

"Naw. Sounded just the same as always."

"All right. What car is missing?"

"The Mazda."

"Okay. Apart from Jennifer Kemp and the lassie Geraldine, can you think of anywhere else she would go if she felt she was in trouble of any kind?"

"Mestre, of course. She's got her fuckin' passport wi her…"

Emma came back in. "All right, Mr. Mortimer. Mr. Gilmour's body has to stay in situ for the moment. This is now a crime scene. My female colleague has gone to speak to Mrs. Gilmour. There will be police and forensics operatives here all night. Is there somewhere you can go for the next few days?"

Mortimer passed his hand over his brow. "Er… no really. No unless a hotel? Can I no stay here the night? My room's on the second flair. I'll no be in anybody's way. Hell, this is *mah hoose*. I live here."

"I'm afraid not. This is a crime scene and nobody can be allowed to stay here without reason. You wouldn't get much sleep here with all the comings and goings anyway," said Emma.

"D'ye think I'm gonnae get any sleep anywhere? Maitter where I go?"

"I'm sorry, sir, truly. But you'll have to make alternative arrangements. Excuse me, I have to speak to the paramedics for a moment. Jack – can I speak to you in five minutes?"

"Sure."

Emma closed the door behind her. Mortimer said, "What the fuck is aw that aboot?"

I said, "When a place is designated as a 'crime scene', the area's taped off and an officer is put outside to restrict access. No-one gets into a crime scene without reason. Not even the poor bastard who lives there, I'm afraid. The officer will have a scene log and will have to note everybody in and out, detailing who they are, reason for access, time in, time out, all that kind of thing. The body has to remain in place while the SOCO team do their work. Once the harvest of evidence is completed, then it gets removed. Real bummer, I know. You'll need to stay at a hotel for a few days. Got a favourite?"

"Aye, the Dalmahoy. This is a pisser. Right, I'll phone the noo, if you're talkin' ti *her*."

I left the room and went back to the lounge. Naturally, Emma wanted to know everything Mortimer had told me. So I repeated our conversation as accurately as I could. Emma listened, nodding her head occasionally. When I'd finished, she said, "Why did you think she might be somewhere else?"

"Well, she *is* somewhere else, Em," I said. "As in, no here. I just wondered if she went that somewhere else before Thursday p.m., like Thursday morning, or even Wednesday night. Maybe she's been elsewhere and Gilmour disturbed a burglar or something."

"There's no sign of burglary."

"There's been an almighty struggle in the kitchen."

"Yes, there has. But no indication that somebody burgled the place. No sign of forced entry or anything. There was a key in Gilmour's pocket. Mortimer said it was for here."

"How seriously have you guys pursued that line?" I asked her. "There's an alarm in the Gilmours' if anybody tries to break in," I said. "I don't know how sensitive it is, or what would set it off, but maybe somebody was trying the windows or something and that was enough to do it, and Gilmour came up to investigate."

She nodded, a sceptical look on her face. "Maybe. We'll check the grounds in daylight. But the obvious facts are that Alex Gilmour has been found murdered in here and Ruzena Mortimer has absconded. Her car has gone too, so possibly not abducted. It doesn't look good for her at the moment."

"No." I nodded.

"The one big plus we have is that the CCTV footage is recorded. There are two cameras…"

"I know," I said. "At the gates. One covering the gates themselves and one covering the house."

"Right. So, Shirley's gone back to the office with that. Hopefully, we can get a clue as to what's gone on from that."

"Let's hope so."

"Hey, anyway. We'll see what that and the path report brings, hopefully tomorrow. Meantime, we'll check the Edinburgh addresses. She hasn't booked on a flight – not from Edinburgh or Glasgow."

"All right," I said. "If there's anything I can help you with, you know where to get me."

"Sure."

"I'll say goodbye to Mortimer. Any problems with me speaking to him tomorrow? I'm a face he trusts."

"None at all."

Douglas had booked a suite at the Dalmahoy, and was about to pack a case. He was not best pleased.

I drove home and made myself up a bed in the study. Didn't want to waken Phyllis. I lay a long time, having me a mull. I don't know why but I kept wondering if Ruzena had lammed from Manderley on Wednesday night or early Thursday morning. At that point, I had no suggestion why she might have done, but the possibility wouldn't leave me. She hadn't moved from the house all Thursday while I was watching it. Maybe she had a day in with a good book. Maybe not. Cards on the table? I didn't think she'd killed Gilmour. It wasn't an impossibility but it didn't gel with me. She was tall and slim, pretty lightweight. Didn't strike me as capable. However, psyched up, under threat, in danger of her life - of course, she might have had the vim. Still didn't ping with me. But, if she hadn't done it, who had? Somebody else in the house. How had they got in? And why was Gilmour there at that time of night? And, most of all, where the blue fuck was Ruzena now?

9

The murder weapon was, indeed, a sharpening steel. It was six and a half inches long, and weighed five ounces. The blade was two centimetres in circumference at the handle, tapering to a sharp point. Before it was found in Alex Gilmour, it had been in Mortimer's family since 1929, having been a wedding present for his grandparents. Ruzena Dolezal's fingerprints were not found on the handle. The prints that *were* found were Alex Gilmour's (which might have been, as DI Wood suggested, because Gilmour was the one who sharpened knives) and those of one other, unidentified. The other prints suggested strongly that someone other than Mrs. R. Mortimer had killed their handyman. Which was a dim light in a dark place for Ruzena. Very dim. But more than she had had the previous night, wherever she had been. Or still was.

Jean Gilmour had been inconsolable, when Shirley Honeyman told her of her husband's death. Understandably. But she had come up with the gold that the burglar alarm for Manderley House had gone off in their place just after half ten. Alex had got in the car and driven up there. That was all she could say about that. When he hadn't come back by half past eleven, she had rung his mobile. And the cops found a missed call from Jean Gilmour on it for that time. In the clear light of day, a pantry window was found to have the same unidentified prints on it as the steel. But it had not been broken. The cops' thinking was that, just possibly, the would-be intruder had deliberately used enough force to set off the alarm but not to break the window, knowing it was enough to work the thing. Emma told me this over a mug of joe in my office above the Chinese takeaway in King Street. She'd come in, later that morning, just before noon.

I said to her, "So, Gilmour arrives, opens up the house, goes in to switch off the alarm and investigate. Leaves the door open. Intruder enters. That how you see it?"

She swivelled in her chair. "It's a possibility, I suppose. But, to be that, it would need the intruder to know that the Gilmours had an alarm in their place – *if* Gilmour was the intended victim. Not very likely."

"And that Mortimer was in England. Maybe even that Ruzena wasn't at home either. If she wasn't."

"M-hm. You see, it doesn't really work out if you think it through. Nothing has been taken from the house. That we know of. So the motive wasn't burglary. Not yet. The CCTV was switched off from 2214 hours, by whom we don't know. Mrs. Mortimer would seem the likeliest culprit. Earlier footage shows a car at the gates earlier in the day. Vauxhall Corsa at about quarter to four. Driver rings the intercom..."

"Ah! I saw that! Gilmour went and spoke to him, guy drove off. Yeah, I saw that. Apparently, that's what they do. You can't just get in to Manderley."

"Right. So it's parked sideways on and the plate is hard to read but we'll get there. Driver's a young male in a dark hoodie and jeans."

"How did the intruder get in?" I asked.

"Ah. Ladder found at the rear of the property, against the internal side of the fencing. Quite a few prints but none the same as the ones we already have. Personally, I think there might have been two ladders. One to get in – you know, slide the second ladder over at the top. On the way back out, it's not so important to rescue the second one. Anyway. That's how he did it. Whatever else he did."

I looked at Emma. "Hang on. You don't think Douglas Mortimer did this, do you?"

She gave a long, slow smile. "What would make you say that, Jack?"

"Because Mortimer arrived home late last night. Because he would know that there was an alarm in the Gilmours' place. Because he would know exactly what would be needed to set off the burglar alarm without breaking or damaging anything – and who else would? Because I know the way your mind works. And because I know you can't rule *anything* out at this stage."

"And what would Mortimer's motive be?"

I shrugged. "Anything. Jealousy? Maybe he got it into his head that the local affair Ruzena was having was with Alex Gilmour."

"Maybe," said Emma. "Like you say, Jack, I can't rule anything out just yet. But Mortimer isn't Public Enemy no. 1 at the moment. We need to identify these prints on the steel and the pantry window, maybe even the ladder, eventually. They're not his."

"No trace of Ruzena yet?"

"None. Jennifer Kemp and the Geraldine Hunter girl have been interviewed. Nothing there. So it's donkey work time for us detectives. Shirley and Jim are talking to the two Polish girls at the moment." She put her mug on the desk and stood up from the chair.

"Anything I can do?"

"Whatever you can, Jack. You work in your own mysterious ways anyway, so anything you can come up with will be welcome."

When Emma left, I sat back in my chair and thought about all of that. I didn't think for a second that Mortimer had killed Gilmour, but I could see why Emma couldn't rule out the possibility. Ruzena was the puzzle, the unknown quantity. If she hadn't killed Gilmour, and it looked like she hadn't, where was she? When had she left? And why? What was all that about? An enigma.

I tried to get inside her head, but I couldn't. A young woman of great beauty and some fame. Clever, intelligent – could speak several languages. Cultured, at least to a degree. She was a reader, a music lover, a connoisseur of art. Witty, according to her husband. Kept herself fit. The exact opposite of the older man she had married. Married because he amused her. Or so the story went. Slovakian by birth, she had lived much, if not most, of her life since childhood in Italy; a town in a highly industrialised area of Italy. During her husband's recent absence, she had gone shopping with her friend and PA, and had called on an old flatmate. So she hadn't forgotten old friends in her fame and success. A good quality. Maybe she was a good woman. But where the fuck was she now?

The thing was, I couldn't get into her head at all; I didn't know enough about young foreign models. I knew Bel Thorn, the working name of Isobel Thornton from Lanark, a model who lived at Stonegate Farm now, on the Edinburgh bypass, with her rock star partner. I'd worked for her and her late old man a couple of years back, trying to trace her brother. But Izzy was an altogether more grounded kind of lassie. And she was local. I shared cultural, historical and regional influences with her. I shared very little with Ruzena. Hence the difficulty in identifying with her.

I had been mulling over the possibility that, if she *had* been fucking around, then it must have been because modelling was such a brain-numbing and time-consuming way of earning a living, especially for a woman of her resources, that she needed something to jazz her life up a bit. Rather than snout or coke, or peanut butter on rice crackers. But that was precisely what music, art and literature did for her. Yeah? Did it for me, anyway. But I didn't really know anything about the woman. I'd seen her in the flesh once. Anything else was hearsay.

And *had* she wafted on Wednesday night, maybe Thursday morning, as my mind kept casting up? And, if she had, was it because she knew – or suspected – that the owner of the prints on the steel, whoever that was, was on his way to Manderley House? And she didn't want to see him, for whatever reason?

That wouldn't leave me alone. What might that reason be?

I called Emma's moby dick. She was obviously still driving, by the background traffic noises. "Jack?"

"Is it kosher for me to talk to the women you guys have interviewed? Kemp and Hunter? Plus the two Polish lassies that work for Mortimer?"

"Okay by me, Jack. If *they'll* talk to *you*. Usual proviso – don't do anything or say anything to fuck up the investigation."

"As if."

"Aye. As if. Let me know if there's anything that strikes you."

"Wilco. Roger and out."

Next, I rang Mortimer's number. "Douglas, it's Jack Black."

"Aye, Black. What can I do for you?"

"I need to know the addresses of the lassies that work for you. The Polish lassies. I'd like to have a wee chat with them. See if anything comes up."

"Like what?"

"I've no idea at the moment. But one of them might remember something that helps us find Ruzena. It's worth a try."

"Aye, I suppose it is. I've got them on my phone here, I think."

"Text them to me, if you don't mind. And I'll be talking to Jennifer Kemp and the Geraldine one, the old flatmate too."

"The polis have talked ti aw these lassies, Black."

"I know that, but I don't ask the same questions the police do. I get different answers that way."

"Aw right."

"Thing is, to introduce myself, I would have to say what my interest in the case is: that you hired me to do a job for you."

"Aye?"

"Yeah. Is it okay to say what job? It might be the key that unlocks things for us."

I expected some resistance. I got none. After a second or two, he said, "Aye. Do whatever you huv ti. I just want to see Roozh again, Black. I just want her back."

"Well, I'll do all in my limited power to see if we can arrange that."

"Will you go to Mestre for me?"

"Why don't you go yourself?"

"A' you jokin' me? Mah hoose is crawlin' wi cops. Ah cannae just leave the country. I doubt they would want me ti, anyway. An' I'd rather wait around here an' see if Roozh gets in touch."

"Why don't you phone Mestre?"

"Cos I don't speak fuckin' Slovakian. Or Italian. An' they don't speak English."

"Just ask for Ruzena. Surely they'll recognise your voice."

"That's aboot aw I can say ti them is her name. An' if she's no there, they're gonnae get in a blind panic as well, in't they?"

"Mmm. Maybe. I see what you mean."

"Will you go to Mestre for me?"

"If you want me to."

"I'll pay of course."

"Of course."

"How will the polis deal wi that? Her bein' in Italy, if she is? Interpol?"

"Oh," I said, "I think Interpol have got weightier matters on their mind. Maybe not even Europol will be involved. The police here will contact the local force over there – I'm not sure which one; there are four or five forces in Italy – and request their assistance. That will have been done already, I'm guessing. But I'll go if you like and see what I can see."

"The day?"

"Not today, Douglas, no. Let me talk to these women today and we'll see how things go from there. But rest easy – I'll help all I can. And she might turn up anyway before tomorrow."

"Thanks, Black. You're a decent man."

"I'll call you later tonight, if you like."

"Yeah, sure. Let me know."

"How is life at the Dalmahoy?"

"Bearable. Mind and let me know how ye git on."

I promised him I would, and rang off.

10

I got a space in Spottiswoode Street this time. *Mirabile dictu.* And, equally wonderful to relate, Jennifer Kemp didn't live on the top landing but also, like Geraldine Hunter, on the ground floor. Twice I hadn't had to scale the heights of an Edinburgh tenement block in just a couple of days. Almost unheard of.

I got there about half two in the afternoon. I had no way of knowing whether Jennifer would be at home or elsewhere. Come to that, I had no idea whether she had a huge, hulking husband who might resent my presence, or a repulsive teenager who would sit and smirk throughout an interview. Turned out, she had neither. She answered the door immediately I knocked, as if she had just been passing it.

"Mrs. Kemp?"

"Miss Kemp."

"Miss Kemp, my apologies. Hello." I did the ID card shtick. "My name is Jack Black. I'm a private investigator. I wondered if I could talk to you about Ruzena Mortimer?"

"The police have spoken to me about Ruzena," she said. "I suggest you take it up with them."

"I know they have, Miss Kemp. I'm working with the police in West Lothian. I'm helping them on the case. The reason I'm here is I was asked to investigate Mrs. Mortimer before her disappearance."

"By the police?"

"No, no," I said. "By her husband. Douglas Mortimer."

"Really? Why?"

"He was concerned she might be having an affair."

She looked sceptically at me, and said, "Rubbish," very disdainfully.

"No, it's the God's truth," I said. "Call him."

She sighed. "You'd better come in."

A bijou little flat for one. Maybe a couple, at a stretch. The living-room was spotless but with a whiff of the monastic. Or, perhaps more appropriately, the conventual. White walls, wooden flooring, tiled fireplace, grey rug in front of it, grey settee facing it, grey chair at the side of it, T.V. She sat in the chair and motioned me to the settee. I sat.

"And why should Douglas think she's seeing someone else?"

"Same reason anyone thinks these things," I shrugged. "Thinks she's changed. Little things. Worries if it's because there's someone else. It's the old, old story. I've seen it a hundred times in my career."

"He should know better," she said.

"Oh? Why?"

"Because she thinks there's nobody like him."

"Oh? I wonder why that is."

"That's something you'd have to ask Ruzena."

I nodded. "I saw them together on Monday, there. And, you're right, her whole demeanour was as if she thought there was nobody like him."

Kemp looked snootily at me and said, "There you are, then."

"Do you know where she is just now?" I asked.

She shook her head. "I don't."

"Ha she been in contact at all in the last, say, thirty six hours?"

"Nope. I told the police that. I saw her on Tuesday. We went shopping and had lunch. Here in town. And I last saw her on Wednesday. She had a shoot at the Castle. After she finished, we had a pub lunch." Her eyes narrowed and she pointed at me. "You were there!" she said. "In Deacon Brodie's! You were there, wearing a beard, right? Following her?"

"Yep," I said. "Well spotted. This is my first week on the case. Monday, I saw the Mortimers together in Queen Street and the Balmoral. Tuesday, I saw you and Ruzena shopping – Harvey Nics, Jenners, most of George Street. Wednesday I watched the shoot and followed you guys into Deacon Brodie's. After you left her, Ruzena went up to Montague Street and spent some time with Geraldine Hunter. Seriously – well spotted! Most people wouldn't have been able to. I'm strictly bona fide, Miss Kemp. I'm working for Mr. Mortimer, but hoping I can prove that Mrs. Mortimer is entirely innocent."

"She is."

"How long have you known her, Miss Kemp?"

"I've been her PA for just over three years."

"How did you get that post? Were you recommended at Brio?"

"No. I answered an ad in the Evening News. Ruzena had advertised for a PA."

I smiled. "Okay. As far as what Ruzena's like," I said, "I know her to be arty, into reading, art and classical music among other things; and sporty – well, interested in running to keep fit, I guess. Her husband also tells me she speaks several European languages and is very witty. Is that a fair character sketch?"

"So far as it goes," said Kemp. "She's very clued-in, is Ruzena. She follows the news and has opinions on just about everything. She's quite a character."

"No just a pretty face, then?" I said, with a smile.

"Far from it."

"Okay, you haven't heard from her since Wednesday. Have you any idea where she might be?"

"None that the police wouldn't have too. Or you, for that matter. Geraldine's place. Mestre. That's about it."

"Did the police tell you that a man was found dead in the Mortimers' home last night?"

"Yes."

"In your opinion, is there any chance, even the remotest…"

"What? That Ruzena killed him? No."

"Even if he tried it on with her?"

"Even that. She's fit and she's quick. But she couldn't kill anyone. And remember, if this was an intruder, she knows the layout of the house and he doesn't. If he was any threat, she could have got out."

"That's a reasonable point."

"Common sense."

"So long as he didn't surprise her."

"Mmm. Maybe. But I still think Ruzena would have had the wit to get away."

I had to wait till after five to get anybody in, in the Montague Street flat. I got up there about half three, quarter to four but couldn't get an answer to my knock. I swithered about heading back out west, maybe checking out the Polish girls, but I wasn't keen. I'd much rather have killed two birds with one in the bush, if you know what I mean. It's a long lane that's as good as a mile. If I drove out, I'd just have to drive back again some other time. I could save myself a round trip of over forty miles if I just sat on my ass in the car till somebody came home from work. So I did just that. I settled down in the driver's seat and went through *Julius Caesar* in my head. I like to do that – play out one of the glover's son's masterpieces in my own wee mental theatre. See how far I can get before I fuck up. Or dry up. I do not too bad with the tragedies and the bigger comedies. Some of the more obscure ones are trickier, right enough. I hadn't done old JC in yonks. I started at, "Hence! Home! You idle creatures, get you home." I'd got just as far as, "Why, man he doth bestride the narrow world like a colossus," when I saw two young women walk along the street and turn in to the appropriate tenement. One was the girl who'd sneered at me that they were strictly hen, the last time I'd come a-calling.

Bingo! Or, more appropriately, 'House!'

I left Brutus and Cassius to get on with it, and stepped out of the yoke, locked up with a flick of my fob and crossed the road. It was the girl I knew that answered the door.

"Hi," I said. "Remember me?"

"Nope. Never seen you in my life. Blow."

Mmm. Direct, at least.

"Last time I was here, I was wearing a beard."

"Oh, I know who you are," she said, her lip curling in contempt. "There's still no man of the house. What is it you want?"

"I'm looking for Geraldine Hunter."

"Why didn't you say that the last time?"

"Because I wasn't looking for her the last time," I said. "Sorry. Didn't mean to creep you out. I just needed to know if a guy lived here, at that time."

"Why? What's it to you?"

I produced the card. "I'm a private investigator. I had a good reason to ask what I did the last time. This time, I need to speak to Geraldine Hunter. Is she in?"

"You're speaking to her. What is it you want?"

"I'd like to ask you a couple of questions about Ruzena. And, yes, I know the police have been here. I'm working with them."

"Who is it, Gerry?" another female voice asked from the hallway. "You all right?"

"Fine, Libby. No probs." She stood aside and barked at me: "Come in, private investigator. You've got quarter of an hour. This is Olivia. Wipe your feet. Through there. Try not to knock the ironing over as you sit down. Fifteen minutes. I'm a busy girl, I'm just home from work and I am famished. Fifteen minutes and then you're out. Okay? Them's the rules. You don't like them, you can do the other thing. So. What is it to be? Speak now or forever hold your peace."

I hadn't been able to get a syllable in sideways. Even when curtly introduced to Olivia, I'd only had time to simper as Geraldine shoved me through the hall to the sitting room. I said, "That's fine," and sat down on the settee without capsizing the neatly folded pile of ironing on the far cushion.

Geraldine shut the door and sat herself. "Okay. Ask."

"Okay," I said, "My name's Jack Black and I work out of Bathgate. I was hired by Douglas Mortimer to find out if his wife was seeing anyone else. I know…"

"So that's why you asked about the man of the house. You thought she was having a bit on the side in here. The obvious assumption if you saw her come in or out of the building, I suppose."

"I knew she'd lived here before and I followed her here on Wednesday. It was an asinine question, I know. My apologies. I'm usually better than that."

"I hope so. Why does Mortimer think she's cheating on him? Just an old man's insecurity, is it?"

"Maybe," I said. "He thinks she's changed. Wonders if … well, you know."

"Do you know Mortimer well?" she asked.

"No. I only met him last week when he asked me to do the job."

"Do you think Ruzena only married him for his money?"

"I guess everybody does, when they first hear the story. I'm not so sure now."

"She didn't. But I'll leave you to find that out for yourself. And why. So tell me what you know about Douglas Mortimer. What you've heard. What you've found out."

"Me? Well, he's a millionaire. He's the head of a huge logistics firm that he built up from scratch, from the time he drove the Co-op van when he left school. He's what unimaginative folk call a 'workaholic'. The firm has depots in several places in the UK – Edinburgh, Birmingham and Canterbury, that I know of. It goes all over Europe … or over most of it … a large part of it, certainly. He had himself a big house built in the countryside outside of Bathgate. He has…"

"Do you know what the house is called?"

"Manderley," I said.

"What does that tell you about him?"

"Eh?"

"What does that *tell* you about him?"

"Err… He told me he named it after the house in *Rebecca* because his mother liked the film."

"And what does that tell you about him?"

"I don't know … that he's sentimental?"

"Maybe. Maybe something else. What else do you know about him?"

"What *else*? Not much. He doesn't have many interests outside work and his wife. He likes pipe bands and jigsaws. So not an intellectual."

"Does everybody have to be an intellectual? Would you say *you* were an intellectual?"

"No and yes, in that order."

"Mmm. Maybe; I've seen no evidence of it so far. So, is that it, for his interests?"

"Uh, he said he liked gaming. Video games. Electronic games. That kind of shit."

"All right. You've known him just over a week. You've obviously formed an opinion of him – even if it's just that he isn't an intellectual. Anything else?" I puffed out a breath. "You think that's a fair assessment of a man you've only met on a couple of occasions? I think you've a great deal still to find out about Douglas Mortimer. Now, what do you know about Ruzena?"

"I'm the one who's meant to be asking the questions," I said.

"Well, you're finding things out by a different method this evening. What do you know about Ruzena?"

"She's Slovakian by birth. She was raised in Porto Marghera and Mestre. She's a well-known model. She met Mortimer at a *Scotsman* do. They've been married about three years. She likes reading, art and music. Including classical music. She runs to keep fit. She speaks several languages and she's very witty, according to Mortimer. According to her PA, she keeps abreast of current affairs and has opinions on most, if not all, of the major items on the news agenda."

"Do you know anything about her childhood?"

"I don't."

"Or her teenage years? Her young womanhood? No?" I shook my head. "How about her time in Edinburgh?"

I shook my head again. "No. Just that you and she shared digs here at one time."

"You've a lot to learn about Ruzena as well. Think about what I've said tonight – I mean, really *think*. It might help you. Now, what did *you* want to ask *me*?"

I looked at her and smiled. "Do you know where she is?"

"No. I told all this to the police. I don't know where she is. I can't think of where she might be if she isn't staying at Jenny Kemp's or at her folks' place in Italy. And no, I certainly don't think she killed that guy. In fact, I know she didn't."

"How can you be so sure?"

"Because I know her. And you don't. That's your fifteen minutes. It's been nice talking to you. But don't come back until you know a lot more than you do at the moment. You're not quite as smart as you think you are, Mr. Black."

I left and walked over to the car, not quite sure of what had just happened. I knew what the guys in Mulholland's would have thought of Gerry Hunter. 'Imagine gaun hame to that wi' a burst poke.' But I was impressed, rather than anything else. She had a sizzling intelligence. And she'd made me think – as she'd said, in a different way from the usual. I liked her. I smiled as I got in the car and drove home. I thought about what she'd said all the way out.

First, she'd asked if I thought Roozh had married Mortimer for his money. When I'd wittered, she said quite dogmatically that she hadn't, that I would find that for myself, and also why she, Gerry, was so sure about it. That was intriguing in itself. If anybody in Scotland would know Ruzena well, it would be Geraldine Hunter; I accepted that. She had shared accommodation with her and known her for longer than anyone else. She would know things about her that others wouldn't. But she hadn't told me why she was so sure. No, no; too straightforward. That was something she obviously reckoned I had to find out for myself. Fuck, this was like being back in school. All right, I'd try to find that out.

Next, she'd quizzed me on what I knew about Mortimer and chided me for making assumptions, based on a very fleeting acquaintance with him. That was a fair point. She'd been at pains to have me consider what Mortimer's calling the house 'Manderley' said about him. And she'd scorned my suggestion of sentimentality. 'Maybe; maybe something else.' What else, I would consider later. She'd been equally scornful of my assertion that he was not an intellectual. And that I was, for that matter. I wondered what she knew.

Then she'd put me through the same routine with Ruzena and said I had a lot to learn about her too. What the fuck did I have to learn? And why hadn't the bitch just told me?

No. That was out of order. Geraldine Hunter was not a bitch. She was a sharp woman who obviously had great affection for Ruzena. I respected that. She must have thought it would be better – not for me, but for the Mortimers – if I found that stuff out for myself. Oh – and what had Jennifer Kemp said? Ruzena thought there was 'nobody like' Mortimer, and the reason for that was something I'd have to ask Ruzena. Jennifer knew something too. I needed to find out what that was. As Gerry had said, I needed to really *think* about what she'd said to me that night.

All right. I'd try.

11

I got back to the office and alchemised some mud, switched on the computer and sat in my chair for a slurp and a ponder. Just what was it la Hunter wanted me to find out? For there was something at the back of all that short, sharp interrogative technique, for sure. She knew something that was material, and she thought I ought to know it too. But it wasn't for her to tell me what. What could that be? What sort of information would be germane to my inquiry but that she wouldn't, or couldn't, tell me?

Something confidential. Had to be. It stuck out like a green polar bear.

What else? Something Geraldine Hunter knew, as an old and trusted friend of Ruzena Dolezal Mortimer, but that it wasn't her place to divulge. Maybe it was relevant to the police inquiry too, of course … but, no. I thought, on balance, not. If it was something the cops had to know, she'd have told them. She was a responsible citizen. The bossy-ass schoolma'am routine was for my benefit only. There was something about Douglas, or Ruzena, or the Mortimers as a couple, that was important.

What? I reached into the top drawer of my desk and pulled out the bairn's fidget spinner, a toy she had craiked to get because all her pals had them. They were marketed as aids for people with trouble focusing or fidgeting; they were supposed to relieve nervous energy or stress. They were also reputed to help kids with autism or ADHD but they did fuck all of the kind. Juliet had none of the above troubles and got bored with hers rapidly because all it did was spin. Her father, on the other hand, liked to spin it now and again on his thumb and think while he did. Diff'rent strokes for diff'rent folks, I guess. I gave it a birl and watched it whirl.

Maybe Roozh had posed for nude photos - or worse - when she was younger and 'needed the money'? Could it be as obvious and as clichéd as that? That Ruzena was being blackmailed for some youthful indiscretion? Nudity? Porno? Drugs? The standard things? Somehow, I didn't think so. I couldn't have given you a logical reason for that thought but it just didn't light anything up for me. If some sad-sack sleazeball had got a hold of some dirt like that and threatened to … send the negatives to Mortimer if she didn't come across with mega bucks, I had the feeling she'd just say, 'Fuck that,' and *tell* Mortimer. Show him the photos, for that matter. Nope. It wasn't that.

In fact, it had to be something that *involved* Mortimer, didn't it? Geraldine had asked my opinion of him first, before she went on to do the same as regarded Ruzena. What did his calling the big hoose 'Manderley' tell me about him? And not that he was sentimental. What, then? Add to that the fact that Jenny Kemp told me that Ruzena thought there was nobody like him.

I needed to know more about Douglas Mortimer than my old man had told me. Or, possibly, than my old man had known. Maybe something that hadn't been true when my father knew him. In his younger days. And I had more to learn about the beauteous Roozh, as well.

I clicked on Google and searched for Douglas Mortimer. He was there. One paragraph that spoke, in the starkest terms, of the rise and success of Mortimer Logistics. 'Founder and Chief Executive Officer: Douglas Mortimer.' There were a few others of that name, who mattered less than nothing to me. Oh, and there was the character from the movie, 'For a Few Dollars More'. Facebook had a couple of dozen Douglas Mortimers but not the Bathgate one.

Okay. I was going to have to search elsewhere for the dope on the Doug.

The Google piece on Ruzena was no more helpful. In fact, it told me less about her than her husband and her PA had. There were a couple of cheesecake photos but that was it. Anything else I found out about these two, I was going to have to find out for myself.

Just what did I know about Douglas Mortimer? Only what old Jack had told me, and what I'd learned from the man himself over the last week. In his sixties. Successful, hard worker. Limited interests other than work. No pals. Well hung. Originally from the Windyknowe area of Bathgate…

Hold hard! Windyknowe! Who did I know from Windyknowe? From Windyknowe and old enough to know and remember Douglas Mortimer? Why, none other than Andra, 'Sky Blue', Green. What this man didn't know about Bathgate and its denizens wasn't worth knowing. He'd helped me out before, had Sky Blue. A fascinating man, in his seventies by then, he suffered from the optical condition called 'macular degeneration', whereby the vision gradually deteriorates from the centre of the eye and usually results in total blindness. SB could only see from the very lower reaches of his eyes and had to tip his head up so that he could see what was directly in front of him. He saw things differently, you might say. He was a kind of role model for me, in that regard.

I checked my watch. Half past seven. It might not even be necessary for me to go to Windyknowe, though that was no distance at all. At that time of the evening, Sky Blue Green was often to be found in Mulholland's.

Na, sod it. That would keep till the next day. I still had time to call on the Polish girls. Finish the day's work, like I'd told Mortimer I would. They lived centrally. Five minutes would take me to Jana Zielinska's place in Stuart Terrace, just along the Edinburgh Road from my little cell. Radka Bartoš lived in Boghall Drive. Half an hour with each woman – my work here is over. Okay. I locked up, walked along the Edinburgh Road and was soon chapping at Jana Zielinska's door.

She was in her thirties, small and what my mother used to call 'pale and interesting'. Jana was as pale as a Victorian heroine. And as timorous. Just my presence at her door appeared to intimidate the life out of her. I had a hell of a job to persuade her that I wasn't a threat, wasn't 'after' her in some way. She couldn't understand why I was there, asking questions just like the police had done. Her English was okay; it was just her meekness that was the problem. Fortunately for her, her man was there and he was anything but meek. His English was better than the majority of Bathgate folk's. When Jana got spooked at the door, she called him. Stefan. He appeared in the doorway behind his wife and said, "What is it you want? Explain yourself."

"I'm a private investigator, sir," I said, "working for Mr. Mortimer. I only wanted to ask Jana here one or two questions, and then I'll leave you in peace."

He took my card, gave it the squinny and spoke some Polish to Jana. Then he handed it back to me. "The police have asked the questions."

The perennial retort. Occupational hazard, I guess, like having to be a selfish and acquisitive sociopath if you're a Tory. I explained that I was here to help Mr. Mortimer find his wife. They let me in and I asked Jana about Mr. Mortimer. He was a very good man. A very hard working man. What about Mrs. Mortimer? Very famous lady. Model. Very beautiful. What were they like to work for? Very nice people. Very generous. Jana really appreciated them letting her work for them. Could she tell me anything about Mrs. Mortimer that might help me find where she was? Did she have a friend, for example, who sometimes came to the house? No; no friend. It was like getting blood from a stone. I asked her about Radka. Did she get on with Radka? Yes, Radka was a very nice girl. She had been working for the Mortimers before Jana. How did Jana get the job? An advert in the paper.

I thanked them and walked along to Acredale, boarded the yacht and set sail for Boghall.

Radka Bartoš lived in the ground floor – hey! another one - of a block of flats in Boghall Drive. The tenement faced an elliptical patch of council grass. Radka was younger, maybe twenty, twenty-one. She was pretty, if that matters a fuck, but tied her hair straight back and wore no make-up, as if to downplay her prettiness. The term, 'self-effacing', might have been made for her. Her English was impeccable, but she told me no more than Jana had. The Mortimers were fine people. She'd got the job through an advert in *The Courier*. Douglas worked very hard and Ruzena was often away, modelling around the world. She could think of nothing that would help me trace the missing Roozh either. (I hadn't expected either of them to be able to do that. But that question was my only 'in' for asking stuff that might lead, via any kind of circuitous route, to information about her possibly having a lover. Hey ho. The job's like that sometimes. I thanked Radka and drove home.

It was still only nine o'clock when I sat down at my desk with Black Jack 2 on my lap, so I called Sky Blue's landline. He answered after three rings.

"Jack, how are you son?"

"Great, Sky Blue. Not drinking tonight? I thought you might be in Mulholland's. Or the Royal."

"Na, fuckin' skint, Jack. Don't have any money till the morra, so there was nae point goin' oot. Like they say, you can only pee wi' the cock you've got. What can I do for you this time?"

"Well, sir, *you're* a Windyknowe man, aren't you?"

"Aw ma days."

"So what can you tell me about Douglas Mortimer?"

"The millionaire? Nae mair than you probably know yersel, Jack. He's five or six year younger than me, so I didnae run aboot wi' him. Well, I don't think many did."

"Well, just think aloud for me. What can you remember about his younger days in Windyknowe?"

"Okey dokey. He's an only child an' his faither was a right bad article. Ran away fi Bathgate when he kent he'd got Mary Mortimer up the duff…"

"Ah, right! So Douglas was brought up by his mother only?"

"Yep. She was aff travellin' folk, I think. She worshipped that laddie. Worked in Woolies after he went to school, but had a hard time when he was just a bairn. Faither was a man called Matheson; Charlie Matheson. Belonged Belvedere, worked in Wolfe's shovel works. But, like I say, got Mary pregnant one night after a session and just scarpered. Bad get. Anyway, Mary Mortimer was as poor as a church mouse when Douglas was a kid but she scrimped and saved and sacrificed to give him everything she could. If there was something the other kids had, an' Douglas wanted it, Douglas got it. Didnae matter how expensive it was, she always found a way. Begged, borrowed or stole, I suppose."

"Or worse, maybe."

"Aye, maybe that tae, Jack. It was said once or twice aboot her. But *anythin'* the laddie wanted, he got. Mostly things likes a, say, the school camp, or the shows at the Gala Day, maybe; the pictures or a fitba' match, things like that. But his togs were ey the best a gear and they went a holiday to Whitley Bay or Scarborough every year."

"That would cost, in those days," I said.

"Ma point. She treated him the best she could. That's why Douglas worked his conkers aff when he left the school. He wanted to provide for his mammy because she had provided for him when he was a bairn. He said he was gonnae make her live like a lady."

"And did he?"

"Nah, never got the chance. Mary died when she was only in her forties. Ta'en a stroke. Douglas was beside hissel'. That's the main reason he didnae really pal aboot wi' anybody, Jack. He only had one thing on his mind – makin' money. He wanted to give his mother somethin' back for aw she done for him. It was sad, really."

"Yeah, it is."

"So what's aw this aboot, son? You helpin' the polis wi' this cairry-on at the big hoose?"

"Aye, in a way, Sky Blue. Okay, I'll let you go in a sec. Is there anything about Mortimer you can remember, anything out of the ordinary, anything unusual? In any way? I mean, did he collect anything unusual? Or do anything unusual as a hobby? Anything."

"Na. He was a borin' laddie, Jack, to be honest. He just worked. Didnae go to the dancin' or chase lassies, wasnae a great drinker, wasnae into music. Mind you, like I say, he was a bit younger than me, so I rarely had anythin' to do wi' him, you know?"

"Ah, that's grand, auld yin, thanks a lot. If anything else strikes you, give me a ring, will you?"

"Will indeed, Jack. Cheers."

Sky Blue, eh? Rare were the occasions I sought a contribution from him and came away with nothing. This was precisely what Geraldine Hunter had wanted me to find out – Mortimer's fierce devotion to his mother, his sense of gratitude for all she had done for him, his great love for her that drove him to try and elevate her out of hardship and have her 'live like a lady'. Something more than just sentiment, then. A strong sense of loyalty. Decency. Humanity. I was impressed. By Mortimer *and* by Gerry's teaching method.

But there must be something else. Ruzena Dolezal, I had no doubt, would think such qualities in her husband admirable but that would not, in itself, be sufficient grounds for her to think there was 'nobody like him'. Which was what Jennifer Kemp had said. For a wife to think there was 'nobody like' her husband took more than just his undying love for his mammy and gratitude for what she'd done for him. In my view, at least. There had to be something else. Something else which, *along with* his loyalty, his decency and his humanity, rendered him non pareil. Peerless. Unparalleled. – Or maybe Roozh had had direct experience of his humanity etc. in a different matter all together! Something different, something more personal. Oh yes! I liked that. In fact, I admired it from several different angles. I wondered what that something might have been.

I put the cat down and flexed my neck. Well, Jennifer Kemp and Geraldine Hunter had given me some powerful food for thought – as befitted the two women who knew Ruzena best. The other two had given me nothing of any substance - the two Poles, Jana Zielinska and Radka Bartoš. Not their fault, of course. Just the way it was. But disappointing, just the same. I texted Mortimer.

Spoke to all women. Need to talk to you but bushed tonight. Can I come to Dalmahoy tomorrow a.m.? Will call before. JB

He replied within a minute.

Fine. DM

I had a quiet hour or so with Phyllis, watching TV and catching up on what was happening in her world and Juliet's – the real world, in short. Then we went to bed. I read some *Julius Caesar*, just to see how accurate I'd been in Montague Street, before we clicked out our lights, kissed and turned over.

Geraldine Hunter! What a dame! Superbly done, I had to admit. I smiled with my eyes shut. And Jennifer Kemp. Loyal and true to Ruzena, both of them. Pity about the Polish girls, Zielinska and Bartoš. Just as loyal, I was sure. But more guarded. Maybe understandably. Some dick turns up at their door, shows them a card and starts asking questions when they've probably already been spooked by the police doing the same…

Wait a minute …

Bartoš …

Bartoš wasn't a Polish name.

At least, it didn't strike me as one. Granted, I'm no expert in the Polish language but that letter, that final letter, didn't look Polish to me; that 'š'. The diacritic mark on the 's' was called a 'caron', I was sure; made the 's' sound like 'sh' when pronounced. But it wasn't Polish. The 'sh' sound in Polish was represented by the digraph 'sz'. I knew that much from my dealings with all the Polish people in that carry-on the year before. So where did the name 'Bartoš' come from?

I slipped out of bed and into the study, switched the pute back on, typed 'Bartoš' into Google.

Abracadabra!

It is a Czech or Slovak name, derived from the name 'Bartholomew'. A quick search for 'Radka' truffled up the nugget that it is the feminine version of the name 'Radek', meaning 'joyful', both Slavic names common in Bulgaria, Germany and Slovakia.

Well, what do you jolly well know? The merest glimmer of why Ruzena Dolezal might think there was nobody like her husband crossed my mind. I put everything off and went back to my farter.

12

Dalmahoy is a hotel, once a country house , on the A 71near Edinburgh. Its actual address is in Kirknewton, so it goes down officially as West Lothian but it doesn't think of itself as being as common as that. Nowadays it's a hotel and 'country club' – which basically means it's polluted with golfers. The grounds are a big deal too, included in some inventory of significant national gardens. Whoopy doo. The hoose was, and still is grand, associated with the Dalrymple family, descendants of the Earl of Stair, till it was sold in the mid 18th century to the Earl of Morton. It's been extended since it was converted to a hotel. I can't be doing with it. It has pretensions to grandeur that the staff fuck up all the way along the line. But I could see why Mortimer would want to stay there. Rural and quiet. Ish. Gave him a chance to wear the breeks, cape and deerstalker he'd probably bought in Stewart Christie's.

He looked like he'd aged ten years in the twenty four hours since I'd seen him. When he met me in the foyer, he said, "Any news?" His look of savage disappointment when I had to admit that I had none, was heartbreaking. We strolled through the corridor to the Douglas Lounge.

"No wonder you like it here," I said. They've even set a lounge apart for you."

He didn't laugh. "D' you want to order mornin' coffee or somethin'?" he said. "Mind you, the service is as slow as fuck the day. Must be short staffed."

"No, you're fine," I said. "How do you find the meals and things?"

"Adequate. Na, they're fine, really. Sorry, I'm just no interested. So you've no found nothin'?"

"Nothing about Ruzena."

"No fi Kemp or the lassie Hunter? The Polish lassies?"

"Nothing about where Ruzena might be now, no."

"So what have you found oot?"

"You know the Polish girls, as you call them?"

"Aye. Have they sais somethin' aboot Roozh?"

"No. None of the women had any idea where she might be. Jennifer Kemp suggested Geraldine Hunter's place or Mestre. Geraldine Hunter suggested Jennifer Kemp's place or Mestre."

"Well, if she wisnae in Kemp's or Hunter's, you'll need ti check oot Mestre for me."

"The police will be checking Mestre. But!" I said, seeing him about to interrupt, "I can go too, hang about the area, see if there's any sign of her. First though, I need to talk to you about something."

"Aboot what?"

"The girl, Radka Bartoš, that cleans for you."

"Eh? What aboot her?"

"She isn't Polish, is she?"

"Is she no? What is she then?"

"I'm guessing, from her name, Slovakian. Both her Christian name and her surname are Slovak."

"So? Slovakian, Pole, what's the odds?"

"Slovakian," I repeated slowly and nodded meaningfully at him. "Like Ruzena."

He looked bemused. "So? There's millions a Slovaks. Like there millions a Poles."

"How did you meet her?"

"She answered an ad I put in the paper for domestic help."

"How many lassies answered the ad all together?"

"Aw fuck, I cannae mind. I interviewed five. Picked the best two."

"What kind of things did you ask them?"

"What the fuck is this, Black? What have these lassies got ti dae wi' Roozh bein' missin' an' Alex Gilmour bein' kilt in mah hoose? "

"Well, Douglas, briefly… Both Jennifer Kemp and Geraldine Hunter scoffed at the notion of Ruzena being unfaithful. Jennifer said it couldn't be true because Ruzena thinks there is nobody like you. Those are the words she used. Nobody like you. Geraldine said I had a lot to learn about Ruzena and that I shouldn't underestimate *you*. She said I had to think about that, think hard. They both meant that there were things I didn't know about you, and that maybe I should know. What do you think they meant?"

"I've nae idea. An' it's irrelevant. I need ti find oot where Roozh is. Will you go ti Mestre and see if she's there? Ye need ti go soon, the day if you can. I'm climbin' the wa's here wi' worry. Will you go? The rest can wait. I need ti know aboot Roozh."

"I'll go, I'll go."

"Good. Whatever it costs, I'll pey. D' you want ma caird?"

"No. I'll pay and you can square me up when I get back."

"Right. Brilliant. Will you go the noo, then? Jist go the noo – I'm desp'rate. We can talk aboot other shit later. I need ti find ma wife."

I shook his hand and left to try.

13

Mestre was easy enough but, as things turned out, I couldn't quite go there and then. A phone call to the Easyjet desk at Edinburgh Airport got me a flight to Marco Polo for the next day, though. Online, I contacted the boutique hotel, Antiche Figure, a little place Phyllis and I had stayed at before when we holidayed in *La Serenissima*. Once, back in the 15th century or thereabouts, the building had been a palazzo. Nowadays it's restored and full of what its literature calls 'the most modern comforts'. It was ideally situated for me, on the Fondamenta San Simeon Piccolo, next to the wee green 18th century church of the same name. A few steps away was the Piazzale Roma, the terminus for buses from Mestre and the mainland, the only stopping place of the motor vehicle in the civilisation of Venice. I got myself a room for a couple of nights. I reckoned that was more than enough to find out about Ruzena and indulge my regard for the city, and also long enough to be absent from home, wife and wean.

So, I flew out the day following, with only hand baggage. The flight to Venice Marco Polo is three and a half hours. I took my Kindle and read a detective novel. Sometimes it's good to compare fact and fiction. But it didn't stop me hating air travel. I always have. I don't care how good my reading matter is, or how tempting the food and drink, or how diverting the in-flight entertainment. I'm still stuck in a tin tube with a hundred other folk, hurtling through the air at thirty thousand feet with their combined farts and body odour being recycled endlessly through the air conditioning.

I have to say, though, that when the plane approaches Venice, the view from the right hand side of the fuselage is something well extra. You're cruising over those palazzi, churches and cathedrals with their rooftops, steeples and domes going back half the civilised era. That's quite a bird's-eye view you got there, of the Grand Canal, the inverted capital S, snaking through the floating city. Quite a startler. Almost makes the previous three and a half hours worth it.

I got a taxi from Marco Polo to the Piazzale Roma, and strolled along the Fondamenta towards the hotel in broad afternoon sunlight. I love Venice – well, I love Italy, but Venice is perhaps my favourite city in the world. And I know it's a confection, a museum piece, whatever you want to call it to underline its difference and separation from the modern world and its realities, but that's one of the main reasons I love it. No cars. That alone is special. And the history, the art, the culture that seeps from the stones into the air… Why wouldn't I like it? *La Serenissima*. The most serene one. The quietest.

Certainly, that particular fondamenta, that particular area of Santa Croce, can be bustling at times. Apart from motorised traffic's wheelprint in the Piazzale, there is the railway station of Santa Lucia directly opposite the hotel, so people are coming and going for much of the day. But everything's relative, and this *was* Venice.

I dropped my bag in the room and strolled back along the fondamenta, turned left at a footbridge into the Fondamenta Tolentini - grey flagstones, white footbridges, dark red and brown buildings and always the green canals - and strolled a bit more till I got to the Osteria ae Cravate on the Salizada San Pantalon. We'd eaten here before, Phyl and I, and I got on well with the patrone, Sigfrido. He liked that I spoke my fractured Italian to him. I liked the way he cooked. Today, there was no sign of him. Maybe too early. I ate a bog standard plate of pasta and clams, then headed off to the piazzale and caught a bus to Mestre.

Mestre is everything Venice is not: recent, industrialised, polluted and cheap. It has its attractions, though, I suppose, to be fair – the Palazzo Podestarile, for example, and the Duomo di San Lorenzo on the main square. But I wasn't interested in any sights.

The Dolezals lived in the centre of town, on a street called the Viale Giuseppe Garibaldi. I got a taxi to take me there. They lived on the first floor of a block of flats with the shape and colour of a block of strawberry ice-cream on pillars. At ground level, there was a row of shops. An art shop and a store called Benvenuti were a couple I noticed - I wasn't paying that much attention to the commercial side of things. The tenement would be shaded from the Venetian sun by the grove of mature and leafy trees outside it. I rang the Dolezals' doorbell.

A thickset man in his late forties, brick-coloured and bald, wearing a blue T-shirt and jeans, opened the door. "Si?" he said.

I said, "Cerco Ruzena Dolezal. È qui?"

The man looked at me with some distaste and said, "No, non è qui. Abita in scozia. Perché la cerca? Chi è?" Which translates as, "No, she is not here. She lives in Scotland. Why are you looking for her? Who are you?" His Italian accent wasn't much better than mine.

I told him I was a private investigator, hired by her husband to see if I could find her. He snarled that the carabinieri had been there, also trying to trace Ruzena, and that he wanted nothing to do with private investigators, whoever hired them. Then he told me to fuck off. 'Vaffanculo, pezzo di merda,' to be precise. Which literally means, 'Fuck off, you piece of shit.' No possibility of misinterpretation there.

I produced my card and tried to reason with him in my not-quite-up-to-the task Italian, but he wasn't interested. He turned and roared, "Paolo!" into the house.

Paolo appeared. In his twenties, brick-coloured and balding. In a black T-shirt and jeans. And just as thickset as the man I assumed was 'il suo padre'. Papa favoured Paolo with a rapid volley of Italian to the effect, I gathered, that this bastard – me – was pestering him and maybe they should loonder the shit out of me.

Paolo strode past his father and gave me a violent shove in the chest, knocking me backwards into the veranda's reinforced glass balustrade. "Andare e non tornare!" he spat. Then he shoved me again. "Andare e non tornare!" Go and don't come back.

"Hey!" I said. "I don't want any trouble. Non voglio nessun problema."

"Andare e non tornare!" He swung a vicious kick that only missed my ass because I skipped out of the way. "Andare e non tornare!"

"Chiamerò la polizia" I shouted. I will call the police. I retreated as I shouted, though.

"Eccelente!" spat Paolo. "Ci salvera!" Excellent. It would save them doing it.

He shoved me along the verandah. I took the hint and got off the property, through the door to the stairwell. He bade me arrivederci with a final, "Andare e non tornare!" And he slammed the stair door shut. Graceless cunt.

I knew the two of them would be watching me from the veranda when I emerged back on to Viale Giuseppe Garibaldi, so I strode purposefully away, in the direction of Via Palazzo, towards the crossroads. I could hear, "Non tornare!" in Paolo's dulcet tones as I walked. So could passing Mestrians. One or two looked up. I did too, and gave the Dolezal chaps the middle finger of my right hand as I stalked towards Via Palazzo.

A left turn headed off the street into the Piazzetta Maestri del Lavoro, so I took it, turned onto the Via San Girolamo after a while and headed south on that, parallel to Palazzo. I turned right on to the major Via San Rocco and then right again into Palazzo. Back north on Palazzo and I was back in Joe Garibaldi Street.

There was a bar cum trattoria directly opposite the flats. Eccelente, as Paolo had said. Two or three shops down, a newsagent was still open. I bought a *Corriere della Sera* and sauntered into the trattoria, ordered an espresso doppio and sat not actually *in* the window but near enough to it that I could still keep an eye on the block where the Dolezals stayed. Then I impersonated an Italian, perused the paper and sipped my java.

Every so often I flicked an eye at the flats opposite as I pretended to read. It was the quiet time of evening and little was happening, but I sat on, just to see if anything developed. I had nothing else on hand, anyway. So I kept drinking coffee, watching the tenement and pretending I understood the *Corriere*. The guy behind the counter, the 'barista', to use a word I despise, was a jovial guy who smiled a lot and was called Enzo. Short for 'Lorenzo'. The things you find out, even with limited Italian.

After a couple of hours of precisely zilcho, I decided it was time to draw stumps. I was dead beat and needed my chariot. I stood up and walked to the counter, asked Enzo if he had a number for a taxi firm. All smiles and bonhomie, he said he would call me one – where was I going? I told him to Venice. He told me to sit down and finish my mud; he would ring right away. One slurp later, he cheesed over to me and said, "All busy just now, signore, but he ring me back when ready. Is okay?"

I said it was okay and went back to my post, watched the road. Traffic was minimal but, ironically, a taxi sailed past the window as I sat. Seconds later, something happened. A car pulled up at the kerb outside the block of flats and a young man, maybe Paolo's age, got out and walked briskly into the tenement. Within seconds, he was padding along the veranda and ringing the doorbell of the Dolezals' place. Paolo emerged, swinging a jerkin on, and they left together, coming out of the street door a few seconds later and getting into the car. The new guy squealed the yoke around in a U-turn and they headed off.

Shit! If the taxi came now, I could follow them, see what was going on. I looked over my shoulder to the counter, just as the phone rang. Enzo lifted it, nodded, gabbled a volley of Italian at 78 r.p.m., and put the phone down again. He looked up, clocked my gaze, smiled and raised his hand, fingers spread. "Cinque minuti, signore!" Five minutes. I had no chance of knowing where Paolo and his associate had gone and, in five minutes, they could have gone anywhere. Looked like I would have to be back in Mestre early the following day, to check the flat again.

I got out of the cab in the Piazzale Roma and it was blue night. The Grand Canal slipped by, black and streamered with lights. I walked along the fondamenta and turned off into Tolentini again. I wanted some quality Venetian chow in the Osteria ae Cravate before I retired. It was only ten o'clock.

I love walking in the back streets of Venice at night time. Night brings back the quattrocento. You're walking through wells of darkness lit only fitfully, and that wanly, by seemingly random lamps and dimly glowing windows. The shells of buildings are dark, looming presences. The canals are smeared with pale imitations of the lights on land. Perspective melts. In the distance, lights float in the mid air. Being me, I love to imagine turning a corner and meeting Shylock wringing his hands and wailing over his ducats, or bumping into Iago, sneering his discontent. It's like in that movie with the dwarf – astonishingly, beautifully atmospheric, but vaguely menacing, too. It's so quiet that your footfalls are quite audible. And so are everyone else's.

Which was why I heard them before I saw them. As I passed the Campo, I heard footsteps coming from behind me, ringing in the little square around the church of San Nicolo. Apart from my own, there had been no sound of feet before that. It's not illegal for people to walk around the area of the church, but nevertheless, I tensed. 'Don't look back,' I told myself. I had a feeling. Just before I passed an osteria called the "Bacareto da Lele" – unfortunately for me, closed at that time – a gruff voice, heavily accented, growled, "Hey, Glasgow boy."

I spun round. Paolo and his friend. It was the friend who had spoken.

"I'm not from Glasgow," I said. "I am Scottish but not from Glasgow."

"Liar. We know where you are from and what you want."

"You know nothing about me," I started.

Started but didn't finish. Paolo made a breenge at me and I sidestepped him, shouted loudly for help – "Aiuto!" as I tried to run. And then the friend grabbed me in a bear hug and slammed me against the wall of the closed eatery. There was no-one around. I kneed him in the gumdrops and he grunted in pain but, as he let me go, Paolo weighed in with two rapid jabs to my kidney. I grunted and slumped a little. Then Paolo made the mistake of stepping in a little too close and, Glaswegian or not, I gave him a perfect Glasgow kiss: my brow introduced at speed to the bridge of his nose. He howled as his nose cracked and pished blood down his lips. The pal manfully ran at me, sore nuts or no. I stood to the side and tripped him. His stumbling momentum carried him forward and he fell into the canal. He made a surprisingly quiet little splash. More like a 'plop'. I turned and ran like the devil towards the Grand Canal. I heard Paolo shout, "Enrico!" as I pelted along the fondamenta.

Two middle-aged couples were sauntering towards me and starting to look puzzled by the rammy. I half turned as I ran, pointed back and said, "Rapinatori! Rapinatori!" Muggers.

I reached the corner with the Fondamenta San Simeon Piccolo, and immediately slowed to a walk. From here, it was a minute's walk to the hotel, and it was busier. People strolling, couples hand in hand. I walked as if I, too, was simply taking the night air. And I got to the Antiche Figure without any further incident. I said hello to the clerk on the counter and took the lift to my room. There, I ran a bath, stripped off and stretched myself out in the hot water. My kidney was still gowping, but I was safe. It was Enrico in the canal and not me; he was alive where I might not have been.

But how the fuck did they know where to find me?

I got out of the tub. Eventually. Felt a whole dig better. With one of the hotel's vast, white towels wrapped around my waist, I lay back on the bed and texted Mortimer.

Phone me as soon as.

He could afford the price of a call. It was all his bill, anyway. He rang me back in precisely two minutes.

"Black? You find her?"

"Douglas. No. But did you get a call from your in-laws tonight? Any of the Dolezals phone you, say about seven o'clock your time?"

"No. Why?"

"You sure? Paolo or his old man didn't ring to see if you'd hired a private eye?"

"Naw. I told you, their English isnae that great. So you spoke ti them?"

"Aye. I was at the flat in Garibaldi Street. I spoke to her old man. At least, I take it it was her old man. Stocky bastard, bald?"

"Aye, that's Tomas."

"Right. He told me the police had been there asking about Ruzena and he didn't want to speak to a private eye. He called me a piece of shit and then he shouted on Paolo. Paolo came to the door, shoved me around a bit and then told me to fuck off and not come back."

"Aye, sounds like Paolo."

"But they never phoned to check my story?"

"I tellt ye. Naw. Did they no say anythin' aboot Roozh?"

"Tomas told me she wasn't there; she lived in Scotland. But listen. I sat in a caff for a couple of hours and cased the place. Paolo fucked off in a car with a mate. I had no idea where he'd gone at the time, but I found out. When I got back to Venice, the two of them jumped me in a quiet back street. Paolo's got a broken nose and the other cunt went in the canal. I was wondering how they knew where to get me."

"Naeb'dy phoned me, Black, I'm tellin' ye."

"All right. One more thing and then I'm getting some kip. I might try and get back tomorrow. The thing that intrigued me is, when they jumped me, it was the other one who spoke. He said, 'Hey, Glasgow boy.' Not 'Hey, Scottish boy.' Glasgow. Who the fuck mentioned Glasgow? I certainly never did. I told Tomas I was hired by you. He would likely know from my accent that

I'm from the same neck of the woods as you, anyway. But not Glasgow. I never mentioned fucking Glasgow. Why would he make that assumption? I'm beginning to smell something I don't like, Mr. Mortimer. Any thoughts on that?"

After a pause, he said, "Come home, Black. I need ti tell you something. No now, no over the phone. There's something you should know."

"Something you could have told me yesterday, obviously."

"It was mair important you try an' find Roozh."

"I'll be in Scotland tomorrow."

"Aye, well, I've cancelled Canterbury for this week comin'. It was just dull shit anyway."

I hung up and tossed the phone aside. I knew it! I knew there was something iffy about Radka Bartoš, for a start. Now the Glasgow reference. That was a weird one. But the Dolezals hadn't checked on me with Mortimer. How did they know where I was billeted …?

Ah! Enzo the smiler. One may smile and smile and be a villain. I knew not how, but he was working with the Dolezals. Now. I thought it out slowly. I'd sat in the trattoria, reading the paper and drinking the coffee, for about two hours. Nothing happened. It was only when I'd asked Enzo about a taxi that Enrico the Wet came calling at Casa Dolezal and whipped Paolo away. And where were they going? Venice. For why? To boot the shit out of me. And how did they know I was going to Venice? Because I'd told Enzo. Plain as your Auntie Beenie. I'd no idea how the Dolezals got word to Enzo to keep cavey on me, nor how Enzo had told them my destination but it had been done. I assumed Enzo had called Tomas and Paolo before he called the cab.

And now, *now*, Mortimer says he has something to tell me. *Now*, when I'm a thousand and a half miles away. Fucking pillock. All right, sod Mestre, I'd be at Marco Polo in the a.m. just as betimes as I could manage it. And I'd prop a chair up under the door handle that night, just in case Enrico got out of the canal, patched up Paolo's neb and they both came in quest of me.

They didn't.

14

You'd think, wouldn't you, that, if there was a seat on the flight out of Marco Polo that afternoon, and I wanted it, that would be a perfect fit. Na; doesn't happen like that with airlines. There *was* a flight to Edinburgh that afternoon, and there *was* a vacant seat on it. The problem, apparently, was that I had a return ticket for the day after. So, the obvious thing, I told the woman at the desk, was to let me fly to Edinburgh that day and let her try to fill my booked seat the following day. Twenty four hours' grace. Maybe somebody would need to get to Edinburgh the next day? Well, they could have my seat. Worked out all round. Except it didn't. My first problem was that it was a different price to fly that day as compared to the following. Moreover, I wasn't an EasyJet Plus flier. Apparently, if you're one of them, you can do anything. Carte blanche. Carta bianca. Presumably, you can sit up front with the driver and screw the air hostess of your choice, if you want. If I'd been an EJP, I could have taken the seat on the flight for a minimal change fee. I think. You see, my Italian wasn't really up to all of the detailed jargon she was spouting, and my patience was wearing very thin. Eventually, I just bought the single ticket I had to, and added it to Mortimer's bill. That klutz was the reason I was having to do this anyway.

We took off and the city of my dreams sank away from us as we climbed into the air. This time, I didn't bother with the Kindle. I was too busy wondering just what Douglas Mortimer was up to. What had he to tell me? And why couldn't he just have told me before I flew out to Italy? Or, maybe *instead of* flying out to Italy? Because, since my conversation with him the previous night, I was starting to suspect I had been shunted offstage for some reason. What that reason might be, I could not imagine, but the possibility that I had been stiffed remained a distinct one. His anxiety to have me establish whether Ruzena was in Mestre had seemed logical and natural at the time. Was there something ulterior, though? I guessed it all depended on what he had to say to me. And I could not think what that might be.

Except that Radka Bartoš was party to it; I was certain of that. Mortimer's reaction when I mentioned her Slovakian nationality, a nationality she shared with Ruzena, had been pure bluster. A snow job. Wherever Radka fitted into the nature of things, Mortimer hadn't wanted to discuss it with me. The fact that Ruzena was still missing simplified matters for him. He wanted me to check out Mestre. The fact he'd asked me before that night made it less of an obvious ploy, but a ploy it was, notwithstanding. I thought that then and I saw it now. Ah well, I'd find out in a few hours' time. Hey ho.

Anyway, more importantly, where *was* Ruzena? Was she safe? And had she killed Alex Gilmour?

The flight passed. They generally do, although my temper is never sweet by the time they're done. I cleared customs, walked briskly to the car park, picked up the yoke and headed west for south and Dalmahoy.

I bit Mortimer with my blue tooth on the way, told him I'd be there in thirty. So, once I had parked the car and when I walked in under the porte-cochere of the Dalmahoy, he was there to greet me.

"Let's dae this ootside," he said. "It's a braw day for it."

I smouldered but said, "All right."

We walked round the building and out into the significant gardens, well out of earshot. He put his hands up and dipped his head deferentially. "All right, I know. I'm a cunt."

"Thine own lips have said it."

"I ken what you must think a me."

"Bet you don't. All right, so what do you have to tell me?"

"Come over there and sit on the balcony. Naeb'dy will hear us."

We did. I said, "Okay, Douglas, what's the story?"

He sniffed. "What do you know about human trafficking, Black?"

I shook my head. "That it exists. Not much more than that."

"Never come across it in your line of work?"

"Actually, I have, now that you mention it. A few years ago now. An elderly London couple asked me to try and trace their daughter. She'd been missing for over twenty years. Went missing up here. I found her. She'd been abducted and forced to live as a slave by a Lithuanian couple. They lived in the countryside between Blackburn and Longridge."

"I remember that in the papers. Mind a your name too. First time I heard it."

"Well, that's the extent of my knowledge. Why do you ask?"

He ignored the question. "Would you say there's a lot ae it aboot? Here in Scotland? In the UK, even?"

"I have no idea, Douglas. What's this all about?"

He sniffed again. "Well, sir, I have a *good* idea; a *very* good idea. I ken what I'm talkin' aboot. There's an abundance ae it in Scotland. Must be thousands a folk trafficked for wan reason or another. Labour – slavery, like the lassie you mentioned. Sex. Beggin'. Sellin' organs. You wouldnae believe the extent ae it. Thing is, though, it's no a case a folk bein' snatched aff the streets in Africa or India and brought ower here against their will. Maist a the folk it happens ti, they come willin'ly. An' how is that? Because they're sellt a dream. A dream ae a better life. But nothin' fancy, nothin' like *we* would call a dream life. They're just lookin' for a decent hoose and a reas'nable income. But they get ti here an' their documents are aw ta'en aff them. So they cannae move. They're kept in appallin' conditions mair often than no, an' they're no given the kind a job they were expectin'. They're slaves, like the lassie you dealt wi." He stopped and shook his head, sniffed again. He was close to being emotional. "Damnable work, entirely."

I just said, "Yeah. Must be." I wanted him to go on. There was something hefty on his mind he had to shift.

He said, after a few seconds. "But most a the folk that's trafficked ti Scotland arenae fi Africa or India or places like that. Maist a them are fi Eastern Europe. Romania. The Czech Republic. An' Slovakia."

"Right."

"There a city in Slovakia cried Kosice. You heard ae it?"

"Yeah."

"Well, there a part a Kosice, a ... suburb, cried Lunik IX. An' this place seems ti be a shanty town, a hellhole aw thegither. Folk's packed inti it like rats. The hooses are shite. There nae gas, water or electricity. Or nearly nane. Because the folk's got fuck all ti pay for them wi. Unemployment's nearly a hunner per cent. An' the folk's health is just the pits. They've got... hepatitis, T.B., meningitis ... Christ knows whit aw. An' naeb'dy gives a flyin' fuck aboot these folk. For the simple reason that maist a them is Roma. What we used to cry 'gypsies'. Know what I mean?"

I said I did. For, certainly, Roma people have been marginalised and maltreated for most of history. Hitler was reputed to have exterminated half a million of them in the 1930s.

"So," Mortimer continued, "you can see that folk in Lunik IX would be desperate ti get oot. They would jump at any chance ti try an' make a life for theirsel's somewhere else. Stands ti reason. An' that's where the traffickers come in. They offer folk the chance ae a better life in the UK, and that's somethin' they folk could only dream aboot. So they jump at the chance. An' they get trafficked."

"You've obviously studied this a lot," I said.

He shook his head again. "Wheesht the now, Black," he said. "Just let me tell ye."

I sat back. "Sorry. Go ahead."

"I got tellt aboot a guy fi Slovakia – no Lunik IX, I'll come back ti that – but a guy fi a place called Modra. He answered an online ad for a job as a waiter in a restaurant in London. He phoned up and the guy promised him a great life in London. But first he had ti front up wi ten grand for travel and accommodation and things like that. So he borrowed it fi a moneylender in Slovakia. Well, ye ken what's comin'. He got fuck all job as a waiter. He got flung inti a hovel wi five other guys, an' he had to dae gardenin', handyman stuff, paintin' an' decoratin' – whatever the bastard that was in charge a him told him. An' the cunt kept his visa an' papers an' stuff. An' the poor sod got paid fuck all. Fed twice a day, that was what he got. The cunt that put him through it aw got done, though, for traffickin', an' got sent ti jile. But the guy that was trafficked's nae better aff. He still hasnae a job an' he cannae go hame ti Modra because the moneylender's lookin' for his dosh. Boy'll get filled in. That's the kinda cunts we're talkin' aboot here."

"Sure."

"But, ti get back ti Lunik IX. The vast majority a folk trafficked fi there is young lassies. An' wheens a them gets brought ti Glasgow an' they take pairt in sham marriages wi Asian men, men a loat aulder than theirsels." He stopped. This was obviously a big deal to him. But I'd gathered that already. I'd never heard him wax so voluble about a serious topic before. "The trafficker – usually somebody they ken, by the way! – buys local Roma girls and flogs them on ti Asian gangs in Glasgow. You know why these bastards want the sham marriage, eh?"

"Because the so-called husband can apply for British citizenship," I said, "if he's married to an EU citizen."

"Zackly. Mibbies Brexit'll pit a stoap ti that, but we need ti wait and see. But, the now, these cunts can become British because they're merrit ti a lassie fi the EU. They need ti stey merrit for five year – that's how long they've got ti be resident afore they get a passport. Soon as the bloke's got the passport – divorce. An' what happens ti the lassie then? Sexual exploitation. The trafficker tries ti maximise his profit, so the lassie's forced inti prostitution. Same wi younger lassies – therteen, fourteen. They traffick theym an' prostitute them. Bairns, man! Bairns. These bairns git ti UK an' they're locked up, raped, thumped, humiliatit... They have ti have sex wi mibbies five , six, seven aulder men a night. Then, in the mornin', they have ti clean the place, make breakfast for the bastart that's keepin' them, be nice to the traffickers. It's a fuckin' scandal, man. That's what women is trafficked for. Sex. 'Fact, it's sex when they're young; then it's slave labour when they're aulder; an', if they git to auld age, it's forced beggin'. An' a lot a these lassies are fi Slovakia."

"Like Ruzena," I said. "She's from Kosice, originally."

"Aye."

"But she wasn't ..."

"Naw, she was one a the lucky wans. She spent maist a her girlhood in Italy."

"But Radka Bartoš wasn't. Am I right?"

He looked at me. His eyes were moist. Then he nodded. "Aye. Radka was trafficked. Fi Lunik IX. Jist acause she's Roma."

He shook his head in disgust. I let him be for a moment or two.

"It's a scandal, right enough, Douglas," I said. "In fact, it's an atrocity. 'The evil that men do', as Antony says. But why have you told me all this? I'm assuming that you rescued Radka?"

He sniffed and nodded. "Aye. She's the cousin a one a the drivers in Edinburgh. Stewart, the manager, told me Silvester had been upset about his wee cousin coming to Glasgow.

Thought she was gettin' a job in a supermarket but they never heard fi her. Ach, long story short, I made one or two inquiries, fund oot she was bein' kept in Ardbeg Street in Govanhill. Went there. Guy wanted ten grand for her, said she was supposed ti be marryin' a guy fi Bangladesh. I paid him the money, got the lassie free. Noo she lives oot in Boghall and cleans for me. She's as happy as a pig in shit, and the family are tae."

I smiled at him. "Good for you," I said. "That was a humanitarian thing to do."

"Aye," he said on an inward breath. "Aye. Radka was the first."

15

I was stunned. Genuinely. I had known that Mortimer had something major to tell me, just by the fact that he was so clued up on the topic. His rescue of Radka Bartoš had been a genuinely impressive revelation. I had seen where he was going just at the end of his narrative. But that there were others … !

"The first?" I said. "Fucksake, Douglas, are you telling me you've saved more folk than just Radka?"

He told me the second part of his story in a much more matter-of-fact manner. Evidently all the emotion was now under control. He said he had spoken to the guy Silvester when Radka was liberated. After the profuse thanks and the protests that they would find a way to pay him back, Silvester told him, in response to Mortimer's question, that the problem was rife in Slovakia, particularly in the Roma community of Lunik IX, and that young girls were the most lucrative humans to be trafficked – for obvious reasons. He told Mortimer that these lassies were bid for at auctions by rival gangs; that the girls were paraded naked and obliged to have sex with one of the traffickers so that all could see how good she was at it. Price was determined on a combination of factors: age; appearance (voluptuous bodies were at a premium because they were so rare), even whether a girl was a virgin or not. The price generally was around two or three thousand Euro. The girl might have been 'married' off to an Asian chancer looking for UK citizenship or, even more commonly, whatever lie she was told as a lure, she ended up in prostitution.

Mortimer told me he was shocked to the core by Silvester's revelations. What could he do to help? Silvester said there was little he could do – the girls were so many, what could one man do, no matter how rich, no matter how well-intentioned? Mortimer told him he would do whatever he could. There was a lot more jaw-jaw but the upshot was that Silvester had family still living near Lunik IX. If they had any fears over a particular girl being trafficked, they would tell Silvester and Mortimer would see what he could do to get her free. Buy her from them, basically. And that's what happened. Through Silvester's family connections, they got a guy called Grigor from Kosice to bid for four separate girls on four separate occasions. All were liable to be carted off to the iffy nuptials scenario – maybe in Glasgow; maybe elsewhere in the UK . Mortimer bought them all, brought them over here and made sure they were established safely, well away from Glasgow – two in London, two in Birmingham.

"Over how long a period of time?" I said.

"Radka was … five year ago noo."

"It all must have cost you a bit," I said.

"Twinty-odd thousand," he said dismissively. "Peanuts ti me. But it means these lassies ha' been saved from all the garbage they would have faced. I just wish I could save more."

I was moved – and flabbergasted - by the generosity and humanity of this man whom I had previously, if I'm honest, scorned a little. But I saw completely now what Mesdames Kemp and Hunter had meant. Why Ruzena thought there was nobody like him. Why I had had a lot to learn about him. I was, however, still a little puzzled as to his motivation. It couldn't simply be because they shared a nationality with his wife.

"Jeez, I don't know what to say, Douglas," I told him. "That's quite a story." And then I knew. Something Sky Blue had said just came back to me. "You try to help these lassies because your mother was Roma, wasn't she?"

He looked at me and nodded. "Aye. 'Mary the Gipsy', they used ti cry her. When they were bein' nice. Gipsy. Gippo. Tink. Pikey. Folk can be awfu' cruel. If I can spare half a dozen or a dozen lassies what my mother went through, I will."

"I think that's one of the *noblest* things I've ever heard. And that's not a word you'll hear me use much. Noble is what it is, though. You've rocketed in my estimation, Mr. Mortimer. I don't know that there is *no*body like you, but there's precious few. But, am I also right in thinking that this has got you into some bother and that that's why you're so concerned for Ruzena's disappearance?"

"Zackly that, Black. You see, it's organised crime that's at the back ae aw this. In Slovakia *and* here in Glasgow. There's Asian gangs in Glasgow that organise the marriage farces. I'm thinkin' they'll no be too happy if they've got word that somebody's buyin' lassies that they could be exploitin'. The money they make oot a these lassies is phenomenal, so they'll no tolerate anybody interferin', I wouldnae think. I'm feart that some gang in Glasgow has got wind a this and managed ti trace it back ti me. I heard last week that Silvester's contact in Kosice, Grigor, the guy who did aw the biddin' for me, got a hell of a beatin' up. Last I heard, he was still unconscious."

"Have you told the police?"

"Naw!" he said. "Naw, I want as little folk as possible ti ken aboot this. That's why I never tellt you eether. Then you sayed aboot the guy in Venice callin' you 'Glasgow boy' an' Ah kent. Kent as sure as day. Some Glasgow gang's efter me. An' they ken aw aboot me. Ken I'm mairried ti Roozh, ken she's fi Mestre. They've been there lookin' for her."

"Are you thinking that somebody like that has come here on Thursday night to harm Ruzena – kidnap her, maybe? – and killed Alex Gilmour in the process?"

"Jist that. She's no here an' we've heard nothin' *fae* her. I'm worried sick."

"So we have to tell Emma Wood, Douglas," I said. "This is a police job, mate. You need the resources that they have at their disposal. And you and I start right now by calling your in-laws in Mestre and establishing just what's happened over there."

"I've told ye. They've got nae English, an' I cannae speak anythin' else. I can only communicate wi them through Roozh."

"Well, today you communicate with them through me. My Italian's about as good as Tomas's. Maybe Paolo speaks it better. You phone and hand over to me. We'll find out what the Glasgow connection is there, and whether they know where Ruzena is. Then we phone Emma Wood."

So we did. Mortimer rang the Dolezals at Mestre, said hello to Tomas and said he had a friend to speak to him before he handed the phone to me. I introduced myself again. Got called a piece of shit again, for what I'd done to Paolo. I told Tomas that, maybe if Paolo and his mate hadn't jumped me, it wouldn't have happened. I asked him if he knew where Ruzena was; Douglas was very worried. He said he didn't and that *he* was very worried. Before I came calling, two Scotsmen had turned up at the house in the Viale Giuseppe Garibaldi, saying they were from Glasgow and had business with Ruzena's husband, but neither he or Ruzena were at home in Scotland. Were they holidaying with the family in Mestre? Or, if Ruzena was there, did she know where her husband was? Tomas might not have been the cutest pair of knickers in the drawer but he was instantly suspicious that these fuckers meant no good to either Mortimer or Ruzena. He said Ruzena was not in Mestre, nor did he know where she was. The Weegies had hummed and hawed but had eventually split.

I asked him if they were Muslim. Well, I knew the word, 'musulmano', and didn't know the term for 'Asian' or 'Pakistani'. They were white Scotsmen. Then Tomas asked *me* where Ruzena was; did I know whether she was safe or not. I told him the state of things but that Mortimer was involving the police. Tomas was a bit more gracious when he hung up than he had been at the start of the conversation.

I gave the phone back to Mortimer. He switched it off and said to me, with a look of real worry, "Have they kidnapped her, do you think, Black? Or, fucksake, even worse?"

I said, "No. I think that's very unlikely, for the simple reason that Ruzena is too high profile a person for them to do that."

"They'll be thinkin' that's a guid thing, though," he said. "They could get millions out a me, through it. Blackmail. Easy dough."

"It's possible," I said, "but unlikely. The publicity would be immense and that's the last thing these people would want. If it *is* a Glasgow gang, like you think, they may well want some compensation – they may even fancy a wee slice or two of revenge. But taking Ruzena would swing a spotlight on them that they'd much rather do without. That's how I see it."

"Where the fuck is she, then? What's happened ti her?"

"I think she lit out because whoever topped Gilmour has been bothering her. Threats, maybe. More likely, vague insinuations about they would do to you, questions about you, things like that. I mean, I take it she knows all about what you've done for these lassies?"

"Oh aye, everythin'. We spoke aboot that a long time at the *Scotsman* do."

"I think they've started bugging her, maybe as a ploy to get to you. And, now that I think of it, I think *that's* what's been on her mind this last wee while. Why she's been different. What's been on her mind is concern for you, not the fact she's shagging somebody else."

The look on his face was childishly hopeful. "You think so?" he said.

Instantly, I was ashamed of all my cynicism about how Mortimer and Ruzena had become a couple. You'll remember it, I'm sure – the opening chapter is full of it. All those jokes about him being as thick as shit in the neck of a bottle, having a brain like a nematode worm, of being just a dunderheid from Windyknowe; of how curious it was (nudge, nudge; wink, wink) for a beautiful young model to fall for a graceless old guy from Bathgate with only several million quid to recommend him; of how they'd met and pound signs had lit up above Ruzena's head; about how they had absolutely nothing in common; of her letting him screw her – job done, married in no time.

Geraldine Hunter had been on the money (sorry for the pun). Douglas Mortimer was a man with depths. He was a decent, humanitarian bloke who had liberated five young women from a fate worse than death. Unlike many millionaires, he did not hesitate in using some of his money to help others. And he had kept all this under wraps for the five years he had been doing it. His motivation? Apart from just helping unfortunates, he wanted to do something in memory of his beloved mother. And he helped some people, representatives of whose race were the worst treated in world history.

This was why a glamorous young model, from roughly the same part of the world as those women he rescued, if not from the same background, had fallen for him, thought there was 'nobody like him'. I was beginning to think that way myself. I'm not the kind of person who prejudges people normally, who has preconceptions about someone because of their background. I know we're all unique; my old man dinned that into me over the years. But, well, we all fuck up from time to time. I've been wrong about folk before. Just never quite *this* wrong. But I was happy to be wrong, in Mortimer's case. And his absolute devotion to his young wife, as just revealed by his juvenile hope that I'd been right in saying she'd been 'different' because she was worried for him, sealed it all for me. I'd have done anything for such a guy.

"I think it's the likeliest scenario," I said. "Now. We need to call DI Wood."

Emma was as thrilled as you might imagine. She had been on the point of lowsing until she took my call. She and Jim Bryce came out to Dalmahoy before they made their way home.

She listened in silence in Mortimer's suite as I introduced his story for him, editing and polishing the delivery, before allowing him to deal with the salient points. Thereafter, I took over again and finished up with my trip to Mestre, and my phone call to Tomas and the story of the Glasgow boys.

She breathed heavily down her nostrils. "God almighty!" she hissed. "Why didn't you tell us this three days ago, Mr. Mortimer? Three days! Three days in which we might have found your wife. What were you thinking?"

"I wis thinkin' I wanted Black here ti get ti Mestre and see if Roozh was there. That wis ma thinkin'. It seemed ti me that that was the obvious place for her ti be. Apart fi that, I didnae think aboot it bein' tied up wi' the traffickin' thing in any wey. No till jist recently. It jist never occurred ti me. I've eywis tried ti prevent anybody kennin' aboot this stuff aboot savin' the lassies because I didnae want any fuss wi folk thankin' me or sayin' what a great guy I wis for daein' it. Far less, bad feelin or revenge comin' ma way."

"All right," said Emma, "we start now and hope it's not too late. First, I need the name and address of the man you spoke to to get Radka liberated."

"He wis cried Bashir Ahmed," said Mortimer. "I met him in Ardbeg Street in Glasgow. I don't know if that was where he lived. I hae ma doots. It looked kinda threadbare for a guy a his means. Or what I took ti be his means."

"Would you recognise him if you saw him again?"

"Defin*ai*tely."

Jim got that down in his PDA.

"Right. That's where we start from in Glasgow. And we'll have to get the Italian guys to call on the Dolezals again."

Jim said, "Sounds, ma'am, like the Dolezals are do-it-yourself kinda guys, judging from Jack's experience."

"Well, the Italians can get more detail of the Glaswegians from them."

"The intermediary guy in Kosice as well, Em," I said. "Supposing he's well enough to be questioned, he might come up with something useful."

"Good point, Jack. Right." She heaved a huge sigh. "We'll get on with this first thing tomorrow. I hope, for everybody's sake, Mr. Mortimer, that we haven't prejudiced a good outcome by delaying so long."

"What about the murder?" I asked her. "Any news on that front?"

"Come with us, Jack. I'll speak to you outside."

"Sure."

"But come back, Black," said Mortimer. "Will ye?"

"Sure."

"Oh, one thing that will please you, Mr. Mortimer," said Emma. "Your home will no longer be a crime scene by tomorrow. The team have worked extremely long and hard to get it all done. You should be able to return home by noon."

"Aw, that's great news, hen. Inspector, I mean."

Outside, standing by the police car, Emma said to me, "What the *fuck* were you thinking about, Jack?"

"Woah, woah, woah," I said. "I only found out about the trafficking thing and the Glaswegians tonight. That was a complete revelation to me. That's when I told him that he had to tell you all that shit. I had to go to Mestre for him, try and find Ruzena."

"Why did he start telling you this, then? There had to be a reason, a prompt."

"Yeah. There was. The girl, Radka, was the prompt. That's not a Polish name, Bartoš; it's Slovakian. That's where the whole thing started. I thought there might be a connection with Ruzena and when I brought the subject up on Saturday, he blustered and said Mestre was a priority. I get to Mestre and the Glasgow boy thing happens as they try to weigh me in. When I mention it to Mortimer, he tells me to come back. He's got something I have to hear. And that was it. I'm being straight with you. I called you guys right away."

"All right, Jack. It's a great thing to have done and I can see why he might not want it talked about but, fuck! When your wife goes missing after your handyman's found murdered in your kitchen? You not think that might have crossed his mind?"

"Not before tonight for me," I said. "Mortimer says not for him at first either."

"Yeah, I guess," she said. "Okay. We're onto this tomorrow. Be seeing you."

"Aye, see you, Jack," said Jim.

"Sure to."

I went back in and Mortimer was sitting in the chair with his head in his hands. He must have heard me enter again for he said, without looking up, "What have I done? What the fuck have I done? What a stupid bastard."

"You're anything but *that*," I said.

"If anything's happened ti her, it's aw my fault."

"Nothing's your fault. You're a thoroughly decent man, a philanthropist for fucksake, who didn't realise what the right thing to do *was*. If anything has happened to her – *if*, mind – it's other people's fault. But hey. We don't know that anything has, yet. Have you tried to contact her recently?"

He took his hands away and looked up. "Ev'ry hour *on* the hour. Ring her and text her."

"Here's a suggestion. Text her and suggest, if she's having any difficulty, to contact *me*."

"What guid wid that dae?"

"Who knows? Worth a try. And tomorrow we'll see how the police investigation goes."

He pulled his phone out and did a slow Dance of the Thumbs. "Right. That's me sent it. Doot if it'll make ony diff'rence, though."

"Chin up," I said. "You be all right here tonight?"

"As aw right as I've been this far."

"Good. Home tomorrow. That's a positive. Call me if there's any problem."

"I will. You're a good man, Black."

"We're both good men, Douglas. There's no many o' us left."

"Here. I near forgot." He lifted a thick brown envelope from a small table. "Yer expenses this far."

"I haven't asked for anything yet."

"I'm aware a that."

"It looks like far too much," I said. "How much is there?"

"Five thoosant."

"What!!! Far too much."

"Take it. Venice isnae cheap. Ye've earned it an' mair. Get Roozh back for me an' it'll be a life changin' amount ye get. An' I'm *no* jokin'! Noo, git hame to your wee faimly."

I drove to the office and put Mortimer's packet of money – a hundred Bank of Scotland £50 notes – in the safe till I could bank it the following day. Then I drove home for some down time with the ones I loved. But I was determined to do what I could to find Ruzena for Mortimer. He was a good man, and he loved her. Easy as that. One two three.

16

Next morning, I sat in my little hutch above Cho's Chinese Takeaway with a cafetiere of the finest Jamaican mud, whirled my fidget spinner and thought hard about how to find Ruzena Mortimer. I was missing something, surely. For her just not to be there when Mortimer got home, and for her not to get in touch… There was something obvious about that – maybe even glaring – but I wasn't seeing it. I was convinced she wasn't dead; that wasn't it. Like I'd said to her husband, she was too well-known for the baddies to risk anything like that. So… what? There were no three Cluedo cards that said, 'Bad Glaswegian bastard, with the candlestick, in the library.' You could put the Black Baby money on that. Even though there had been, 'Some cunt unknown, with a sharpening steel, in the kitchen.' Made no difference. Ruzena wasn't dead.

And no way had it been Roozh who iced Alex Gilmour. That idea just whited out in every colour on the chart. So… if not her, somebody else – for the moment, it didn't matter who, precisely. And had that somebody else abducted her? It seemed the obvious suggestion. But no… That didn't gel either. She had her passport and her phone with her, which suggested to me a degree of planning. Something she would not have had time for if she was kidnapped. Well… Unless the kidnapper(s) intended to take her abroad. Like to Mestre. But no; no. I'd seen her home to Manderley on the Wednesday night and kept a weather eye on the place for all of Thursday and there had been no sign of her. I came back to what I'd thought before: something or someone had made her decide to get the fuck out. Therefore, she must have had a reason – threats maybe. So. That's the premise I would work on. She had to have packed and gone by herself before the intruder arrived and certainly long before the murder took place.

But, if that was the case, why hadn't she told Mortimer where she was going and why? And why had she switched off the CCTV? That was a poser. I slipped me a slug from the wonderful mug. Waiter, waiter, percolator. Savoured the roll of coffee round my mouth. Ah! Dat am de stuff. All right; okay. She hadn't told Mortimer because it would have been dangerous to do so; and probably because she'd been warned not to. In fact, it *had* to be because she'd been instructed not to. Some threat against her husband. Close circuit TV for the same reason. Had to be that – it was the only way the long division worked out with no remainder.

You'd think, though, that she'd call him once she was established safely wherever she had headed, wouldn't you? Obvious thing to do. 'Hallo, darling, sorry I got outa there like shit out a goose but the reason was…' Similarly, if Douglas was distracted enough to be calling and texting her every hour on the hour, why in the name of Launcelot Gobbo wasn't she answering?

Because she was being prevented from doing so?

But that flew in the face of my near certainty that she had scarpered early and alone. So it had to be that she had been warned before; threatened – or, *better*, that threats had been made about what might happen to Mortimer if she told him what was going on.

Aye; I liked that.

I sat and poured me a new shot from the cafetiere, thought long and hard. Was there any other reason she could be blanking DM's phone contact? Nothing came to me. So. Had to be. Had to.

However, this was an intelligent and resourceful woman who thought there was nobody like her man. She loved him; she had excellent reasons to love him as a human being as well as a husband. And she had had time before she left. Therefore, she would have left behind some kind of communication, no matter how cryptic. Bet your sweet ass she would.

Where, though?

Where else?

The house. The big hoose. Manderley. That was where Mortimer had been returning to, from his jaunt to Birmingham; that was where any message would be. Sure as fishes swim and birds do fly. Sure as the Devil's in London.

In her rooms? The most obvious place. But the polis had checked there. Shirley Honeyman went through them with Douglas. Somewhere else? The lounge? The kitchen? There had been a lot of activity in the kitchen that night. His rooms? The bathroom? Hell, the SOCO team would have searched the whole house.

Fuck it. So would I.

I put my mug of java on the desk and dialled Mortimer .

"Black? I'm just gettin' ready to drive back ti Manderley."

"Call me Jack, will you?"

"Aye, of course, if you wahnt. Didnae like ti. I thought maybe you'd think it was cheek."

"Bollocks. Okay if I come over to Manderley?"

"I'm no there yet."

"No, I know. Text me when you're home, would you?"

"Aye."

" I want to look over the house, see if Ruzena left any clues. I know the police have done that, before you say it, but I should have a looksee too. I look differently from the cops. That all right?"

"Come over. I'll text ye when I get there."

I started in Ruzena's suite of rooms. Her bedroom looked like it was ready to be photographed for a magazine. The bed was made up and the place was spotless. I slipped on a pair of surgical gloves and went through the drawers in her dressing-table, with Mortimer's permission. Nothing of note, apart from the fact she liked ordinary M&S knickers. I was getting to like this couple more and more. There was nothing in the bathroom cabinet bar toiletries and cosmetics. I spent more time in the sitting room. A copy of Daphne du Maurier's *Rebecca* was beside the pile of magazines on the table. I lifted it up.

"She's been reading some literature recently, anyway," I said.

Mortimer looked at the book. "That?" he said. "Naw, that was on ma desk in ma office. I fund it there the night a the … business, y'know? I wondert why Roozh had pit it there. I just brought it back up here."

"But that's significant," I said. "Did you not think it was meant to tell you something? Because it is. Why would she leave a book like this in your office except to mean something?"

"Mah mind just disnae work like that," said Mortimer.

I waved it in Mortimer's face. "Christ, Douglas," I said, "it's *Rebecca*. You must see that this is meant to tell you something. *Rebecca*? The novel the film was made from? The house in the book is called *Manderley*. It has to be a clue she's left us."

"What clue?"

"I don't know just now. I only read it once, years ago. Can I hang on to this?"

Mortimer shrugged. "Sure."

I said, "I'll read it later. I don't know exactly what she meant but I'll get it." I opened the book. It was an old paperback, a 1986 reprint that she had evidently bought in a second hand bookshop because the flyleaf bore the price, '50p', in pencil. It was a fair while since I'd read it. But it had to be important.

I went through the rooms downstairs too, until I came to his office. By God, but it was a stark and joyless wee room. I couldn't help compare it to my study at home. Not fair, I told myself; you're two different people. Desk, chair, PC, table, cupboard. I was aware of Mortimer sliding open the drawers in the desk for me. I was looking at the chalkboard, thinking. He straightened up and became aware of my silence. "Aw right?" he said.

"You going to Paris this week?" I said. "Or sometime soon?"

"Paris? Naw, how?"

I nodded at the board. It was as it had been the last time I saw it, with one exception. Beneath 'London' and 'Canterbury', over the smudged cuffwork the name was no longer 'Birmingham' but 'Paris'. I'd never actually seen anyone's eyes grow as large as Mortimer's did. He said, "Jesus Christ! I never seen that. I've never peyed any attention …"

"There's the clue I'm looking for," I said. "That's not your writing, is it? It has to be Ruzena's."

"Aye, it's hers. When wid she dae that?"

"Well, it has to be before she left. Does Paris have any special significance for you two?"

"Eh? Aye. Oh aye. We've been three or four times. Roozh loves it, the hotel we go ti, there. Hotel du Louvre."

"Place André Malraux," I nodded.

"You ken it?" said Mortimer.

"I know where it is," I said. I've never stayed there. Too dear for a private eye."

"You think that's where she might be?"

"There's a bloody good chance. Anywhere else in Paris important to you?"

"Well, we like lots a places in the city. But the hotel's why we go, really. Sentimental attachment, I suppose."

"Well," I said, "sentimental or not, that's the clue we need. I suspect the book is another one but I can't work out why at the moment. Where did you find it?"

"There, in the middle a the desk. Right bang in the middle."

"So you couldn't miss it. Did it never *strike* you…?" I said.

"Never," Mortimer shook his head. "Sorry. I just thought she must a been readin' it an' left it doon. Absent minded, like."

I nodded. "Any chance a makin' us a coffee?" I said.

Over a coffee, in the lounge/drawing room, I listened to Mortimer talk of how he and Ruzena had gone to Paris for the first time together, happened to stay at the Hotel du Louvre, and had a wonderfully romantic time. They had walked by the Seine hand in hand, checked out some galleries, gone to the third stage of the Tour Eiffel and had an angel's eye view of the city of light, loved Montmartre, loved l'Opéra, loved each other. The city of lovers was 'their' place. And the Hotel du Louvre was their lovers' nest there.

"That's where she is, then," I said, "for whatever reason. I don't know what the *Rebecca* thing is yet, but it's something all right. The fact she'd placed it so deliberately on your desk tells us that. But leave that to me. I'll work it out."

"Will you go and talk to her, Jack? Bring her back?"

"Why don't you phone the hotel now and speak to her?" I said.

"Ah cannae speak French," he snorted. "You phone it."

"The staff on reception will speak English," I assured him. "Call her."

"Don't know the number."

"Give me your phone."

I jiffied it up on his browser. 0033 173 111 234. Dialled it. Put it to 'Speaker'. Passed it over to him. "Just ask to speak to Mrs. Mortimer," I said. "But slow down the speed you talk at and try not to sound too like Paw Broon."

"Eh?"

"The reason many folk find Scots difficult to understand is that we speak too fast and we speak from back in our throats."

"You think this Frenchie will find me hard ti understand?"

"Fucksake, Douglas, I find you hard to understand. Slow down. Speak clearly."

I heard the phone answered in French. Mortimer looked at me in panic. "Ask if he speaks English," I said.

"D'you speak English?"

"Ah, yes sir, I do. Good morning. This is the Hotel du Louvre."

"I'd like to speak to a Mrs. Mortimer. I believe she is staying at your hotel. This is *Mr.* Mortimer. Her husband." God help him, he was trying. He wasn't quite enunciating like Alvar Liddell, but he was doing okay.

"One moment, sir."

Douglas turned his beaming face to me. "She's there! Jack, you're brilliant."

"I know."

After thirty seconds or so, the guy on the far end of the phone said, "One second, please, sir, while I connect you."

"Hallo?"

"Roozh, is that you? It's me, Douglas..."

Ah, let me a draw a veil of tact over what they said to each other. They were both extremely emotional, but extremely glad that the other was safe. They had worried so much, each said. But when Mortimer asked Ruzena why she had lit out the way she had, and said nothing, she told him she didn't think it was safe to discuss it on the phone. Would he come to Paris?

"Should I go, Jack?" he said. "What aboot Inspector Wid?"

"Go," I said. "Get the first available flight. I'll tell Emma Wood what's going down."

I heard Ruzena, puzzled say, "Douglas, who is Jack? Why did you want me to text him? What is going on?"

I said, "I'll let myself out."

"No," said Mortimer, holding a hand up. And he explained to Ruzena that Alex Gilmour was dead and DI Emma Wood was investigating the murder. Jack was Jack Black, a private detective he had hired to help him.

"Alex is *dead*?!!!" Ruzena gasped. "Oh, my God! That is awful..."

I slipped discreetly out of the room. I sauntered into the kitchen and poured my coffee down the sink. It was rank. I rinsed the cup out and had a long draught of cold water. Then I rinsed the cup again, dried it and left it on the worktop. I looked around. The Environmental Health guys had done a good job. You wouldn't have known someone had been plunged in here not so long before. I've always had a kind of morbid fascination for that kind of thing. I lifted the spoon Mortimer had used for the coffees, and rinsed it under hot water. I looked around the floor. No blood left. Obviously. Worktops, cupboards, sink – all shiny and new. Just like it was before the murder. Well, no; maybe not *just* like it.

When I put the spoon in the circular metal cutlery drainer on the draining board, it scraped something on the bottom; moved it a little.

Oh aye.

I removed the spoon again and tipped the drainer up over my left hand. A small, round, silver disk fell on to my palm. It had a capital 'S' stamped on it. I replaced the drainer and looked at the disk. Obviously, Environmental Health hadn't found this, lying in the bottom of the drainer. Nor had anyone else since, I thought. Those cleaning lassies deserved a talking to. I tore a square of kitchen towel from the roll on the spindle and laid the disk on it to look at it more closely without getting my paw prints all over it. It was about half an inch in diameter and looked like a charm from a bracelet or a necklace. 'S'. Nobody in this house had the initial 'S'. Douglas or Ruzena. Mortimer or Dolezal. None of the staff had, either. Alex Gilmour. Jean Gilmour. Jana Zielinska. Radka Bartoš. Therefore it must follow, as the night the day, that it belonged to a stranger. I hoped whatever amount of water it had encountered since it became lodged in the drainer had not washed away any prints. For prints there had to be.

It was then that Douglas came in. "Jack, she says you'll need ti go ti Paris."

"Come and look at this, Douglas," I said. He did. "Have you ever seen this before?" He put a hand out to lift it. "No!" I said. "Leave it on the paper. Recognise it?"

"Never seen it afore."

"I thought as much. This, my friend, may be the wee break we've been looking for. It was obviously missed in the clean-up by the Environmental Health guys. I don't suppose you were doing the dishes before I got here, were you?"

“Nae chance,” said Mortimer. “I just got here in front a ye. The polis an’ whoever must just a baled oot this mornin’.”

“Ah. Explains it. And Jana and Radka haven’t been yet, of course.”

“Naw. Where was it?”

I pointed. “In the cutlery drainer. We leave it where it is until the cops come and collect it. Which is the first item on our agenda today. I’ll call Emma now; she’ll want it checked for fingerprints. What were you saying about Ruzena?”

“She said that it was you that had ti go ti Paris. She says it’s too risky for me. An’ she wouldnae say much mair on the phone. Too risky, she says. She says you’ve ti call her on yer mobile an’ arrange ti go an’ see her. What the fuck…?”

“She didn’t know about Alex Gilmour?”

“Naw. She’s pretty cut up aboot that. An’ for Jean.”

“As I thought, then. She vamoosed before our friend ‘S’ arrived.”

“Will ye go, Jack?”

“What, to Paris? Venice and Paris in the space of a few days? Aye, naturally I will. But all in good time. First we get the fuzz present.”

17

Emma arrived with Gerry Vaughan – Jim was on his day off. Vaughan's okay but is basically just a plodder. Bryce has personality and occasional flashes of insight. Plus he's handy at various things to do with fighting and wielding firearms. It's a good job Emma's as sterling as she is. She slipped gloves on, and gave the 'S' disk a keek.

"It looks like something I've seen before. On a bloke. Tony's nephew, Michael, has a necklace thing, a black leather cord with a silver cross – sterling silver – and a charm like this. Sterling silver too. Only with the initial, 'M', of course. It was a present for his Confirmation or something; I don't know, I'm not religious. But Michael's charm is the same as this. Bag it, Gerry."

Vaughan put gloves on and lifted the disk, dropped it in an evidence bag and sealed it.

"Where did you say it was – in the cutlery doodah?"

"Yep."

She breathed in sharply. "That's not like Environmental Health. Maybe somebody put it in after they'd gone?"

"Naeb'dy been near it," said Mortimer. "This mornin's the first time I've been in the kitchen since the business, an' naebody else has been here."

"No biggie, Em," I said. "The drainer was just on the draining board. If there was no reason for them not to be cleaning up there…"

"Don't like it," Emma shook her head. "How did it get *in* there?"

I thought aloud. "The guy is struggling with Gilmour, Gilmour grabs at his neck as the guy stabs him with the steel, pulls the charm off, the disc flicks up in the air and lands in the drainer."

"It would make a noise as it landed," said Vaughan. "Both metal."

"Did you see the mess the kitchen was in?" I said. "Pots and pans all over the floor, dishes broken… You think two guys in a life and death struggle would hear this wee thing plinking into the drainer with all that commotion going on? Not on your life, mate."

Emma breathed in again. "Maybe, Jack, maybe. Anyway. We need to get it checked; that's for sure. Now, Mr. Mortimer, tell us about getting in touch with your wife."

"Come ben and we'll get a comfy seat," he said, and led the way to the lounge/drawing room again.

"'Come *ben'*?" I whispered in his ear as we walked. "What did I say about Paw Broon?"

Settled on comfy chairs, Emma asked how Mortimer knew Ruzena was in Paris, which necessitated mentioning the chalkboard message and the significance of Paris to the Mortimers, before the bigger question of why Ruzena was there and what she had said to Douglas.

"She wants Jack to go?" said Emma. "Why not you, her husband?"

"She says I might be in danger if I dae," said Mortimer. "She says she didnae tell me onythin' direct afore she went for the same reason. But I cannae think what that wid be. She wouldnae tell me. I'm worried noo."

"We need her back here," said Emma shortly. "She needs to be here to tell us what she knows about the death of Mr. Gilmour, quite beside any threat to you, Mr. Mortimer."

"She says Jack has ti go," he said. "Mibbies you can persuade her," he said, now looking at me.

"If *I* can phone her, I'll stress the importance of her returning," said Emma.

Mortimer shook his head. "She's no the kinda lassie that'll give in ti bullyin' or anybody tellin' 'er what ti dae," said Mortimer. "It's best if Jack goes."

Emma puffed out a breath of impatience and looked at her feet. "All right," she said, "are you up for that, Jack?"

"Trip to Paris? Mais oui. Bien sûr."

"That mean 'aye'?" said Mortimer.

"It does, Douglas," I said.

"Right. I'll pey yer flight *and* an overnighter in the hotel."

Emma shook her head. "If we can get him on a flight today, we might be able to get Mrs. Mortimer back here tonight. Willing to try, Jack?"

"Absolutely," I said. "If you're willing to accept that the likelier scenario is that we come back tomorrow."

"You know what I'd prefer. But, all right. Tomorrow would be acceptable. Can we phone her back just now and see what she says?"

"I'll gie it a bash," said Mortimer.

While he dialled Paris again, Emma said to me, "And what's the significance of the book?"

"Haven't a clue," I said. "I'll ask her."

"What's it called – *Rebecca*?"

"Yeah. The house in the novel is called Manderley. It's why Mortimer called this place Manderley. The film was his mother's favourite."

"Oh. That sounds intriguing. I take it the mother's dead?" she whispered.

I nodded.

Mortimer got Ruzena on the line, said to her I was willing to come over to gay Paree. He also told her that the police were present and that they wanted her back in Scotland. He listened for a while and then held the phone out to me. I took it.

"Hello?"

"Mr. Black? Will you come to Paris?"

"If that's what you and Douglas wish."

"It is."

"Then I'll try to be with you as soon as I can. Today, if possible."

"Thank you."

"Will you agree to return to Scotland with me and speak to the police?"

"Let me speak to them now."

I handed the phone to Emma. Emma said she hoped Ruzena would return as soon as possible with Mr. Black. She listened. Then she asked what danger she thought Mortimer was in. She listened again. Mortimer looked at me with a look of puzzlement. I nodded reassuringly and waved him to be quiet while the women spoke. The upshot was, Ruzena agreed to return if I flew over and accompanied her. Today if possible, tomorrow at the latest. Vaughan was deputed to organise my flights. Ruzena would make all clear when she got here.

"She wouldn't say what she thought the danger to you is," Emma said to Mortimer.

“Naw, she’s refusin’ ti say it ower the phone. She wis the same wi me; says it might be dangerous. I donno what the hair ile the danger can be, but she’s a sensible lassie. We’ll jist need ti thole it till she comes back.”

And, two hours later, I was on flight FlyBE 3055 out of Edinburgh and headed for CDG. Returned from Venice Marco Polo one day; heading out to Paris Charles de Gaulle the next. I could put up with that kind of lifestyle, I guessed. Bar the flying part.

18

I got a cab from CDG into the heart of Paris. The Place Andre Malraux isn't a big, fuckoff square, unlike so many in the centre of the city; it's just the area at the confluence of three or four impressive streets of Second Empire architecture: among them the Rue de Richelieu, the Rue Saint-Honoré and the splendid Avenue de l'Opéra, with that dome of the Palais Garnier closing off the vista. There's a couple of fountains, and the Hotel du Louvre dominates the southern side of the square. There's a fair helping of greenery around too. The smaller Rue de Rohan leads you away from the square towards the Musée du Louvre. I wouldn't be taking in any culture on this visit. I like that the square is named after a writer. There's not enough of that in general, I think. The taxi pulled up at the front door. There was a very Parisian looking eatery across the street, the Café RUC, with a huge guy in an orange top and shades sitting at an outside table with a coffee and a cigarette. I paid the cabbie and went into the hotel.

Revolving door. Marble floored lobby with dark marble pillars. Chandelier. Soft lighting. Plants. Reception on the left. There was a uniformed guy just finishing a telephone call. I walked up and tried my French.

"Bonsoir, je cherche Madame Mortimer. Elle m'attend."

"Eh bien, monsieur. Puis-je avoir votre nom, s'il vous plait?"

"Bien sûr. Je m'appelle Jack Black."

He raised an eyebrow and I half expected the shit I regularly get about there being an actor of that name. But he said nothing, merely lifted the phone and punched a couple of digits into it. Then he gabbled a bunch of French, in the midst of which I picked out my name. He listened, nodded, said "Oui, oui, certainement, madame." He put the phone down and spoke in English. "Madame Mortimer is expecting you, as you say, sir. If you will follow me, please."

He came from behind the counter and crossed the foyer to a staircase with a black wrought iron handrail and climbed the stairs in front of me. Along a railed corridor above the foyer and round a couple of turns, he stopped and knocked on a door.

Ruzena Dolezal opened it. "Monsieur Black," he said to her and then stood back, ushering me in.

"Merci," said Ruzena.

"Merci," said I.

The guy ghosted, and then I was in the room and she had the door shut. It was a luxuriously appointed pad, with a large bed – king size, queen size, I don't know – a three piece suite round a small table, two sets of French windows onto the balcony with a view of the Louvre, and a door which led, I assumed, to the ensuite bathroom.

It was a rather surreal experience, being face to face with this striking looking and much photographed young woman. She was dressed in slacks and a white shirt, her hair pulled back in a scrunchie. I smiled gormlessly at her.

"Mr. Black," she said, "please sit down, and make yourself comfortable. Did you have a good flight?"

"I did, thanks."

"Would you like a drink?"

"A coffee would be good."

"I'll ring down."

"Thanks."

She then said, "How is Douglas?"

"Concerned for your safety, as you can imagine. Which is why I'm here. Why did you leave Manderley so hurriedly?"

"Because *I* was concerned for *Douglas's* safety."

"Why don't you tell me about it?"

She rang down for coffee and then sat down facing me and said, "About a month ago, I started getting texts from a stranger. They were in Slovakian. At first, it seemed innocent – well, I don't know about 'innocent'; it seemed not dangerous is what I mean. All that worried me was where the person had got my number. The first one said, 'A certain Slovakian model's husband has been doing corporal works of mercy.' In Slovakian. I thought what a generous thought that was. I texted back – I didn't know if it was a man or a woman – and asked how they she had got my number. The answer came back, 'You can get anything if you know the right people.' I texted back ..." She stopped and opened her handbag, took out her phone, saying, "One second, please, Mr. Black," thumbed through it and read, simultaneously translating, or so I guessed. " 'No, seriously, how did you get it? I'm not angry. I just want to know. And how did you know about the works of mercy?' And the reply to that was, 'Never mind. You may not be angry, but we are. However, we will not let the sun set on our wrath.' And that's when I started to think something might be wrong."

"But you didn't tell Douglas?"

"No. I wish now I had. But I was … where was I? … in Cologne, I think, and it slipped my mind that day. I had hours of work still to do."

"I take it they left it at that for a while, then."

"Not so long. The next day, while I was in the airport, I got another one. She read her phone in between talking to me. 'Your husband is bored. He has been outside for a smoke five times in the last hour. He should make the best use of time, because the days are evil.' That one really got to me. I thought, they're watching him – why? So I sent, 'I didn't think he was so fascinating he merited so much observation.' Trying to sound offhand, you know? And I got back, 'Not only him. That blue top you have on is very becoming.' And then I started to get genuinely scared."

"Why didn't … no, scrub that. It's obvious. You didn't contact the police because you were in Germany."

"Yah. If I had been in UK, I'd have contacted immediately. I looked around but I couldn't see anybody I thought was watching me. But it was a creepy feeling. The next text said, "Corporal works of mercy come at a price." And I thought, O-ho, could this be to do with something that Douglas has done without many knowing…"

I said, "He told me about the girls."

"Ah. Did he? Well, I wondered if it was to do with that."

"Had to be."

And then I got this one. 'He should know better. Render unto Caesar.'"

"Now that's interesting. Most of these texts have a smack of the scriptural about them, don't they?."

"Mmm. I thought that too."

The door went, and she rose to admit a flunkey with a tray of coffee and stuff: pastries, shortbread and the like. He set it down on a table and she bunged him a note before he left. Then she played mother and poured two cups. I said, "Just black, thanks," stood and took a cup, then sat down again.

Ruzena sat too and said, after biting a coffee biscuit, "I wouldn't know why they are using parts of the Bible; I'm not that clever. But I know I was really scared now. I tried not to look as if I was, because some creep was probably watching me. I wrote back, 'I don't know what that means.' And, by return, I got, 'You will, soon enough. For there is nothing covered that shall not be revealed; neither hid that shall not be known.' And finally, just before I got on the flight, I received, 'Say nothing to your husband if you want him to be around for a while yet. Or anyone else, including the police. Remember - we are watching you both.' The word 'nothing' was in capitals. And it finished, 'Beware Glaswegians bearing gifts.' I suppose like the Three Wise Men. They wanted me to be too scared to tell Douglas. Anyone."

"Precisely what they wanted, Mrs. Mortimer. But still you should..."

"I know, Mr. Black, I know. But when the one you love most is threatened in that way ..."

"Sure. And did the texts continue like that?"

"No, no," she said animatedly. "Something like a fortnight passed before I heard anything again. Slightly less than that. Roughly ten to twelve days, maybe. So, I assumed – I hoped – that it had been a crank. You know, maybe somebody in the departure lounge that day saw me and ..."

"The first text was before the airport," I said. "They knew about the trafficked girls that Douglas liberated. 'Render unto Caesar the things that are Caesar's and to God the things that are God's.' I think that's how that goes on. They were saying Douglas had no business interfering to rescue the girls. Then they referred to 'Glaswegians', which makes me think of Bashir Ahmed, the guy Douglas bought Radka from. The line about Glaswegians bearing gifts isn't the Nativity. It's a parody of a line from Virgil. It wasn't just a troll at the airport."

"Oh, I know that *now*," she said, "but for a while, I clung to the hope that it was just a crank who'd got to hear about the girls and wanted to make me sweat a bit."

"Okay. And how were you with Douglas, once you got back? Did you act as if nothing had happened?"

"I tried to, but that business was always at the back of my mind. Once or twice, Douglas said to me I was miles away, asked me if there was anything wrong, you know? But I laughed and brushed it away. I didn't want him to have any worries. If you know what he has done to help those girls, Mr. Black, you will know what a wonderful man he is. I didn't want him to worry. And, for a couple of weeks or so, nothing else happened and I started to hope, like I say, that it was just some stalker or something. And then, well … and then, this."

She thumbed the phone a second and handed it to me. A text in English. I read, 'He saved others; himself he cannot save.' I pursed my lips and nodded. "Somebody is intelligent," I said. "Virgil and now the Bible again."

Ruzena said, "Matthew; verse 27, chapter 42."

"That's impressive," I said. "You knew that one?"

She shook her head. "I knew it was Matthew. I had to look up chapter and verse. I read the Bible every night."

"I didn't notice a Bible among your books," I said.

She looked startled. "Have you seen my books? Have *you* been in my rooms?"

Shit. Douglas's reason for hiring me was something I had no intention of sharing with her.

"Oh yes," I said as suavely as I could manage, "I asked to see your stuff in case I got a wrinkle about what might have happened to you. The police will have checked your place out but I like to do it too. I think differently from the police sometimes. I was the one who saw you had written 'Paris' on Douglas's chalkboard."

"You were?"

"I was, yes. The writing was different from the other names up there. Anyway, I didn't see a Bible among your books."

"I carry a pocket one with me. But there is a King James one there."

"Right; okay. When did you get this text …?"

"Last Wednesday. Turned my heart over. I thought, shit, he's back. And then the …"

"Wednesday what time? Wait…" I checked the screen. "21.43, right. Evening time."

"Yes, after I got back from Edinburgh. I had a shoot at Edinburgh Castle that day."

"Sure. Somebody probably followed you around Edinburgh and waited till you were home."

She put her hand out and I gave her back the phone. "Then the call came. A phone call." She puffed her lips out and stopped. I waited, let her collect herself. "That same Wednesday night, about an hour later. I had just showered and was reading before going to bed. The phone rang and I answered it. A Scottish voice said, "I've just been thinking. I don't want you around to spoil the negotiations." She tilted her head. "I think that's how he put it. 'Negotiations'. With Douglas, he meant. He said he knew Douglas was due back in Manderley on the Friday. He said he would call on Douglas to … I think it was 'enter into negotiations', he said. Oh, I forget all of what he said, but it was all on that theme. He wanted to talk to Douglas. He had to … what was it? … 'settle an outstanding debt' or something very like that. Douglas owed him 'big time'. This Scotsman was out of pocket and wasn't happy about it, wasn't willing to let it go. I said he should come to the house like anyone else might, and discuss it man to man. Then he said Douglas was back on Friday. I should 'get to fuck' out of there by the morning. Women always screw things up, he said. If I didn't 'get to fuck', he would make Douglas regret it. I said where was the fairness in that? He said Douglas hadn't played fair by him, so they would be even. Then he said very plainly I had to go by morning – the Thursday morning. And I hadn't to tell Douglas, hadn't to contact him in any way until all this was over and settled. And he said, 'You know what this is about. Leave it to the men to deal with. And I fucking mean it, lady. If you don't, I'll deal with him and then I'll come and deal with you. Pack up and get to fuck.' I don't remember what I said to that exactly, but I said something about he needn't be so aggressive and he more or less repeated what he'd said before. And said if I so much as tried to contact Douglas by phone – calling or texting him – they would know. And he said, 'You might want to put on more than just that one light at the side of the house.' Then, just before he hung up he told me to sleep well. And rang off. I was frantic. I put every light in the house on. I didn't know what to do. Where was he? He had to be outside, watching the house, surely."

"He had driven past minutes before, probably. Why didn't you immediately tell the police or phone Douglas and tell him?"

"Why? Because the caller said he would know if I did. And he would hurt Douglas. That's why I didn't contact him."

"There's no way they would know if you phoned his mobile."

"They can trace these things now, can't they?"

"Well, the *police* can do it, via the service providers. They can … anyway, it can only be done *after* the event. There's no way they would have known if you'd phoned Douglas that minute and warned him."

"Have you never heard of hacking? You know, like those journalists did on the Murdoch paper… what was it? The *News of the World*? Hacking into someone's phone. I bet you know how to do it. Wasn't there a private investigator charged with doing just that?"

"Indeed there was. But he was a crook, not just a private investigator. I'm just a private investigator, and not a crook."

"But you know how to do it, yes?"

"In theory. I read how to do it at the time of the hacking scandal you're talking about .But I could only hack into voicemails on landlines with a random number generator. Mobiles are easier, if the owner hasn't changed the default password – usually four zeroes or 1234. I couldn't tell you were calling Douglas, or he was calling you, and listen in. I doubt anyone could."

"I didn't know that – and I couldn't take the risk. They might have killed him. They killed Alex, didn't they!"

I puffed out a breath. "All right. What *did* you do?"

"I got dressed at once, packed a grip and put all the lights out on the way out of the house. I thought I could maybe at least leave a clue for Douglas, something they couldn't harm him for. So I wrote 'Paris' on the board. And I put a copy of *Rebecca* on his desk, so that he would know I was thinking of him and Manderley. He called the house that after the house in the movie. It was his mother's favourite. Then I locked up and drove away. There was nobody around when I did. I took the Mazda. I thought less people would look at it. I thought, I could be followed to Edinburgh or Glasgow airports. I'll try Newcastle. And that is what I did."

I steepled my fingers at my lips and nodded. "Okay," I said. "You did what you thought was right. I doubt if anything you did would have resulted in harm to Douglas, but…"

"Somebody killed Alex Gilmour."

"True. Oh – did you put the CCTV cameras off at Manderley before you left?"

She looked baffled at the question. "No…"

A sudden thought eeled into my mind. I stood up. "Ruzena," I said, "do you know if there's a window on this floor at the front of the hotel?" She wrinkled her brow. "One that looks out on to the Rue de Rohan? At the Café RUC?"

"Uh … yes," she said.

"Show me." I beckoned with my hand.

She stood up, went to the door. I followed her. She led me along the carpeted quiet of the corridor to the windows on the building's façade. I said, "Let me, please." And I stepped passed her, stood at the long net curtain and looked. Then I beckoned her again and said, "There. On the pavement in front of the café. Seen him before?"

The guy in the shades was still there, still smoking.

She looked and nodded. "Once or twice. He sits there sometimes. I guess he likes the food there."

"Or he's keeping an eye on your comings and goings."

"You think? But no, he can't be. I've gone out and come back and he hasn't been there at times. Most times, in fact."

"But I'll bet there's always been someone there."

She thought. "Not always. Often, I'd say, but not most times. I think. I wasn't looking so closely."

"The times no-one was on the pavement, someone was somewhere else close to the front door, looking."

"You think?"

I nodded. "I know. Have you eaten in the hotel?"

"Most nights."

"Been watched then too. They will know everywhere you've gone, everything you've done while you've been here. Done a lot of sightseeing?"

She shrugged. "Just the usual. Montmartre. Place du Trocadero… you know."

"Sure. And you've had a tail at them all."

"So Douglas will have been followed too?" she said.

"Douglas now has the police on his case. I suggest you go back to your room and get packed. We fly back tonight. Call Douglas while you're at it. He misses you."

"What will you do?"

I smiled. “Practise my conversational French.”

19

The massive dude in the shades had taken them off. They hadn't been strictly necessary for a fair old while, afternoon sliding into evening as it was. But he was on what must have been his twenty seventh coffee. By the time he got home, he would be speeding like a bullet. And pissing like an elephant too, I assumed. I sauntered out of the hotel door, my cellphone in my hand. I stood and looked around, looking up at the sky appreciatively and breathing deeply. Tam the Tourist lining up a shot. Then I crossed the road to the RUC side and went through the motions of taking a tourist pic of the HdL. Couple of shots. Turned the phone sideways and took another. Knelt down and took one more. I stood up and turned to the side, skipped through the snaps in the photo gallery. Looked up, smiling. Your man was watching me and drawing on a weed.

I nodded. "Braw night," I said. "How ye daein'?"

He looked at me and shrugged, as if I'd spoken Chinese. So. Not a Glaswegian bearing gifts. I beamed like I'd just had an idea and put my thumb up in the air, said, 'Smile!', lifted the phone again and took his photograph. Immediately, he stood up and scowled, said, "Non, non, non! Interdit! Effacez-le maintenant!"

I said, "Quoi? Baise ça, mon brave. Vous êtes enregistré pour la postérité. Partez maintenant, avant que j'appelle les flics!"

I wasn't a hundred percent sure about the accuracy of all of that, especially my subjunctive after 'avant que', but it got my message over. He'd ordered me to delete the photo. Fuck that, I'd told him; now he was recorded for posterity, he should bugger off before I called the cops.

He took a deep breath and swelled visibly. His fists balled. Big fists. I thought, I'm going to get my sweetbreads stuffed down my throat here. But there were people passing by; people sitting at tables behind the RUC windows looking out on to Rue de Rohan; there were people standing on the pavement outside the hotel entrance, and there were people walking along the streets on either side. It wasn't as if we two were alone in a deserted backyard. He breathed out stertorously – you don't hear many doing that, these days – and barked some French at me, probably to the effect that I was a hateful Scottish cunt, and then he stalked off towards the Avenue de l'Opéra. Much to my relief.

I watched him pull his phone out of his pocket as he went. That meant either: A) that a substitute was being summoned to take over caretaker duties; or B) that a posse was being organised to kick seven different colours of shite out of me. Therefore, speed was of the essence, I told myself. Hopefully, by the time I got back to Ruzena's room, she would be packed and ready to rock.

She was, in a headsquare and glasses. No make-up, too. A smart move. She just looked like an attractive woman, rather than a well-known model. I told her she should go to the airport now, separately from me, and wait. Terminal 2E, since we were travelling Air France to Edinburgh. We would call a cab for her and get it to come to the back door, by the Metro station - Palais Royal Musée du Louvre, Line 1 (yellow). I would keep the key for an hour and hand it to reception, before cabbing up, myself, and meeting her at CDG. And so it was done.

The lackey on reception agreed to Madame Mortimer's request, ordered a taxi and told us it would be there in five minutes. I stood with Ruzena till it came – in exactly five minutes – and saw her off. I looked around when the taxi pulled away but what was I looking for? Any of the bods going past could have been in the gang. How would I know? I tutted and went back through the hotel and up to Ruzena's room. I sat on one of the comfy chairs and tried to think about things. It was unlikely that the smoking dude in shades and his mates would come to Roozh's room, but you never know, I told myself. I'd give it an hour.

I was trying to concentrate but my attention wouldn't stay at peace. Ruzena had left a Paris Metro map, so I amused myself by scanning that for a while. These schematic maps fascinate me – you can get them for the underground in any major city. I like the colours. I like to savour the names of the stations, too; roll them around on the tongue of my imagination, appreciate the resonance, wonder what the hell they mean. All that comes from my childhood.

As a boy, I'd been fascinated by the schematic map of the Tube, originally designed by Harry Beck in the 1930s. I used to pore over it in my room some nights, shut my eyes and visualise riding the tracks under the coiling guts of the city: circuits of cables, pipes and wires; then riding instead a map of the mind: grids of vibrant coloured lines, blue and yellow and red and green, silver and lilac, meshing and locking at cogs with talismanic names, names I'd known through a process of osmosis over the years, but one or two of which were still resonant. Harrow-on-the-Hill. East India. Elephant & Castle. Barons Court. Peckham Rye. I researched other cities' underground systems, noted names I liked there too: Mount Eden, Temple, Diamond Hill. Maybe that shows the sort of mind I had as a child; how it worked. Still did. Still does.

I skiffed the Metro map. Stalingrad. After the battle, no doubt. Maybe it was opened about then. Cosmonautes – were there any French ones? Garibaldi – the Italian revolutionary or the biscuit? Belvédère – I wondered if that was as pretty as Belvedere in Bathgate. Magenta and Solferino, two battles the French were involved in during the Second Italian War of Independence. Some thinkers and revolutionaries: Voltaire; Robespierre; Mirabeau. Couple of writers: Anatole France and Avenue Emil Zola. I liked old Avenue's work. Choisy-le-Roi. Choosy the King. No wonder he got guillotined. I would take the map back home with me, keep it beside the other schematics I had.

A knock at the door startled me off the chair. It was the guy from Reception.

"Mr. Black, may I come in?"

I said sure. Well, it was no skin off my nose and, in a way, it was his hotel.

When I closed the door, he said, "Monsieur, there are two men downstairs who want to talk to Madame Mortimer. I am very suspicious of them. When she arrived, she asked us to notify her if anyone came asking for her. I told them I would ring the room number. But I rang the number of another room, a room I know to be empty. I told them there was no answer. They asked if she had gone out and I said I do not know. Then they asked if she had left her key. I had to say no. They asked me to ring again in case she had simply fallen asleep. I said I would do better than that. And so I am here. I am suspicious of them, Monsieur. I wish no harm to come to Madame Mortimer. She is a gracious and generous lady. I think it best if you go now, and I will take the key downstairs, say to these men that this is a strange occasion, that Mrs. Mortimer is not in, but her key was left in the room."

"Sure thing, if you think that's best. Is there a way I can get to the back door without going through the foyer?"

"Bien sûr, Monsieur." He opened the door and pointed away along the corridor. "Go this way and you will find another escalier, staircase, to take you down."

"Thanks."

"Of course, Monsieur. Please convey my regards to Madame Mortimer."

"I will. She will be pleased."

We got out into the corridor and he shut the room door. I walked quickly in the direction of Reception. He said, "Monsieur…" but I put my finger to my lips and held up my other hand, walked to the iron railing and looked over. Two guys were standing at the counter. One was the peach whale who had been sitting outside the Café RUC. I swayed back and returned to where the clerk stood.

"You were right to be suspicious," I said. "I thank you again and I'm sure Madame Mortimer will, too. Now – this way?"

"Oui, Monsieur. Et bonne chance."

I padded away along the corridor. Tufted, expensive silence. Not a sinner about. Down the stairs and along cheaper corridors to the back door again. Out into the Paris evening air. Busy. Best plan? To forget a cab, take the Metro to Châtelet-les-Halles and change to the blue line north for CDG. Which is what I did. My French is easily good enough for transactional stuff like that. The RER (B) line to the airport took thirty five minutes. I texted Ruzena and told her I was on my way and to make *her* way via the most populous parts of the airport to the appropriate departure lounge.

Charles de Gaulle is a huge fuckoff airport. Terminal 2E is a vast tubular building, kinda wooden in look, with miles of walkways, yards of bleak travelators and miles of uncomfortable metal seating things in rows under hideous modern roofing, curved, with square skylights; but I knew roughly where I was going. I was delighted to see Ruzena, still in her headsquare, sitting in one of the seats. She had a magazine on her updrawn knees and was looking at it. I sauntered up to her and said, "Dobrý večer, pani Mortimerova."

She looked up startled, saw it was me and gave me a winning smile. "Mr. Black! You speak Slovak?"

I sat beside her and said, "No, of course not. I had to look that up this afternoon."

"Everything all right before you left?"

"Well, two men came to Reception looking for you, including the one who was at the RUC this afternoon. That guy… Raymond, is it? … came to tell me. I sneaked out the back way and he took the key. He seemed a good guy."

"He was very helpful. He knew I wanted informed of anyone asking for me. I had to tell him about your arrival, so he would know I was expecting you. He was very watchful for me."

"Good. Well, we're on our way, at least."

Two armed cops strolled by. Ruzena said, "The armed police are very visible. It makes me feel better."

"The intention," I said. "After Charlie Hebdo and the Bataclan, here in Paris. There have been three terrorist attacks in England in the last few weeks, remember. Manchester and London."

"There was another in London last night," said Ruzena. "A white man drove a van at some Muslim worshippers leaving a mosque in Finsbury Park. Tit for tat, I think."

I hadn't read that or seen it on the TV news. I'd been so busy working on the Mortimers thing. "Christ on the cross," I murmured and shook my head. Where the fuck was the world going these days? 'Ay me, what fray was here? Yet tell me not, for I have heard it all. Here's much to do with hate.' Ah, but the glover's son got it right when he went on to say, 'but more with love.' The stories of the goodness, the selflessness and the overwhelming generosity of ordinary folk who helped the victims of the atrocities gave me hope that mankind would get it right yet. Even in times of horror, people are generally good.

"Have you checked in?" I asked her.

"Yes."

"Right. Have you eaten?"

Ruzena said, "No. I thought I would wait for you."

"Okay. Let me check in and then let's eat."

We went to a snack bar called La Terrasse and ate. She said, "How did they *know* I was in Paris? I never used my phone till today."

"Somebody followed you when you left Manderley," I said. "Presumably the one who warned you to get to fuck. He followed you to Newcastle, saw that you were heading for Paris and then contacted someone on the continent. It's a big concern, obviously. I mean, the criminal organisation. I know it's a concern for you."

"They contacted a cell in Paris? Or a couple of people in Paris?"

"One or the other. Organised crime has tentacles everywhere … Ruz … ena."

"What is it?"

I was looking out of the snack bar. The two guys who had been in the foyer of the Hotel du Louvre were making their slow way down the vast hall towards us. You couldn't miss that gorilla in peach. They were checking everybody sitting in the seats, stopping and checking out the shops and eateries.

"Okay," I said. "You go to the Ladies over there and stay in it till I text you, all right? The guys from the hotel are here. See the fat fuck in the orange top? Right. Take your case. Wait till I text."

"What are you going to do?"

"I'll think of something. Go."

She slipped off her stool and picked up her case, crossed over the walkway to the Ladies'. I waited till the door closed behind her and I went into the WC in the snack bar. Into the cubicle. Sat on the pan, bag at my feet. Lifted out, from beneath a change of clothes, my false beard and a baggy bunnet. I changed my shirt, stuffed the old one into the grip, gummed on the whiskers, slipped on the bunnet. Hey presto. Did you say hipster? All I needed was a man bun. Stood up, flushed the toilet, opened the cubicle door, walked out. Checked myself in the mirror. Fuck, *I* didn't know who it was. Walked back over to our place and sat, waiting for our pursuers. Not one person in La Terrasse gave me a second look, despite the fact I'd gone into the can looking like a Bathgate private eye and emerged from it looking like I played keyboards in a psychedelic rock band.

It was my photographic model himself who stepped into the place, turned his head slowly round and checked out everybody sitting. His eyes met mine. I held his gaze for a second then looked away as if I assumed he was looking for a friend. He looked at the couple next to me, his eyes swept the back wall, he left. Some watcher. Thick as thought could make him. Not as observant as Jenny Kemp, that's for sure. His buddy had gone into the newsagent cum book shop next door. My man went into the Gents'.

I texted Ruzena to meet me right then outside the Ladies'. She came out and looked around. I waved. She looked. Peered. I said, "It's me."

She guffawed and said, "How did you do that?"

I said, "Easy. I think it's time we went through security, don't you?" and nodded at two armed police strolling that way.

"Yes. Our flight is in an hour. Let's go."

We sauntered behind the cops to security, I peeling off the whiskers as I went.

20

The chat on the plane was easy, covered a lot of topics. I had to do a fair bit of small talk, which is generally a trial for me, but I managed. Ruzena asked me a lot of things, as if she was really interested in what kind of guy this was that her husband had hired. Was I married? Yep. Had been once before; didn't work. Married again, deliriously happy with a seven year old daughter. How did I become a PI? Easy. What I'd always wanted to do. Just did it. Had I never thought of joining the police, working with the CID? No. Who was my favourite writer? Shakespeare – *are* there any others?

You know what I think? I think she was doing what savvy women do when they want a guy to feel relaxed and important – encourage him to talk about himself. I turned it round on her, though. "That's enough about me," I said. "Who the hell cares about me? Tell me about yourself," I said.

"There's not much to tell," she said. "Just a poor Slovakian girl, born in Kosice, devout Catholic, fond of animals, not bad at school. My father lost his job and we moved to Porto Marghera so that he could work in the oil refinery. Then got the apartment in Mestre."

"Does your brother work in the refinery too?"

"Pavol? Yes, he does."

"I thought he was called Paolo? Ah – the Italian equivalent. Makes sense if he's living in Italy, I suppose. I went to see them at Douglas's request. Looking for you."

"So I believe!" she laughed.

"What about your mother?"

"She is a wonderful woman. Just a housewife, but so capable. Very practical. Can put her hand to anything. Joinery, decorating, electrics..." She laughed. "All the home repairs are done by Mum, not Dad."

"And how did you get into modelling?"

"Oh, that was my aunt. My mother's sister. She said I was a beautiful girl, when I was about fifteen, and she sent away photographs of me to various agencies. But no joy. Then someone told her that an agency in Bratislava was having an open call session. And ... what do you say? 'Hey presto'?" She laughed.

“And it all started from there?” I said.

“Sure did.”

“I wonder then, why your family stay in that flat. I would have thought a successful model would have bought them a luxury place on the Grand Canal.”

She giggled. “I bought them a place in Pavlovce, where my mother comes from. They use it as a holiday home.” She leant in to me confidentially. “Or maybe they rent it to other people as a holiday home, eh?” She rubbed her thumb and forefinger together. “Plenty of Euros.”

I laughed politely. “Did you know about Douglas’s heroics in saving those girls the night you met him at the *Scotsman* do?”

She brought her brows down jocularly and gave me a smile as arch as the Rialto. “I had heard rumours,” she said. “And so I wanted to meet this man who performed such corporal works of mercy. I asked one of the journalists to introduce me.” She laughed. “I think we hit it off.”

“I think you did, at that,” I said.

Stilted stuff, but it helped to pass a flight.

I drove Ruzena back to Manderley, to be engulfed in the warmth of Mortimer’s welcome. I split the scene as soon as I could. No wish to gooseberry on anyone’s happiness. However, not before he said to me, “Mind what I said ti ye, Jack, about the reward. You’ve got a fair bit comin’ ti ye now, man.” He beamed at Ruzena, his arm on her shoulder. “Because my wee wife is back safe an’ sound. An’ that means the world ti me.”

“There’ll be time for talk like that later,” I said. “For tonight, just enjoy the fact you’re together again.”

“We’ll hae a wee drive the morra,” he said, “eh love? To Newcastle and get the Mazda. A wee day trip.”

“Of course, darling.”

I said, “I think you might find that DI Wood wants to talk to Ruzena tomorrow.”

“Aw, right. Well, we’ll go efter she speaks to her.”

“Ok, glad you folks are happy again. I’m out.”

And I drove home, glad to be back in the company of my own wee family. I like being in romantic cities as much as the next man, but I can do without physical threat and air travel.

And being separated from the ones I love. So I peeped in on Juliet as she slept and my heart filled as I watched her. Then I spent the night close to Phyllis on the sofa, with the TV off, just talking and relishing her proximity. We spoke, of course, of how the Mortimer case was going. Phyl asked me why Ruzena had taken off in such a precipitate way, and I told her the conversation Roozh and I had had in the Hotel du Louvre.

Phyllis creased her brow. "So she bailed out because she was terrified of what was going to happen to Mortimer?"

"M-hm."

"But how was that going to help him? And it still doesn't explain why she didn't phone him or text him – *or* why she didn't answer his."

"She said the threat was that, if she did, Mortimer would be hurt. Or worse, she assumed."

"Baloney. How would the guy threatening her know if she phoned him or not?"

"She said she thought that they could trace these things nowadays. The guy said he would know if she did. She was frightened they'd hacked her phone. Or his."

"I thought you said this was a bright woman."

"Aye, she's bright. That doesn't mean she knows anything about I.T. or technology or anything like that. Lots of folk don't."

"You'd have to be particularly dense to think that, though."

"You think?"

"I do. Mind what I said the other night?"

"What?"

"That there was something else in all of this. That either *she* was up to something or that *he* was, something not really related to what he hired you for. The adultery thing. You remember that?"

"I do, love. But you didn't suggest what it might be."

"Well, I don't know, do I? But I still think that's what it is. Something else."

"Well, you're right to a degree. She's been different from the usual for a wee while for the simple reason that she's been feart that her man is going to get a doing."

"Mmm."

"You don't sound convinced. Well, it seems to me that the lovely Ruzena..."

"Oh," snapped Phyllis suddenly, "fuck Ruzena!"

"No thanks."

She pushed me back in the sofa. "Well, how about me, then? I could be doing with some of your expert attention too, you know."

"Okay. You talked me into it. Jezebel."

The next day I spent in the office. I had a cairn of paperwork to get through and thought I might as well get on with it. Some mindless correspondence and filing might clear my head of the stresses of the previous few days. So I clerked away, drank coffee and listened to some Einaudi on the player, trying not to be irritated by Bugsy the Budgie when he chirped along with it. At lunchtime I strolled up the street and bought myself a pack of sandwiches and a copy of the Herald. Some crossword with my lunch seemed the mere coupon (4,3,6).

Just the ticket.

I passed the time of day with one or two and, by the time, I got back to my little cell, I was as relaxed and refreshed in mind as I had aimed for. More coffee. Lunch. Crossword. Happy as a big sunflower. I was just filling in the boxes for 'Unknown quantities reveal hitherto unknown qualities' (6,6) – 'hidden depths' – when the door was knocked, opened and Emma stuck her head around it.

"Jack. Busy?"

"Not too. Pull up a couch and tell me what's on your mind. Java?"

"Aye, go on then." She sat. "I've just interviewed the Mortimer woman. She's a rum one, isn't she? I'm wondering if it's just that she's foreign."

"Jeez, Em," I said. "You sound like a UKIP candidate."

"Ah, you know what I mean. Different background, different culture."

"Sure. What's not gelling with you?"

"All the texts and phone calls she got. Her reaction to them."

"Aye, I know what you mean." I handed her a mug of coffee. "Phyllis was just talking about that last night. I told her Ruzena was wary in case one of their phones was bugged or something."

Emma sniffed. "Have you seen her and him together?" she said. "Christ, I didn't carry on like that with my boyfriend when I was 15."

"Ah, but your boyfriend hadn't saved five Roma lassies from prostitution, had he?"

She gave me a look. "You think that's what it is?"

"I *have* seen them together before," I said. "Once. She was all over him like shit on velcro."

"My point. I know she's young but… come on. He's in his sixties. What's that all about? And it's not the trafficking thing, either."

"Are you saying, as my mother used to put it, that she is too sweet to be wholesome?"

"I am. Anyway. I've just left them and they're on their way now to Newcastle to pick her car up from the airport." She sneered. "Hand in hand. What did she tell you about the night Alex Gilmour died?"

I repeated what Ruzena had said to me.

"That sound right to you?"

"Like I said, I guessed she suspected one or both of their phones were bugged. She seemed genuinely scared when I spoke to her."

"I don't buy that," said Emma.

"You don't think it's possible to bug someone's mobile? You can get a device off the Net for fifty bucks."

"That's not what I mean. Somebody calls *you* up, right? Tells you they're going to have words with Phyllis. But you've not to contact her, or to warn her, or she'll be hurt. What's the first thing you do?"

"Get the number traced."

"All right. What's the first thing you do, if you're not Jack Black?"

"Notify you guys."

"Of course.

"But she was specifically warned not to contact the police either, or Mortimer would get a Chinese burn."

"Jack! For fucksake. Do you think she believed that?"

"I thought she did."

"All right. If you say so. What else did she tell you when you were over there?"

I summarised my whole time in Paris with Ruzena. She nodded, sipped her coffee. Said, "Mmm," and not much more.

"So," I said then, "what's new? Find Bashir Ahmed? Identify the young guy in the Corsa?"

"Glasgow guys have come up with a photograph of Ahmed. Not sure where is at present." She took out her phone and skiffed through it. "Image of the young guy isn't clear enough to be any good. The Corsa was stolen." She handed me the phone. Bashir Ahmed was maybe 45 to 50 years old, I'd say, with a pock-marked dial. "It's definitely the man that Mortimer dealt with in Ardbeg Street, though Ahmed has no obvious connection with the property, which is owned by a guy called McGilveray. According to the paperwork. Ahmed is known as a shopkeeper - one or two wee corner shops in Govanhill. But the staff say he is back in Pakistan at the moment, apparently."

"Do you think the young guy in the hoodie is the one who killed Gilmour?" I said.

She shrugged extravagantly. "Who knows? Who fucking knows? He must be a likely suspect." Things weren't working out for Emma and she wasn't liking it.

I didn't go back to desk flying when Emma left. I sat back in my chair and thought about what she'd said. And about what Phyllis had said the night before. Ruzena was a bright woman. Young and cultured. Arty. Fluent in several languages. Up to the minute with the news agenda. And she had an iPhone. In her mid 20s, with all that going on in her napper, was it likely she wouldn't know how a Smartphone works? That she believed some intimidatory lout would be able to monitor what she said in a call or text to another iPhone? That she wouldn't know that these things are logged by the service provider and can be accessed by the police in the right circumstances and with the right authority – but *after* the event? No, of course it wasn't. Hell, now that I remembered, I'd said almost exactly that to her while we spoke in her hotel room, in just about those words. And what had her reply been? 'I couldn't take the risk. They might have killed him. They killed Alex!'

That was the line that had swayed me. She couldn't risk anything happening to Mortimer because hadn't they killed Gilmour? They would as readily have killed Douglas, if he'd been there. That, almost subliminal, suggestion that she had done the right thing, the logical thing, and got Mortimer out of danger in the nick of time, as was proven by the murder of his handyman, was what had deflected me from seeing the iffiness of that whole bolt of flannel. For that was what it seemed to me now. Flannel. Equivocation. Bullshit. Mrs. Mortimer wasn't telling the truth. As my wife and my favourite detective inspector had sussed. The burning question now was – why?

I had to talk to someone. Someone who knew Ruzena. Not Kemp, not Hunter, not Zielinska, nor even Bartoš. I'd been there; I needed new input. Who was there? Who was left?

Jean Gilmour was who.

21

Torphichen was my next port of call. Well, why not? Edinburgh, Venice, Paris … Torphichen. I drove up there. 'The Hill of the Ravens' in the old Gaelic tongue. The Statistical Account of 1843 noted that it was 'situated on a sheltered plain, away from all post-roads or thoroughfares, and once a place of great importance as it is of high antiquity,' then consisting 'of only a few cottages, and … (with) … a straggling and deserted appearance.' Its place in high antiquity is denoted by the presence in the village of the Preceptory. Founded in the 1140s at the invitation of King David, it was built some time between the thirteenth and fifteenth centuries, the only house in Scotland of the Knights Hospitaller of St. John of Jerusalem. That's an ancient order that started off caring for sick pilgrims on the Crusades in an infirmary near the Church of the Holy Sepulchre. They ended up, via escorting pilgrims in safety, and fighting off Muslim attackers, as a military order. The Knights of St. John, in fact. The local hospital's name derives from that order. The Preceptory is a mere remnant now but it is still impressive, with its traceried windows, ribbed vaulting, tomb recess and piscina. William Wallace briefly governed Scotland from Torphichen in 1298. The present parish kirk, from 1756, stands on the site of its wooden predecessor, founded by St. Ninian in 400 AD. That's a fair whack of antiquity in anybody's domesday book.

For hundreds of years, Torphichen was clustered around the church and the village square, gradually expanding northwards. The square is still quaint but it must have been serenity exemplified back in the day. Council houses were built after the Second World War in Greenside – where the Gilmours lived – and Bowyett. In the 50s, more council housing was built in Priorscroft and St. John's Place; and the last council stock was built in the 60s in Northgate and Manse Road. Thereafter, all new building was private. But the village still has fewer than 350 houses. There were no more than 750 people resident there, according to the 2011 census.

I remembered it well. Torphichen was one of the places Mad Jack and Pious Peggy used to take me as a kid. I turned off the North Gate into Greenside. The Gilmour place was one of the last ones in the street, facing down Bowyett.

Jean Gilmour was not quite the weeping widow in blacks I had expected. When she opened the door to my knock, she fixed me with a gimlet eye.

"Mrs. Gilmour?"

"Yes?"

"My name is Jack Black. I'm a private investigator. I'm helping …"

"I know who you are."

"You do?"

"I've seen you around Bathgate. What are you helping to do?"

"Right. I'm helping the police with their enquiries regarding the murder of your husband. I wondered if I could talk to you briefly?"

"Why not?" she said, and opened the door. "Everybody else has."

She showed me through to the living room and sat down. I sat facing her.

"I'm truly sorry about what happened to your husband, Mrs. Gilmour," I said. "It must have been a terrible shock."

"It was. But I can't tell you anything more about that night. More than I told the police, I mean. DS Honeyman, was it?"

"Shirley Honeyman, yes. No, what I wanted to talk to you about wasn't so much to do with that awful night. It's more to do with Mrs. Mortimer."

"Oh. That one." She tossed her head in a manner I remembered well. My mother used to do it too. Unimpressed. Disapproving.

"I take it you don't have a lot of time for her," I said.

"I don't, Mr. Black, quite frankly. I don't."

"Can I ask why?"

"Alex and I have worked for Mr. Mortimer since he built Manderley House. He's a good man, Mr. Black, and a decent employer. I have a lot of time for *him*. We both did," she added sadly. "But I just can't take to his wife. I don't care for her, I don't like her. And I don't believe she feels anything for Mr. Mortimer. Other than the desire to relieve him of his wealth."

"Right."

"Oh, I know – she's a beautiful young woman, successful in her own right; a celebrity with her own money. But there's something about her that's just not right… not … genuine! That's the word. She's not genuine. Alex thought so too."

I perked up. "Oh *really*?"

"Oh aye. He used to say to me sometimes, 'She's up to somethin', that one. I wouldn't trust her as far as I could throw her.' Or, 'I wouldn't believe her if she told me my name was Alex Gilmour.' Things like that. No, he had no time for her either."

"Why was that, do you think?"

"Just because she's so false. You can't believe a thing she says or does. Alex used to say she had more faces than the town clock. She's always sweetness and light with Mr. Mortimer – always. I've never seen her short with him or even disagreeing with him. No woman is like that with her man all the time. You fall out with them. Things they do get on your nerves. You can't help it if you're living with somebody. Even though they're hardly on top of each other in that big house. You're bound to snap sometimes. But not My Lady Ruzena. Always billing and cooing at him." She looked aside in disgust. "Make you sick."

"That's interesting," I said. "And when your husband used to say she was up to something, he never mentioned anything specific he thought she was up to, did he? Apart from being after his money?"

"No, just that."

"How does she treat you and the girls who clean?"

She thought for a second. "Lukewarm. That's the word I'd use. Lukewarm. She smiles and speaks nicely but there's no warmth in it. No sincerity. Except maybe Radka. She speaks to her more than any of the rest of us."

"Because she's Slovakian too, maybe."

"Maybe."

"And was she like that with your husband?"

"Aye, more or less. But, because he was a man, she would simper and flutter her eyelashes at him if she wanted a favour. Washing the car. Or cutting some roses. The great model."

"I take it Mr. Mortimer's looking after you," I said.

"Like the gentleman he is. Paying me my wages *and* Alex's at the moment. Says I don't have to go back till I'm ready. Such a genuine person. Unlike his wife."

"I'm truly sorry for your trouble."

"Thank you. Our son and his wife should be over from Canada tomorrow. That will help."

"Good."

When I left, I drove down Bowyett and, rather than pass the Preceptory, pulled in for a wander. The building is only open in summer months and even then only on Saturdays and Sundays, but I strolled through the churchyard and had me a mull over what Jean Gilmour had said. I've told you before I like cemeteries, especially old ones. I like the fact they're a massive *memento mori*. Reminds me that our life is short and swift. We pass over like clouds – just as fleeting, and leaving as little trace. Tara is grass, and look how it stands with Troy. There's a wheen of old, mournful looking trees and a plethora of gravestones. Some of the stones are 20th century, most are Victorian, and one or two go back as far as the mid eighteenth century. But there are headstones even older than that: tilted, weathered, crumbling and delaminating stones, some half sunk into the earth, many with those old symbols of death like draped urns, hourglasses, scrolls, crossed bones and grinning skulls. They go back even further than the eighteenth century. Hell, maybe there's a Knight of St. John under each of them.

In days of old, when knights were bold, the Preceptory stood within the Privilege of St. John, and there is a sanctuary stone in the graveyard marking the centre of this area of sanctuary, one old Scots mile square. All that stuff ended when the Knights were disbanded in 1564 after the Reformation took hold in Scotland. I tell you, what seems like eternity is just a breath in the wind.

I thought about the first time I'd seen Ruzena with Mortimer, in Queen Street. Seemed ages gone, but it was only a handful of days. Then, it seemed to me that she was a woman in love. Unless, I'd thought, she was an actress with the skills of a Helen Mirren, a Maggie Smith or a Judi Dench. I remembered thinking that. So, now the things Jean Gilmour had said were tending to the same conclusion. She was an actress. False as dicers' oaths. False as stairs of sand. False as hell.

All right. That just led me back to the same query. Why? Mrs. Gilmour had not the depth of knowledge of the couple that I had, so her – and her husband's – opinion of Roozh was a simple one; the old one. She was after his money. However, I knew, as she didn't, of the texts and phone calls threatening Mortimer. – Hey! But why had no trafficker turned up to at least argue over the money Morts had cost him? Eh? Aye, think about, then. All that huffing and puffing and nothing done. At least not yet.

I stood and read a gravestone, one of those obelisk ones. An obelisk is a symbol of fatherhood, I read somewhere. In Memory of Ebenezer Oliphant, Schoolmaster of Torphichen, who died, 24th of December, 1861 aged 77 years. His wife, Isabella. Their sons, the eldest of whom, Captain William K. Oliphant, died in Buenos Aires in 1848, aged 42. Fuck knows what a guy from Torphichen was doing over there. In the army, I guess, but I hadn't heard of any British – Argentine wars in the 19th century. But it just goes to show. People are never what they seem. You can never be sure what they're up to. Just what I'd been mulling over, in fact. Ebenezer Oliphant. I smiled – now *that* was a good name.

Anyway. What was it Geraldine Hunter had asked me about Ruzena? What I knew about her; about her childhood, her teenage years, her young womanhood. She said I'd a lot to learn about Ruzena. All right. I'd learned a fair whack in a short time. But I could happily do with learning more. I didn't fancy a drive to Edinburgh. I didn't have Gerry's phone number. But I knew someone who would.

I called Ruzena's cellphone.

"Hello?"

"Ruzena? It's Jack Black. How's the drive to Newcastle going?"

"Oh, fine. I like riding in Douglas's car. He's a very good driver. We should be there soon. Was it me or Douglas you wanted to speak to?"

"You, actually. When I spoke to Geraldine Hunter in the course of trying to find you, she asked me what I knew about you. I assume she was referring to the fact that Douglas has rescued five girls from traffickers. But she also asked what I knew about you when you were young, your background, that kind of thing? I don't know much, obviously, apart from what we spoke about on the plane. Now, I could just ask Geraldine what she means, but I have the distinct impression that that lady won't be cajoled into doing or saying anything she doesn't want to. So I wondered, when you come back up, if I could talk to you for half an hour and see if there's anything in your background that might help find who these bastards are who have been threatening you. Would you consider doing that?"

"Of course, Jack. The moment I'm back, I'll give you a call and set that up. How's that?"

"Brilliant. Thanks, Ruzena. Give my regards to Douglas. Bye."

I rang off and left the Oliphant family to their eternal rest, walked down the churchyard path to where I was parked in Bowyett, and drove back to the office.

The Statistical Account of 1843 was right. You could still see that 'sheltered plain' it referred to, as you drove back to Bathgate. The view on my right was like something some old Dutch master had painted. Tranquil, undulating countryside under wispy cloud. Trees, hills, dales. Cows grazing. Only the pylons looked out of place. But then, there's always one thing that fucks up an otherwise perfect picture, isn't there?

22

Some days are quiet days; others are the opposite. The following day was the opposite. I had barely opened up, lifted the mail from behind the door and set the kettle to boil, when I got a call from Douglas Mortimer.

"Jack! She's away! She's away again! Fuck knows where she is this time. Christ, I don't know, really I don't..."

"Woah, Douglas! Woah!" He woahed a little. "All right. Where are you?"

"Fuckin' Newcastle. Mind, came for her car."

"Yeah, but that was yesterday."

"We stayed owernight. Have some time thegither. We'd a guid night. A meal, a drink and a guid blether. An' then - she was away when I woke up. The Mazda's away tae. We brung it back fae the airport ti the Vermont. Steyin' at the Vermont Hotel, like."

"All right. She was just gone when you got up?"

"Aye. I sleep like a log, me. Woke up. Her side a the bed was empty an' aw her claes wis away. Went doonstairs, says ti the boy on reception an' he didnae ken nothin' aboot it. Looked in the car park. Mah car's there. Hers is away. I tried ti phone her again an' nothin'."

"All right. Maybe you'd best tell the local police."

"Fuck that. I'm comin' hame. Check oot Manderley, will ye? Get back ti me."

"What? Just drive up to the gates and look through?"

"See if the Mazda's there."

"What if she's put it in the garage?"

"Oh aye, right. Tell ye – Jean Gilmour's got the key back. Get it aff a her."

"Sure, I can do that. I'll get back to you."

He rung off. I looked wistfully at the kettle but left and drove to Torphichen .

Jean Gilmour didn't look too stoked to see me again. When I explained what I was after, she told me to come in. "I didn't want the bloody thing," she mumped. "I only took it to oblige Mr. Mortimer. What's the panic this time? My Lady vanished again?"

“Well, actually,” I said, “she has. They were in Newcastle last night and when Mortimer woke up … as you said, gone. The lady vanishes.”

“Seriously?” She stopped in her tracks. She had just lifted the key from a heap of oddments in an old fruit bowl on the sideboard. There was just about everything in that bowl – keys, coins, a comb, a jeweller’s screwdriver – just about everything, that is, except fruit. “She’s done another bunk?”

“So he told me this morning.”

She shook her head. “I don’t know why he bothers with her.”

“Because he loves her,” I suggested.

She favoured me with a withering look and handed over the key. Then she said, “Oh, you’ll need this as well,” before she opened the top drawer of the sideboard and passed me a doofer. “Top one opens the gates.”

On the short drive to Manderley, I gave Ruzena’s number a zap on the bluetooth. Nič. Nothing. Zip a dee doo dah. So she wasn’t answering my calls either, the wee besom.

I rolled up to the gates, fired the doofer at them and they peeled back. When I was halfway down the drive, they peeled shut again. There was no sign of a car at the house. I parked, got out, walked over to the garages and rolled each door up in turn. Only FAB 1 was at home. Douglas’s was still in Newcastle and Ruzena‘s was God knows where. I shut the doors and walked to the house. Opened up. Went in. Closed the door behind me. Stood stock still. That oppressive silence that tells you there’s nobody home, and hasn’t been for hours.

I went in to every room. The longcase clock in the ‘lounge’ – taller by far than the old man himself – sounded obscenely loud in the otherwise silent house. Nothing untoward. Nor in the dining room, ‘the living-room’, the cinema room; the smoking room; the ‘library’ or the kitchen. I stepped quickly and quietly up the stairs. Nothing untoward in Mortimer’s bedroom, ‘office’ or bathroom. Nothing untowarder in Ruzena’s suite of rooms. I checked her fitted wardrobes. Rails of expensive clothes. Didn’t look like much was missing other than the clothes she would have packed for an overnighter. The only sounds in the vast house, other than any I made, were the sonorous tick-tock of the grandfather clock in the ‘lounge’ and the ‘ping’ of the Vienna wall clock in the hall for the hour when I came back downstairs again. Nothing obviously amiss or even missing.

But, now that I thought about it, why would there be? Her decampment had obviously not been premeditated. If she had just decided to bolt while she was on the road to Newcastle, or while she was in the city - more so if the scram was no choice of hers - what the hell *would* be missing? But, unless somebody dogged them from Manderley to Newcastle again, and that was not impossible, how could she have been taken?

Which left the alternative. That she'd taken a powder. Why would she?

These thoughts, as I locked up and turned towards the car, were interrupted by my phone going off in my pocket. Mortimer? Maybe Ruzena – getting back to me? I angled it out. Emma.

"Em?"

"Jack, where are you? I'm at your office."

"I'm at Manderley. Mortimer asked me to check the place out. Ruzena's vanished again. From Newcastle."

"Jeee-sus H. Christ! Well, hang on to your hat. Geraldine Hunter is dead."

"What?!!! How?"

"How long will you be?"

"Stay there. I'll be with you in ten."

Emma was in my wee ante-room when I got there. Like Marlowe, I leave the outer door unlocked when I'm away in daylight hours so that potential customers can park their ass on the wooden bench by the wall, if they wish, and await the master's return. She was texting. She looked up when I opened the door.

"Sorry to keep you, Em," I said.

"No probs," she said, finishing her text before putting her phone in her coat pocket. "Your landlady is a really nice person. She offered me tea or coffee."

"Did she?" I said, unlocking the door. "Aye, Cho's a wonderful woman. Her laddies are great too. They've saved my skin once or twice."

We got in and I switched the kettle on. "Pull up a stool and sing." I hauled two mugs.

"Yeah, right. Geraldine Hunter was killed in a hit and run in Montague Street last night at 11.40 p.m. One witness. Hunter killed by a Silver Nissan Note driven by a young Caucasian male in a hoodie, drove on to the pavement, crushed Hunter against a tenement wall, drove off, almost crashed into another car on St. Leonard's Street, and drove off at high speed away down the Pleasance. Car later found abandoned on Arthur's Seat. Had been…"

"Stolen, yeah. So not an accident."

"Hardly. Hunter pronounced dead at the scene. Five yards from her own front door."

I poured two coffees, brought them over, handed one to Emma and sat down opposite her with mine.

She said, "Think it's the Glaswegians come to call again?"

I took a slurp of coffee and said, "Maybe. In a way. But I am beginning to think that our Ruzena is in on all this shit."

"Say why."

"What you said yesterday - how believing calls to Mortimer could be traced or bugged or hacked was a load a shit. Phyllis suggested that too. I spoke to Jean Gilmour yesterday after you left. Went to see her at Torphichen. She can't stand Ruzena, said her man had been the same. Said they both thought she was as fake as Liberace. The husband had said once or twice that she was up to something. Made me think again. I mean, when you said that, it compounded Phyllis having said it. And then Jean Gilmour – well, I thought, three smart women can't all be wrong. And I went over it again in my head. Came to the same conclusion as you three did. There's something phony about Ruzena Dolezal; about as phony as a phone box."

"So… why make the jump from that to her being involved?"

"Because I phoned her, before I left Torphichen. I said Geraldine Hunter had questioned me about how much I knew about our Roozh, that time I spoke to her. I said to Ruzena I didn't know much, bar what she'd told me on the plane back from gay Paree, and could I speak to her when she got back from Newcastle. She said aye. Hung up. And now Geraldine Hunter is dead. That strike you as fishy, or is it just me?"

"No. It's fishy."

"Fishy as fish sauce. I think Ruzena gave the order for the hit."

"Mmm. Maybe so. So why would she be involved in intimidating Mortimer and killing Gilmour?"

"Gilmour's murder wasn't planned. Certain of that. It just became necessary. You see, I think Ruzena bailed out and left the place for Mortimer to come back to, unaware she would be gone. The intended victim was Mortimer, not Gilmour. But … well, we know what happened. But the stiff was meant to be Mortimer, I'm sure."

"Why not do it herself?"

"Because she would be the Number 1 suspect. If she's away, then she's out of the frame. Same reason she stayed married to him for three years. Let time pass. Make it look like they are happily married. But I'm beginning to think she's somewhere at the back of it. In some capacity."

"So why not arrange it for when she's abroad, modelling?"

"I've thought about that as well. That struck me as the obvious time to have it done too. And the only reason can be that …"

"It's only recently been decided on."

"Give that lassie a coconut."

"So what's the motive?"

"Not sure, to be honest. It *could* still just be the money. I dare say she's his sole beneficiary. But… I don't know."

"What? Come on, don't be shy with *me*."

"I wonder if it's connected to the trafficking thing."

"In what way?"

"Revenge. The gang who organise shipping these lassies to UK for shagging purposes lose a hell of a lot of money when one of the girls is rescued. Not only *that* – Mortimer will be a source of hope for many more. He has to be rubbed out."

"And you think she's involved in a plot to kill her husband?"

I shrugged. "Could be."

Emma nodded slowly for a second or two. Then she said, "I think she might be, too. We need to get a hold of her right away. In connection with the murder of Geraldine Hunter alone."

"You do. And quickly. I'm happy to leave all of that shit to you guys."

"Might not just be us guys. Don't be going too far afield in the next week or so. We may need you."

"Need me?"

"This smacks of organised crime all right. So … Slovakian girls. Slovakian model. Family living in Italy. Europol might be on the cards here. We might need to call on their assistance. If we have to be in Mestre, for example, I want you there."

"Been there, done that, bought the Murano glass paperweight."

"Seriously, Jack. Here in Scotland we're looking for Bashir Ahmed and the young guy, or two young guys, driving stolen cars. Looking for Ruzena Dolezal too. If she's in Mestre…"

"Europol will deal with her. Or the local carabinieri."

"I might want to be there. I've never seen Venice."

I laughed. "All right. But it's a long shot."

"Sure. In the meantime, give the matter some of that grey matter of yours and see what
you can come up with to help us."

"You got it, sister."

23

The next day, the rain was unrelenting. It lashed down. It was Biblical, third act of *King Lear* stuff. 'You cataracts and hurricanoes, spout till you have drench'd our steeples, drown'd the cocks!' I stood at the window of the office and watched it sizzle in the streets, driven every now and then by squalls of wind that dashed it against the glass. Such groans of roaring wind and rain, I never remember to have heard.

I hadn't slept well. Mortimer had phoned me to ask what I'd found out at Manderley, which was nothing, and stayed on the phone for the best part of half an hour, bleating and maundering about his wife and what could have happened to her. I felt sorry for the guy but all I could tell him was that the police were on to it. There are many events in the womb of time which will be delivered. But on and on he went. Eventually, Phyl gave me the glare so I interrupted him, said I had to go but I'd be up to see him on the morrow. And here I was, having thought the case over all night. And wondering what in the devil's name I was going to say to him when I got to Manderley. How I hoped Emma would phone to tell me that Ruzena had been found safe and well, with a light-hearted and perfectly plausible explanation for her second disappearance …

But she didn't. So, at half past eleven, I donned my hat and coat, texted Mortimer to say I was en route, and I headed off to Acredale and the car. The piss was pelting down so that, by the time I got along King Street and into the car park, roughly one minute and fifty-three seconds later, I was drenched. Hey ho, the wind and the rain. I sat in the driver's seat and wiped the wet from my face. It took two minutes to demist the windscreen. Ever have one of those mornings you wish you'd just gone into the Civil Service like all the other grools? Eventually, I pulled out and motored up to Manderley.

Mortimer was quiet. Lugubrious. He was disposed to mirth, but on the sudden a Roman thought hath struck him. Like he was resigned to hearing that his glam young model wife had been kidnapped and chopped into messes for a goulash. He let me in and told me to sit in the lounge – there was a fire on – and he'd bring me a coffee. I opened the lounge door and the heat hit me square in the pan. You could have roasted an ox over that fire. I took off my coat, opened the neck of my shirt and wafted my hand in front of my face. What the fuck…?

Which was the precise interrogative pronominal phrase I used to start my question when he came in. "What the fuck made you put that fire on, Douglas? It's not cold outside; it's just raining. It's lashing down, right enough, but it's not cold."

"Cannae get a heat in me, Jack," he said, handing me a coffee. "There's somethin' wrong wi Roozh. I can just feel it in ma bones."

"Can we sit in a room that isnae like a crematorium furnace?"

"Eh? Aw. If you want."

We moved to the living-room. The rain battered the windows. "What's happened, do you think, Jack? Naeb'dy can have ta'en her this time. I'd a kent. She's away under her ain steam. What's the maitter? What have I done wrong?"

"You've done nothing wrong, Douglas," I said. "You're a good man. You're not to blame for anything. And we don't know what's happened yet, so don't be jumping to conclusions."

"DI Wid would contact you if they fund anythin', wouldn't she?"

"You're the first she'd contact. Put your mind at rest about that."

"What am I gonnae dae?"

"Keep calm and do a jigsaw. Listen to a pipe band CD. Seriously. Try to chill as much as you can."

"Easier said than done."

"I know, but you have to try. Now. Can I talk to you about Ruzena? See if anything comes up that might help us?"

"Of course."

"So. First. Tell me about her family. Mother, father, brother. Are they close?"

"The faimly? Oh aye. Awfu' close. Well, you've met the faither an' brither."

"They didnae act awfu' close to me, I have to say. Tell me how you see them."

"How I *see* them?"

"What they're like – with you and with each other. Start off with … are they proud of Ruzena?"

"Oh aye. Proud as Punch. Mind, they dinnae go on aboot it. She's still just their lassie, an' his sister. But oh aye, they're proud ae her."

"Ruzena told me it was her aunt that got her into the modelling."

"That's right. The maw's sister. Her Auntie Lenka. She's a hell of a nice wumman – well, like the mother, Dominika. The auntie and uncle bide in a place called … what the hang …?"

"Pavlovce?"

"That's it! How the hair ile did you ken that?"

"Ruzena mentioned the place when we were talking on the plane. Said she bought her folks a house there."

"So she did, aye. But they only go there on holidays."

"Okay. What's Dominika like?"

"Wee fat thing. Nice, mind you. Great cook. Cheery body but disnae understand a word I say. Handy aboot the hoose, though. An' idolises Roozh."

"Okay. How about Tomas? Apart from being crabbit with me, what's he like?"

"Crabbit. Well … *dour*. He works away in the refinery there and he likes a gless a wine at night. Don't get me wrong; he's hospitable enough. But no a great socialiser."

"No shit. Proud of Ruzena?"

"Aye. Disnae say much but you can see his chest swell wi pride at times."

"And brother Pavol. Or Paolo as he is now?"

Mortimer shrugged. "Typical daft young cunt. Never says much ti me when I'm there."

"Yeah, I think I'd agree with that character sketch. What about Auntie Lenka?"

"Only met her the wance. In the hoose at Mestre. But a lovely woman. Younger than the mother and quite good lookin' hersel', you know?"

"And she'll be proud, I take it?"

"Very. Oh aye. Smiles at Roozh aw the time. Cannae take her eyes aff her."

"What about her husband, the uncle?"

"Never met him. Tibor, he's cried, an' that's aw I ken aboot him. They never spoke aboot him when I was there."

"Tibor and Lenka what? – It'll no be Dolezal, because that's Ruzena's father's name, isn't it?"

"That's right. D'you know, I don't think I know that eether." He thought. "Nup. I'm sure I never heard it."

"All right. So. Enough about the family. Time to look a wee bit more closely at you and Ruzena yourselves. As a couple. See when you met Ruzena the first time, at that do in the *Scotsman* building…?"

"Wisnae in the *Scotsman* buildin'. It was run bi the *Scotsman* right enough, but it was in the Caley Hotel. Ken, the Caledonian?"

"Right. Did you tell her about the lassies you rescued? Was that how you took her interest?"

"Well, it was the opposite wey aboot. I was talkin' ti wan a the journalists an' another wan brought Roozh over, introduced her. Said she wanted ti meet the Scottish Businessman a the Year – the award Ah won. So I got her a gless a wine an' we got talkin'. I didnae ken who she was. Well, Ah'm no really inti modellin' or that stuff. But she tellt me she'd won an award tae, an' that she was a model and she was fae Slovakia. 'Oh,' says I, 'some a mah trucks go ti Slovakia. Never been there masel, but some a ma fleet has,' kind a thing. An' *she* says ti *me*, 'A wee bird tellt me you do guid things in Slovakia whether ye're there or no.' And…"

"She talked just like you, then," I said and smiled. "A Slovakian lassie speaking English with a West Lothian accent?"

"Well, that's what she says in so many words. Aw right, smartarse?" And *he* smiled. A little, wintry one.

"Good, a smile," I said. "On you go."

"An', well, I was a bit wary at the kick-aff, but she said she heard that I'd rescued a few lassies fi prostitution an' that. So I says, hardly that, I helped some kids a bit but it wasnae a big deal, and she says, how did I think the lassies would feel, and their folks when they heard the news. An' well, I kinna soft-pedalled aw that talk 'cos I don't like talkin' about it. But that was the start a things. We went on ti speak aboot lots a other things." He stopped and breathed in through his nose. "Aye. That was the start."

"Okay. Good stuff," I said. "How about politics? Is she political at all?"

"Naw, no really. She watches the news and she reads the papers but I've never heard her talk aboot politics."

"M-hm. Okay, easier stuff. Like in the old fan magazines. Likes and dislikes?"

"Jist in general?"

"Aye."

"I widnae ken where to start."

"All right. Food and drink."

"Er, she likes Italian food and hates curry. She drinks red wine or a gin and tonic. Disnae like beer."

"Music."

"She likes maist things but she hates Rap."

"Reading."

"Nae idea. You'd ken that better than me fae the books she has."

"Films."

"She likes love stories an' comedies. Historic stuff. But she disnae like Westerns. An' she's no struck on gangster pictures. Or action pictures. Ken, men's stuff?"

"What about you? What does she like about you most and least?"

"Me? Fuck, I donno. She says I'm a guid man. She likes that I dinnae talk much aboot savin' the lassies. She likes ma sense a humour. Dislikes? She says I smoke too much." He guffawed. "An' I fart too much tae."

"Ah! There's a laugh. Good. Lifted your spirits a bit, hopefully. Has Ruzena any interest in the business side of things? I mean, does she ever ask about your work, say? How you started, how you built up Mortimer Logistics, the places your lorries go, the markets you've still to open up?"

He pursed his lips and thought for a second. "Nah, no really. We spoke aboot that kinna thing at the start, but she never asks aboot anythin' now. If I talk aboot the work, she'll listen but I don't think she's that interested."

"Okay," I said. "let me think about all of that and see if anything comes out of it. In the meantime, I'm afraid it's a waiting game. Emma Wood will call you the minute she knows anything. I'll keep you in mind at all times and you can ring me if anything strikes you, okay?"

"Okay."

"Seriously, have you got a big jigsaw you haven't done?"

"Aye, two or three."

"Do one. Occupy your mind. Pass the time. Get the biggest one out and do it. Play 'The Black Bear' on a loop while you do. All right?" I said, standing up. "I'll be seeing you."

"Thanks, Jack," he said, shaking my hand. "You're a top guy."

"Don't I know it."

I hadn't mentioned Geraldine Hunter's death for the simple reason that *he* hadn't, which suggested he didn't know about it. Besides, telling him would have got him as antsy as an ant-hill, and he didn't need any more excuses for that. I piled in the bogie and headed back towards town. It was still pissing down. For the rain it raineth every day.

24

I needed to get that old A game of mine out again, blow off the cobwebs and see if I could do something practical to assist Emma. I fancied a drive to Glasgow, so I drove over to Starlaw and took the motorway west. It's a strange thing – I've mentioned it before – but it seems to me I've only ever had weird or threatening or negative experiences in that city. Now, I know there's roughly a million and a quarter souls moving around the Dear Green Place and I also know that most of them are the salt of the earth. It's just that I cannot remember anything but bad times when I've been in Glasgow. Sod it. I'd be Pollyanna for the day. Or maybe even Pangloss – at least he was the same gender. This would be the day when something exceptional, something wonderful happened to me in Glasgow. I zoomed out the M8: Whitburn, Eastfield, Kirk of Shotts, Newhouse, Bargeddie and the M73 to the M74. Off the 74 at Junction 1A, took the A728; right on to Calder Street, and the tenth on the right from that was Ardbeg Street. Took me 38 minutes to do the roughly 30 miles. Groovin'.

It's a short and narrow street of red sandstone buildings and privet hedges that would look good in an evening sunset, I reckon. This afternoon, the rain had washed all the colours out. Aaaah-ah, we fade to grey. I knew the address where Mortimer had ransomed Radka, but I wasn't interested in checking that out. I was pretty sure it would be a sparsely furnished apartment for rent, unoccupied at the present time. No, what I wanted to do was to check out Bashir Ahmed's shop in Calder Street, not too far along from the corner with Ardbeg. I'd checked on the Web the night before and sussed where it was.

There weren't too many brave souls on the street in that downpour, but the one or two I saw were definitely Asian, from the subcontinent. There were Asian shops perforating the street too: restaurants, grocers, dairies and a travel agent that I saw. Ahmed's place, 'Nakhlistan', on the other side of the street and just along a bit from the Govanhill Library, was open.

It was a bog standard wee shop, a kind of Jannat A'thing I suppose, with the cash register and a small counter with glass display cases of sweets on the right as you went in the door; shelves of booze and fags behind the counter; and the rest of the space taken up by shelves of the kind of groceries that you nip out to the corner shop for at night. There was a young male behind the counter, not in shalwar kameez and bushy beard but in a leather jacket and jeans. He was clean shaven and extremely handsome. He smiled non-committally as I looked over.

"Assalaam alaikum," I said.

"Waalaikum assalaam," he replied.

"App kaaisii hai?" I said.

He said, "Bahut achaa, shukriyaa." And then he spoke some more Urdu and that was me fucked.

"Sorry," I said, "I only know a few words of Urdu."

"Good for you," he said in a Glasgow accent. "Maist folk don't even bother. Why did you?"

"Oh, once upon a time I was a teacher for my sins. I had a lot of kids from Asian families in my classes and I learnt a few phrases just to be able to be sociable to mums and dads and grandparents at Parent's Nights."

"Excellent, ma man. You lookin' for anythin' in particular? "

"Not messages-wise," I said. "I was actually looking for Mr. Ahmed. Mr. Bashir Ahmed."

"Aw. Dad's no here the now. He's in Pakistan. Fam'ly weddin', you know? What was it to do wi'?"

There was a volley of Urdu from behind the stacks of Curly Wurlies, Fry's Chocolate Creams and Aeros. An older man, but still a young one, so I assumed a brother, stood up from behind the display cases. Wee brother spoke Urdu back. Big brother snarled some. Wee brother replied some more, snappishly. Big brother turned to me.

"What do you want Mr. Ahmed for, eh, man?"

"It's a business thing."

"Yeah? Well, he's not here. Tell me, I'm his oldest son."

"Well, it's to do with something he might want to buy."

He swept his arm around. "Does it look like we need any more stock?"

"Not that kind of thing."

Now he calmed a little. "You got a bride?" he said quietly.

"Yep," I said. "When does your father get back from Pakistan?"

"We're not a hundred per cent sure. Maybe not for a week or two. Give me your mobile number, man, and I'll get him to contact you. He phones every night."

"Yeah? Great. It's 07823 555 254. Get your old man to give me a ring."

He punched the numbers into his phone. "Where you livin', man?"

I sang, "Wherever I hang my hat, that's my home. See you guys."

The older one laughed. "Wise man. Take care."

"I intend to."

Younger brother said nothing. He had taken a huff. I took my leave. It was still raining, still overcast. Devenir gris. Aaaah-ah, we fade to grey. Well, I don't know about wonderful or exceptional, but it was a better day than many I'd had in Glasgow. And I hadn't actually lied when I'd told that guy I had a bride. I had a great one. She just wasn't for sale.

On a whim, I drove out to Boghall on the way home, the wipers beating away but not really coping with the rain and the spray from other cars. I was calling on Radka Bartoš again. Just because she wasn't due to be cleaning at Manderley didn't mean she would be at home, I knew. But it was worth the five minutes' drive to check.

I splashed up the steps to her door as a jag of lightning fizzed through the sky. Rumble thy bellyful! Spit, fire! Spout, rain! She answered the door to my knock and looked warily at me.

"Hello, Radka," I said. "I'm sorry to bother you again but I want to help Mr. and Mrs. Mortimer. Can I talk to you for five minutes? That's all it would take, and then I'll try not to pester you again."

"Come in, please."

I went in and she offered to hang up my coat, but I refused. "No, thanks, I won't stay that long. I want to ask you something about when you were brought over to UK. I know it must be a painful time to think about but Mr. Mortimer helped you then and I want to help *him* now."

"Is all right. Ask."

"You were told you were coming over to a good job, in a supermarket, I think?"

"Yes. Is true."

"Can you remember any names of the people involved? Who told you you would get a job in a supermarket, for example?"

"Is something I am frightened to talk about. I do not want trouble."

"Radka, let me assure you, you will come to no trouble, if you tell me. I will make sure of that. I will not be mentioning your name."

"I am not … want to say this."

"You'll be safe, I promise. Look at it this way. Mr. Mortimer helped you. Now is your chance to help him."

"Help him? How?"

"Mr. Mortimer is being pestered by strangers. If one of them is the man who lied to you about a job in Glasgow, we can do a favour for both of you. Please, Radka."

She gathered her courage. "The man who organised this was called Novak. Is all I know. Not his first name. Only Mr. Novak. And I hear the driver who brought me from Birmingham is called Craw. Maybe is the name Crowe. This is the Scottish way of say 'crow', I think."

"From Birmingham?"

"Yes. I am on a lorry from Slovakia to Birmingham. Maybe six people. Two of us are going to Glasgow. In Birmingham, a van picks us up for Glasgow. The driver is called Craw. Is all I know."

"That's a great help, Radka. Now, I'm off and I guarantee you won't be bothered again."

"I hope."

She shut the door behind me and I skipped down the steps. Novak the Slovak, eh? Well, if the Emmaroo was going to work with Europol, maybe that name would grease some nipples. By this time, I was wiped out so I decided just to head home and spend some down time with the loved ones. I Googled 'Nakhlistan' when I got in. The Urdu word for an oasis. Mmm. Then I shut the PC down. The little I had for Emma wouldn't spoil by being kept overnight. It was good – contact made with Ahmed's sons and marriages mentioned; and a positive name for one of the gang in Kosice – but I thought kicking back for the night and passing it on the following day would present no significant problems.

As my mother used to say, “You know what thought did.”

25

I got to Acredale about half nine in the morning having slept like a top or, as my father used to say, having taken a short course in death. I was awake, refreshed, ready to rumble. I bought a Herald for the crossword and a shitrag for the chance to hate the Tories again. I swithered about buying something for my lunch, then decided I would leave that till nearer the time. It was sunny, bright and promising warmth. It had all the makings of a good day. I walked along King Street with a spring in my step and bade everybody I passed a 'Good morning.' Just by the Dreadnought, I met Rab Buchanan, a guy who used to live near me in Boghall, back in my single days. He was built like the proverbial brick shithouse and was a very political animal.

"What about that fire in that tower in London, Jack?" he said. "Fuckin' disgrace, isn't it? All that cheap shite claddin' and nae sprinklers. Only one stair. See when you hear these Tory bastards goin' on about deregulatin' the buildin' industry? See what their deregulation's done – *that* many folk deid. Died a horrible death. Unnecessary death. Makes you puke, man."

"Just part of the inhumanity that's rife just now, Rab," I said. "Profit margins before poor folk. So long as bastards are making money, they don't give a shit about anybody else."

"You said it, Jack. High time there was a revolution in this country."

We shot it for a minute or so longer and, just as I was about to take my leave, I noticed, over Rab's shoulder, two men crossing the road from the car park and heading towards the alley to the back of Cho's. Both tall, both slim, one, the younger, wearing a hoodie with the hood down. The older one dark haired, the younger one ginger. Hands in pockets, looking around. I stopped talking and looked. Rab said to me, "Somethin' wrong, Jack?"

"They two," I said, nodding over his shoulder.

He turned. "Ken them?"

"No," I said. "But they're headed for my place, I'll guarantee it."

"Trouble, do you think?"

"Well, they're no deliverin' the milk, that's for sure."

"No problem," said Rab and called, "haw! You cunts! What ye's up to?"

The young man stopped just outside Cho's front door (locked at the time). They looked in our direction, clocked the size of Rab and took off along King Street towards the Edinburgh Road.

"Come 'ere, ya bastarts!" he shouted and took off after them. I had no option but to join in, since Rab was doing all this on my say-so. I threw the papers to the winds and hared away in pursuit too. Along King Street towards the junction with Academy Street, the two men sprinted, heads back, arms pumping,
legs a blur. A black Lexus with tinted windows pulled out of the car park opposite and turned right. Rab was just behind the youths as they zipped across the mouth of Academy Street. A car stopped with a lurch and a squeal as it turned right off the Edinburgh Road and the driver pumped the horn loudly, then ran his window down and shouted obscenities at the runners.

They gave no fucks. Nor did Rab as he raced along in pursuit. I stopped and let the guy proceed up Academy Street then I took off again, yards behind. The Edinburgh Road was devoid of traffic for the moment, all the way up to the Farl and most of the way back towards the Steelyard. Only the black Lexus, moving slowly, was coming from the town centre. Now it gave a blast on the horn and the two youths looked back quickly, and cut across the empty road to the farther side. As Rab saw what was happening, the Lexus picked up speed and, when he ran across the road too, it accelerated in a blink and smacked into his right leg just below the hip, flipping him into the air where he spun twice before he landed on his back in the middle of the road.

"Rab!!!" I shouted and ran towards where he lay.

But, before I got to him, the Lexus stopped, the two thugs grabbed me and threw me in the back seat, the ginger-haired one got in beside me and the other jumped in the passenger side. The driver pulled away with a squeal of rubber that told me he'd left a centimetre or two of tyre wall on the surface of the road. Now cars were heading into town from the east and the driver – an Asian guy – wrenched the car left across the carriageway and up Gordon Avenue. There was a cacophony of horns, cars stopped and folk got out to check on the supine Rab Buchanan.

Meanwhile, we zipped up Gordon Street and on to Marjoribanks Street, turning left.

The guy next to me slid a blade out of his inner pocket and put the point to my throat. "Don't fuckin' move," he said.

"I won't," I said. I didn't.

Along Marjoribanks, down Hopetoun Street and North Bridge Street, left at the roundabout, along Menzies Road and on to the Whitburn Road. Glasgow bound, for sure.

"Thanks for that, Jamil," said the guy in front to the driver. "That big cunt woulda kilt us."

"You shouldn't have run, man," said the driver. Then he flicked his eyes up to the rear-view mirror and said to me, "What was all that about, man? We were just coming to see you about your business proposition." The older brother from the Calder Street Oasis.

"I'm sorry," I said. "It was my friend who shouted and did the chasing. I had no idea that he was going to do that."

"Yeah? Who is he?"

"I only know him as Rab," I lied. "A hard man but mad as a fucking mongoose. Sorry about that." We were on the M8 now and heading west. "I didn't know who the two guys were," I said. "Your father didn't phone me last night so I had no idea what was going on."

"Yeah."

"Look," I said, "I need a shit. I've had sickness and diarrhoea all night and that running has upset me. Can we stop at Harthill Services? I don't want to mess your upholstery."

"No fucking way," said the front guy. "He'll do a runner."

"No I won't," I said. "One of you can come with me just till I get sorted. Anyway, I want to speak to Jamil and his brother about business."

There was a silence and Jamil said, "All right."

I had no intention of discussing any business proposition with Jamil and his brother; my sole intention was to get the fuck out of that situation, and the old Code Brown trick was my best shot. I'd worked it once, a few years before, in Byres Road in Glasgow. Then, I was being marshalled about by a couple of bonedomed heavies working for a guy I was trying to trace. Maybe Glaswegian baddies just brought out the shit in me.

We pulled off the freeway into what used to be Harthill Services, rebuilt twice and grandiosely renamed 'Heart of Scotland' in 2006. The old place had had ideas above its service station. It was a shithole, the dirtiest stop on the motorway system, folk used to say. The M8 is a short motorway, Edinburgh to Glasgow, and most drivers on it are commuters with no requirement for extensive catering. I hadn't been inside in some time. Now it was simply a BP garage with a couple of amenities: an M & S Simply Food and a Wild Bean Café. Maybe they should have called it, 'Heart Bypass of Scotland'. But, where there was any catering, there would be toilets.

As it turned out, I had no need of them. We parked and the older one got out of the passenger door, opened the back door and hauled me out, saying, "Try anythin' an' yer deid."

I said, "Right," and pointed to the left side of the BP Connect shop. "There's the Wild Bean Café," I said. "There's bound to be a can there."

"Right. Stay close to me. Don't try nothin'."

"You got it."

But he hadn't, of course. I was wondering whether I should give him a hearty dropkick in the jube-jubes, like I did with the gorilla in Glasgow that time, when I realised it would be a lot more simple than that. Much to my delight, lined up at one of pumps was a squad car and a policeman just emerged from the kiosk at that moment, no doubt having signed for his allocation of juice. His mate was in the passenger seat, looking at something in his lap.

I simply walked diagonally away from my escort and towards the cop car. When the thug realised what I was doing, he about turned and legged it back to the Lexus.

"Officer!" I shouted to the cop just approaching his car, "That guy kidnapped me! He and his mates injured a man in Bathgate in a hit and run. See? The black Lexus."

By this time, Jamil, having seen what was going down, had gunned the Lexus and was whizzing across the forecourt towards the road. The goon ran after it, yelling, "Stop, ya bastard!"

"Get in the car!" the cop shouted and I sprinted to it and piled in the back. The cop got in and started up the engine as Jamil battered on to the motorway and tore off westward. The dark-haired bastard, trying desperately to haul the passenger door open, was dragged across the forecourt and left sprawling.

"We'll need to pick him up," said the cop behind the wheel.

"It's fine," I said. "I know the driver of the Lexus and where he works. Did you see the reg? J4MIL. Guy's name is Jamil. Get that other one. They drew a shank on me."

"You'll need to get in the front when we do."

"Sure."

They picked him up off the tarmac, slapped the bracelets on him and the other cop slung him in the back before sliding in beside him. I sat up front with the driver. "You any idea how my mate's doing?" I said. "The guy hurt in the hit and run? Robert Buchanan is his name."

"Find out for you," said the policeman in the back, and he started on his radio.

It impresses me, the number of devices these guys have to manage at one time. Most cops now have a job-issued mobile for placing routine calls for appointments to see people, for general enquiries, for contacting other agencies and things like that. They also have a car radio which is usually tuned to the Force's radio channel. This is for important and urgent calls such as road traffic collisions, pursuits and firearms etc. Besides those, each officer has his own personal radio attached to him. This is tuned to the local area channel and they receive most of their calls and tasks via that one. Like I say, impressive. If the phone rings when I'm changing channels on the TV, I try to answer it with the remote control. That's how co-ordinated I am.

"We'll head that way," said the driver. "This guy should be at Livingston if he was involved."

"He was," I said. And I told them the story.

Turns out Rab was alive but had been removed to St. John's. Something at least. The cop in back gleaned that nugget for me.

"Where do you want us to drop *you*, buddy?" said the driver.

"Take me to the Civic Centre too," I told him. "My name is Jack Black. I'm a P.I. and I work a lot with DI Wood. I'm helping her on a case at the moment."

He looked at me. "All right," he said. "We can do that."

26

The goon we'd captured was called Shane Easton. Figured. Shane is a dug's name, as my father might have said. He was led away for questioning by Shirley Honeyman and Gerry Vaughan. The two Murdochs from Harthill said they had alerted Glasgow to the son of Bashir Ahmed's involvement in the hit and run, in a black Lexus, registration plate J4MIL. They took off to pursue that line of inquiry, with Emma promising to liaise with the Weegie CID later.

That left Emma, Jim Bryce and me in her office. She looked at me and smiled, widened her eyes as if to say, 'On you go.'

"Well, I was just trying to get the grey matter working to see if I could come up with something to help you," I said. "As requested."

"And how did that go?"

"Be you the judge. But first, how is Rab Buchanan doing?"

Jim said, "Just off the blower, Jack. Broken pelvis, two broken legs and concussion. But he'll live. He's tough, they said."

"Good. He is. And is there any word of Ruzena Dolezal Mortimer?"

"Not yet," said Emma. "I've contacted Europol and they've set up a hunt."

"Excellent."

"What happened, Jack?" said Emma.

"Right. I wanted to help you. So yesterday morning I went to Manderley and spent some time with Mortimer, trying to ferret out information we could use. Asked him about Ruzena, what sort of person she was, her level of interest in the Mortimer firm, what her family was like and so on. Got that they're a tight family; the mother, name of Dominika, is a stay-at-home, practical and a good cook; father, Tomas, is dour, works in the refinery and isn't a socialiser. The psycho brother, Pavol by his Slovak name, Paolo now, is a 'daft young cunt', to quote Sir Douglas. There is an aunt and uncle who live in Pavlovce, where Dominika is from and where Ruzena bought her folks a second home. Mortimer has never seen Tibor, the uncle, but the aunt, Lenka, Dominika's sister, is the one who got Roozh started on the modelling career. All very proud of Ruzena."

"Does that help us?" said Emma.

"Don't know yet. I moved on to asking him about the time they met at the *Scotsman* do, and did he tell her about the Slovakian girls he was responsible for saving. He said she knew about it before."

"*Did* she?" said Emma. "Now that might be of interest."

"My thoughts, too. Apparently, after the introductions, she said she was a model from Slovakia, he said some of his lorries go there but he never has, and she said … how did he put it? That 'a wee bird tellt her he did good things in Slovakia whether he was there or no.' Turns out she knew the deal all right, despite his reluctance to admit to his part."

"How the hell would she know?" said Emma. "He tells nobody. Nobody knew, apart from the girls."

"The drivers would know, ma'am," said Jim. "At least, them who did the Slovakia run."

"Why would they?" I said. "Mortimer's direct involvement comes when the girls are dropped at Birmingham. A minibus or something picks them up there. But I wondered before – mind, we spoke about it, Em – whether she was privy to information at the Slovakian end. Now, it seems she might well have been."

"All right. Anything else?" said Emma.

"Tried to deflect his mind from why I might have asked all that by asking about her likes and dislikes. Nothing of any import there. Then I finished by asking if she ever asked about the work: how he started, built it up, the markets he's opened up and any plans for the future. He said she *used* to. At the start. But hasn't seemed interested for a while."

"For the simple reason, maybe, that she got the information she needed some time ago and has no further need of any more?" said Emma.

"It's at least a possibility," I said. "But I did more yesterday. Append! I went to Glasgow, to Ardbeg Street. And, more importantly, to Calder Street."

And I told them of my visit to the oasis, of the younger Ahmed telling me that Father was in Pakistan and of older brother, Jamil as I now knew him to be, throwing a strop, then asking if I had a bride. Of my giving him my mobile number. And of his driving the two yobs Rab chased off King Street.

"*He* mentioned the bride thing, not you?"

"Yep. The shop is called 'Nakhlistan' and it's in Calder Street, like I say. I doubt if Bashir Ahmed is in Pakistan, though."

"More likely to be in Partick than Pakistan," said Jim.

"Aye, that'll be the routine answer to a query about him," said Emma. "So we share this with Glasgow."

"And finally…" I said.

"More?" said Emma. "My, you *have* been a busy boy."

"You asked for my help," I said. "Lastly, I spoke to Radka Bartoš last night. The surname of the guy who is responsible for her trafficking from Kosice is Novak. That's all she knew. Novak. But you guys maybe knew that."

"No, we didn't," said Emma. "Novak?

"As in 'Kim'?" said Bryce.

"Exactly that," I said. "Incredibly common name in Slavic countries. Means 'stranger' or 'newcomer'. Often given to a newcomer in a city."

"How the hell do you *know* these things?" said Jim.

"I didn't. I looked it up."

"Why do you look these things *up*?" he laughed.

"So that I know more than I used to."

Emma looked at me and we both smiled. "Are you thinking what I'm thinking?" she said.

"Oh aye. Now, any chance of a lift back to Bathgate?"

Jim looked bewildered. "What are you both thinking?" he said.

"Great work," said Emma, standing up.

"Thought 'Novak' might be a useful name to run by Europol," I said.

Emma said, "Calling Roos de Jaager at 4 p.m. She is head of the human trafficking unit at the Hague. It might start a hare."

"Definitely working on those tropes, Em," I said. "It's paying off."

"What are ye's *think*ing?" snapped Jim.

Emma looked at me. I looked at her, then at Jim. "Think about it, Jim," I said. "It'll come to you in a flash."

"Flash? Is that a clue?"

I laughed and said, "Catch you in a bit, Jimbob." Then I left.

27

Emma drove me over to Bathgate. She told me she had requested checks at all UK airports to ensure that Ruzena Dolezal was not allowed on any flight out of the country without police knowledge. That, she said, would at least ensure that Mrs. Mortimer had to be hunted in the UK. But she wanted my opinion as to whether there was any way Roozh could circumvent that and get over to Europe? Apart from sailing in a cockle-boat from some obscure bay somewhere on the coast, which nobody could anticipate. What did I think?

I sat and gave that the full lucubration. I thought for a minute at least. “How about she travels to Slovakia in one of Mortimer’s fleet?” I said. “With whatever driver does the Slovakia run, next time he’s headed there.”

“Ah, but she has the car,” said Emma.

“It’s only a Mazda, and Mortimer is minted. He’s not going to care a hoot about that. She leaves it parked in some side street and gets picked up by the truck as it travels through England. She’ll know now that we’re on to her. All that she’ll be concentrating on is getting to Mestre, out of the way. Or conceivably Kosice, Slovakia in general, I suppose. But, either way, we need to check with Douglas when the next runs to those destinations are.”

“Aye, you’re right,” said Emma.

“I’ll do that. Know what I’ve just realised?” I said.

“Tell me.”

“Ruzena composed those texts , the threatening texts she received. However she wangled getting them sent to her phone, she thought them up. Don’t know why it didn’t occur to me before. She reads the Bible just about every night. She was raised as a devout Catholic. She knows all that stuff. One of them, when I mentioned it, she quoted chapter and verse, literally. Matthew, chapter 21, verse 11, or whatever it was. She knows all that shit. She’s organised the hit on Mortimer that went wrong, too. A lot of thought and planning has gone into this.”

Emma dropped me off in the centre of town. She had a lot to work on so I set about getting the details on the Mortimer Logistics runs to Italy and Slovakia. First I walked up the street and bought myself some lunch, then went back to the office. I pulled up a political map of Europe on the PC, as I ate my sandwich and I called Mortimer.

I'll give you a resume of what the guy said to me, the one I gave Emma, actually. It was one of those rambling conversations that Douglas specialised in, but the gist of it was as follows.

I asked him what times, what trucks, what drivers and what routes were involved in his company's visits to Mestre and Slovakia. He said that there were four main runs that his trucks did to Europe. I was about to interrupt him and say I was only interested in Slovakia and Mestre when he started to list them. I drew a deep breath and said nothing, just followed them on the map as he enumerated them. The first and commonest one took in Belgium, the Netherlands, Germany, Poland, the Czech Republic and back through Poland and Germany to Belgium. Another common one was France, Spain, Portugal and back. There was a third which took in the Netherlands, Germany, Denmark, Sweden and Norway before the return; and the one which interested me was the fourth, and often longest, run: Netherlands, Germany, the Czech Republic, Slovakia, Hungary, Romania, Croatia, Slovenia, Northern Italy, Switzerland and finally France on the way back to the English Channel. Not every run did all the countries, but that was the route when they did.

The last one being the one I thought germane to the police inquiry, I asked him what kind of trucks went there and how often. I regretted it. He went on at some length but, eventually, I sussed that he had different kinds of lorries, for example, refrigerated lorries for foodstuffs, and container lorries or pallet lorries for other freight. He still had something called flatbed trucks for machinery or construction steel, but few of them went to Europe other than to the countries just over the Channel. He went on about container trucks carrying televisions and electrical goods, toys, food, computers, DVDs and clothing – some were specially adapted for the transportation of hanging garments. He shifted what he called 'dry bulk': coal and iron ore; food stuffs like grain or sugar; and construction materials like cement or sand. 'Breakbulk' consisted of stuff like wood, steel, machine parts and so on that could be loaded on pallets.

I was starting to be sorry I'd asked him, especially when he volunteered to go on and discuss vehicle and driver documentation required for driving and delivering in Europe: Community licences and road haulage permits, passports, visas and shit like that. I had to stop him and spell out in words of one syllable what I needed, and Emma needed, to know. And that was, whether the run that included Slovakia and Northern Italy (therefore Mestre) ran regularly; whether there were regular drivers on that run, and whether there was a run due to go there in the immediate future.

He said, oh, that was something he'd need to check with the Birmingham manager since Brum was the depot that dealt with that particular run. He thought I'd wanted to know about the European runs in general …

I restrained myself, with some difficulty, from biting his nose through the phone and asked him politely if he could maybe find that information out for me in the next couple of hours. He said, sure, no problem, leave it to him. And hung up.

I flicked the phone off and took a large draught of tepid coffee, tried not to swear. He got back ten minutes later. Said that the run was being done the following day, just Birmingham to Kosice, leaving at 5.30 a.m., and returning via North Italy to pick up iron goods at Port of Venice, as he called it. A seven day run, the drivers being Tony and Vass.

"You got any surnames for those guys, Douglas?" I asked.

"Aye," he said, "Wait the noo." He had evidently written them on a piece of paper. I could hear it being rustled. "Tony Appleby and Vass … Strand… if that's how you pronounce that."

"Spell it."

"S-T-R-N-A-D. Strand, is it?"

"I doubt it. The A and the N would have to be the other way. It's probably just 'Strnad', you know –'stir-nad'. That sounds Slavic. Okay, Douglas, that's great. Much obliged. Oh – are those the regular guys that do the Slovakia run?"

"Aye, I think the Vass guy speaks the language."

"And the reg of the truck?"

"Nae idea, Jack. I don't suppose they've decided which one yet."

"Coolio, Julio. Be in touch."

I Googled 'Strnad'. Czech surname. And 'Vass' would be short for the Czech name 'Vaclav', pronounced 'Vatslaf'. Somebody from the Czech Republic would understand Slovak and be understood by Slovakians. Looked like this could be our truck and our team.

I called Emma and shared the news.

"Brilliant, Jack. Okay, we need to get the Port guys at Devon to give that truck a check."

"That won't do you any good. They'll be leaving from Dover. Nowhere near Devon."

"Dover! I meant Dover. I'm just frazzled. How long would it take a truck to get to Dover from Birmingham, do you think?"

"Googling it now. About four hours. So they'll be looking for a sailing about 9.30, more likely 10 or 10.30, yeah? But it's Mortimer Logistics, a braw bright tartan truck, so they'll no miss it."

"All right. I'll get on to Dover. Cheers, Jack."

"What's the form with the Dover situation?" I asked. "Never come across that. Who does it – local police?"

"Oh, no, no. Not at all. This is a job for Special Branch. I'll get the Glasgow guys on to it. But… interestingly enough, Kent and Strathclyde are the only two Special Branches who work in uniform. So there you go. And, since there is the suspicion of human trafficking involved, SB would be on the scene – drugs, guns, people, anything being trafficked is a Special Branch area – and the UK Border Force will be happy to help them out. That's basically the old customs and immigration services. As you know, human trafficking is a major issue, links to organised crime and modern slavery. So, I'll get on to Glasgow and set up a check at Dover tomorrow."

"Okay, I'll let you go; I know you're busy."

"Thanks for all this, Jack. Be in touch."

I rang off.

I drove to St. John's and visited Rab Buchanan. Ward 23. He looked like Norman Wisdom in that picture – what's it called? – the one where he's bandaged like a mummy in a hospital bed. 'A Stitch in Time', maybe? Rab had a turban on his bean, and his legs were all bandaged up.

"Hey," he said, as I sat down by the bed.

"Hey yourself and see how you like it," I said. "Sorry about what happened, man."

"No your fault, Jack."

"If I hadn't clocked those twelps, you'd never have chased them, and you'd never have got knocked over. So I'm sorry."

"Still no your fault, Jack. You werenae drivin' the motor. I hope they get that bastard though…"

"They're on it now. His name is Jamil Ahmed and he's from Glasgow. I told them about the car and the reg. plate. He'll be getting huckled about now, I would think."

"Crooks, I take it?"

"Big time," I said. "Organised crime, I think. Are you *awful* sore?"

"Na," laughed Rab. "They've got me on the old diamorphine. It's good gear! All I need now is some Jimi Hendrix on the player and I'm sorted. Eh? Been clean all my days, then I get to my age and they put me on the heroin! Never a dull moment knowing you, Jack."

By the time I left Rab and drove back to Bathgate, it was after half four. Emma called me on the mobile as I drove, to tell me that she had had a couple of productive telephone conversations, the first with Roos de Jaager. Apparently, Novak was a name they had heard rumours of before, in connection with trafficking in Kosice. Roos was going to firm up inquiries, now that this person had been definitely identified by a victim. Emma also said that Special Branch would be on their mettle at the port of Dover in the morning, for one of Mortimer's tartan trucks driven by Appleby and Strnad. Their vehicle would be gone over with a nit comb.

She sounded like she felt she was getting on top of the game now. And so, since all of this was serious police shit – Europol and Special Branch – and no input from me was required, I closed up and went home early, for a change.

I sat with Juliet while she did her homework. Clever kid. When it was her bedtime, I sat by her bedside and read her a few chapters of 'Harry Potter'. She had just recently discovered Ms. Rowling's boy wizard stories and couldn't get enough of them. Then I kissed her goodnight and put the light out, went downstairs. Phyl and I had a good old cuddle with a glass of wine and a box of chocolates while we watched the box sporadically and nattered. She was interested in the developments in the Mortimer case and speired the arse out of me about them. It was a relaxing evening, and I was enjoying the unusuality of it. Then my mobile ringtone sounded. She's filing her nails while they're dragging the lake.

Emma.

"Hi, Em."

"Well, Jack. Roos de Jaager's not been hanging about. Her people have uncovered a first name for Mr. Novak."

"Wouldn't be Tibor Novak, would it?"

"Give that man a coconut. Tibor Novak of Kosice, lawyer by profession. Married to Lenka Novak. Second home in Pavlovce – is that how you pronounce it? Uncle by marriage of Ruzena Dolezal, model and wife of Scottish millionaire. Like I say, they'd heard rumours before. Tomorrow, Mr. Novak will be interviewed by the Human Trafficking Unit of Europol. On my recommendation, the Dolezal home in Mestre, Italy, will be under surveillance from tonight. Anything suspicious from Tomas, Pavol or Dominika and they will be questioned."

"Good stuff. Anything of Ruzena? Hide or hair, for example?"

"Nothing at all. I'm hoping the Dover scenario might throw her up."

"Okay. Thanks for the update, Em. Have yourself a cheeky wee Sauvignon to celebrate."

I clicked the phone off and gave Phyllis a resume of what Emma had said.

"Looks like you were right again, honey," she said. "Emma say anything about the Asian guy? In Glasgow?"

"No. I guess that's being handled by Strathclyde just now. She'll let me know when she's got anything."

28

Next morning, I didn't feel like doing the Coffee and Contemplation routine in the office. Don't know why, just didn't. I felt like I needed to get the neurons snapping by doing something different. It was a fine morning, sunny and redolent of good things for the day. I took that as an omen. (No, I didn't; I'm hardly the kind of guy who believes in omens. I just felt like doing something cheerier than sitting in my little cubiculo and drinking coffee, staring at the wall and spinning a kiddies' toy on my fingers.) Al fresco contemplation was the thing, but where? Where had I been recently that was pleasant and conducive to quiet thought? Somewhere local and quiet? Somewhere, moreover, Knightly and Hospitable? I drove up to Torphichen again and parked outside the Preceptory.

I strolled through the churchyard in the sunlight and sat down on a bench by the crumbling graves and the sedate greenery – yew trees, maybe, and whatever else. It was quiet, the breeze shifted the branches of the trees a little, and birds were doing all that avian chirping stuff. I put my head back and let the sun bathe my face. Where had Ruzena Dolezal gone? Was she about to be sniffed out of a tartan trailer by some German Shepherds and armed police? I had thought it likely enough the night before. Now? Less so. It wasn't the way a reasonably famous fashion model would get to the Continent, stowing away among pet food and rubber goods. No. Definitely not.

So, given that airports had been notified, and now the port of Dover had too … I knew there were other ports and many ways to cross the water to Europe. She could have gone from Hull to Zeebrugge, maybe even driven back to Scotland and gone from Rosyth to the same port. She could have gone from Portsmouth to Cherbourg, from Plymouth to Santander, from… where did Newcastle do sailings to? Amsterdam! Newcastle to Amsterdam. She'd vanished in Newcastle – was that where she had vanished to? The Netherlands? Driven from Holland down through southern Germany and Austria to Mestre? A distinct possibility. I pulled my phone out and made a note of that for Emma – in fact, of all the ferry routes I'd just been thinking of. Harwich to the Hook of Holland; that was another one. Hull to Rotterdam. Christ, she could have sailed from Liverpool … what was it? …

Birkenhead … to Belfast, then driven through Ireland and sailed to the Continent from an Irish port. Shit. It was beginning to look extremely unlikely that the Dover Special Branch guys were going to turn her up.

Aye, she would drive. Drive to somewhere comparatively out of the way, comparatively quiet and get off mainland UK that way, then catch a ferry to Europe. That's how a reasonably famous fashion model would do it.

A reasonably famous fashion model. – Maybe she had professional engagements on the Continent! How would I find that out? I could be finding out where she was right this minute if I knew. Who would know? Mortimer. Surely. He'd said … what had he said, when he hired me? That after the Castle gig, she had nothing till after the holiday back home in Mestre? Was that it? When was it he said that – a fortnight ago, just? Maybe jobs had come in since then. I'd best check.

I dialled him. "Douglas, it's Jack. No, nothing yet, before you ask, I'm sorry. Listen up. Could you check in Ruzena's diary if she has any jobs scheduled for this week and next, say? It could be important. The diary in the table drawer in her sitting-room."

"Nane, I'm sure. But, wi' aw this shenanigans, I … I'll check it. Haud on."

I haudit on and heard him pace through the hall, up the stairs and open a door, walk on more padded footsteps and slide open a drawer. "It's no there, Jack," he said. "She must a took it wae her."

"No bother. Don't concern yourself about that. I'm working away here for you. I'll get back to you as soon as." I rang off.

Jenny Kemp would know. Nobody more so. Her P.A. I skiffed through my calls list for her number and, as I did, thought, 'No… Let's call on Jennifer, shall we?'

I rose and walked through the graveyard to where I'd parked the car, got in and tootled out the Bathgate road. It shouldn't take me too long to get to Spottiswoode Street on the Sabbath. Easy like Sunday morning, in fact. I drove out the M8 and the miles went by like quiet days. I thought a half hour's wee chat with Jennifer might help a little, in that white and grey living-room, with perhaps a coffee and a biscuit.

I got there, pulled up, knocked the door and received no reply. I lifted the letter-box lid and called, "Miss Kemp? It's Jack Black! We need to talk!" Nothing. I took out my phone and called her. More nothing. She wasn't *with* Ruzena, was she?

I knocked the other door on the ground floor. After a minute or so, an elderly man in a cardigan answered it. He had white hair combed straight back from his brow, wire specs and a walking stick.

"Pardon me bothering you on a Sunday morning, sir," I enunciated slowly and clearly, "but I was looking for Miss Kemp."

He continued to look at me for a second or so, saying nothing. I thought this might descend to the level of farce, me shouting in his ear and him looking for his ear trumpet. But no; not at all. He was as sharp as Tewkesbury mustard. He said, "Were you?" His voice was cultured and clear. "Then you might have knocked on the door opposite, which is where she lives."

I smiled. "Yes, I know, sir," I said. "But I can't get an answer from there."

"And you think she might be in here with me?" he said, a smirk crossing his face.

"Well, no, not really. I just wondered if you knew where she is, whether she's gone on holiday or something."

"And why would I know something like that?"

"Because she might have told you as a neighbour? You know, to keep an eye on the property and that sort of thing."

"I'm afraid not, young man. Miss Kemp and I exchange civilities when we meet, but we are no more neighbourly than that."

"Ah. Can I ask, when was the last time you saw her?"

"Oh," he sighed. "Well, I should say … on Friday." He wrinkled his brow in concentration. "Yes, Friday. That was the day she was locking up and heading off with a suitcase. She got a taxi. But as to where it took her, I could not possibly say."

"A taxi? Definitely a taxi, and not a lift from a friend?"

"Not unless her friend drives a black cab."

"Ah. Was this morning or afternoon?"

"Mmm, morning, I should think. Perhaps about eleven or thereabouts."

"How was she dressed?"

"Normally."

"I'm sorry?"

"Are you? I wonder why. No, she was not wearing a bathing suit and a Panama hat or anything outlandish; just a light summer jacket – yellow, I think – and slacks. And now, young man, if you don't mind, I have a crossword to finish."

I let the old bastard creep back into his hideyhole. He was educated and sharp, but he was a bigger liar than Tam Pepper. Friday was the day it rained so much I was thinking of building a boat 30 cubits high and 300 cubits long. She wouldn't have been going anywhere in a light jacket and slacks. In fact, I suspected she wouldn't have been going anywhere, full stop.

I left the tenement and climbed back into the bogey. I didn't fancy just sitting there until she turned up but there wasn't a great deal I could usefully do otherwise. Then my phone started. *Watching the Detectives*. She looks so good that he gets down and begs. I checked the caller ID.

"Emma."

"Jack. Mortimer's lorry fine-tooth combed. She wasn't in it."

"Okay. Not that surprised, actually. I've just been thinking of all the ports she could sail from – you know, Newcastle and all points south, basically."

"Aye. We might have to put out a general notice. I thought that earlier. Other thing? Better result. Shane Easton's fingerprints match the prints on the window and the steel at Manderley."

"Yesssss!"

"Aye. Wait for it…! They match the charm disc with the capital 'S' too. Looks like you were right about it coming off in the struggle. He's requested a lawyer. And the Glasgow guys have pulled Jamil Ahmed. Still being interviewed as we talk. They've got the third name though. Hang on… Edward Storie. So. We know the three amigos' names now. And they'll be talking about Manderley too, in case Mr. Easton was not alone that night."

"Excellent, Em."

"What about you? What are you up to?"

"I'm in Edinburgh. Spottiswoode Street. Thought I might have a chinwag with Jenny Kemp. No joy, though. No answer at the door, nor on the phone. And her next door neighbour just told me a pile. I'm wondering if she's with Ruzena."

"Why would she be? She's maybe just down the street."

"Maybe, aye. Anyhoo, that's good about Easton. I'm on my way back. Speak soon."

And I headed back, through the sunny sabbath, to West Lothian. On my way, I bit Mortimer with my Bluetooth and told him that the rashers had someone in the frame for the Alex Gilmour job, a Glasgow man, possibly connected to organised crime through the west. He was pleased to hear that and said, though it didn't bring Ruzena back to him, it was a positive piece of news and part of the same inquiry, which he hoped boded well for the rest of it. I let him think that, if he wanted.

I berthed the yoke in the car park opposite the office. I wanted to just nip in, pull some paperwork for doing at home, then get back to the bosom of my family. As I crossed the road – quiet, it being a Sunday – I saw a man with his back to the wall of Cho's Chinese Takeaway. He looked like a regular guy, maybe six feet high, brown hair, jacket and open neck shirt. He was on the phone to someone.

He looked up as I reached his side of the road, said, "Hang on, he's here," into the phone and then put his hand up to stop me. "Mr. Black?"

"Yes."

"I'd like you to come with me, sir, please. My car is jus…"

"Come where?"

"Not important at the moment. You'll find out, sir. Everything in turn." Then he spoke into the phone again. "Send it now."

"Look, mate," I said, "I don't know you, I don't *wish* to know you, and I'm certainly not accompanying you anywhere in your car. Got that? Now do me a favour and fuck the fuck off."

His phone gave a 'ping'. He said, "Wait a moment, sir. You'll want to see this." He pushed a button or two on his phone, clocked what he saw and turned it to me. "Two of my friends are in Wester Inch at the moment," he said.

It was a photograph of the front of my house. Looked like it was taken from the passenger seat of a car, judging from the level and the way the car would be facing. Juliet was running along the pavement, hair flying, looking at the front door.

Phyllis was in the doorway, smiling at her. Probably just called her in for lunch. My blood froze.

"Beautiful wee girl you have there, Mr. Black," the guy said, turning the phone so that he could see the photo. "They're so vulnerable at that age, aren't they? You worry about them all the time. Mine are grown up now, but I remember that age well. And your wife is a very attractive woman. A face full of character, as my mother used to say."

I said, "All right. Call your friends off and I'll go with you."

He smiled. "Good show. What I'll do is just stand them down a step or two until I see that everything's well at this end, all right? And when I do, I'll 'call them off', as you put it. One second." He put the phone to his ear and said, "Fine. He's coming with me. I'll get back to you as soon as possible." He put the phone in his pocket. "Right, Mr. Black," he said, "my car is just there." He pointed to a Skoda Octavia parked three spots along from mine. "It's a hire car, just to save you trying to memorise the plate and things like that. I know what you private investigators are like." He chuckled as we crossed the road. It was all very civil. On the surface. "An associate got it this morning, via Rentalcars.com. So I suggest you just relax and enjoy the run."

"Relax?" I said. "With your goons threatening to harm my wife and kid?"

"Oh, think nothing of that. No harm will come to them. After all, you've joined me voluntarily. I regret that the photograph was necessary. I agree it was a crude gesture but, unfortunately it was necessary. Now, Mrs. Black and your daughter will be perfectly safe – so why don't you stop worrying and relax on the way, eh?"

We had reached the car. He flicked it open and we got in. "Do you have any idea where we are headed?" he said.

"None."

"Really? You do surprise me. Ah well, you'll guess in a minute or two."

And he pulled out of the car park and hauled the buggy left. West. Of course.

29

We headed towards Glasgow at a fair rate of knots. After Whitburn, my driver set the bluetooth a-sizzling and called someone. The dude at the other end said simply, “Yep?”

“On our way,” was what my driver said.

My driver. It occurred to me that this was precisely what this fucker was: a driver. Somebody’s hireling. I had a fair idea whose, too.

I said, “Well, your boss might have sent *you* yesterday instead of the incompetent buffoons he did send. One of my friends might have escaped serious injury, and one of your gang might have been spared arrest and serious criminal charges.”

“I have absolutely no idea what you are talking about, Mr. Black.”

“Aye, sure,” I said. “Omertà, is it?”

“That’s a Cosa Nostra expression, isn’t it? For ‘silence’, I believe.”

“Go to the top of the class.”

“I am not sure why you would apply such a term to our situation, however. I know of no previous run to pick you up, Mr. Black. Then again, I am but a humble servant.”

“Yeah? You don’t talk like one.”

“Nevertheless.”

“Yeah. ‘Nevertheless’. I don’t know too many humble servants who use adverbs like ‘nevertheless’. Adverbs at all, really.”

He chuckled and said, “We won’t be long now. Oh, that reminds me.” He called another number.

A male voice said, “Hello?”

“No requirement for you still to be in Wester Inch.”

“Right.”

He pressed the red icon on the dash display. “Your family are no longer under surveillance.”

“For the moment,” I said.

“No,” he said, “the photograph was only ever a means of leverage to be used to persuade you. There was never any intention of harming your loved ones. We are not brutes.”

“So why keep your goons there till now?”

"To add to the atmosphere," he said, turning to me and smiling before he concentrated on the road again.

I said nothing, watched as he came off the M8 at Junction 17, on to the Great Western Road. This was a surprise. I had been expecting the M74 and Ardbeg Street/Calder Street again. But I kept shtum and observed. Mr. Omertà would tell me nothing in any case. We turned off and into Cleveden Crescent, an elegant West End address. It consists of some fine houses curving round communal but railed off gardens. Victorian sandstone by the look of it. Tall windows on the ground floor, gardens, shrubberies, flowers. Many had paved the small garden area out front and had benches for sitting in the sun. Some doorways had leaded windows on the inner doors, occasionally also with stained glass. On the built-up side of the crescendo, tidy little railings marked the boundaries of pavement and property, and small lamp standards stood at regular intervals on stone bases. If you wanted to bide here, you'd need between half a million and a million, I reckoned.

We pulled up at a house in the middle of the crescent. "Here we are," said the driver jauntily. A big bald man, dressed in a dark jacket over a blue polo neck and dark jeans, came out and opened the passenger door. "Mr. Black?"

I said yes.

"Come this way, please, sir."

I didn't feel like trying any smarts on this guy, so I got out of the buggy and followed him into the house. It was as well appointed as I'd expected. He showed me into the front room. Through them tall windows, I could see the Skoda still parked outside and Humble Servant seated behind the wheel, looking down at something – his phone most likely.

Pale blue rug. Imitation old-style fireplace with gas fire and several glass vases of dried flora on the black mantelpiece. Framed oleographs of the sort of faux Victorian sentimental cack that stoneheads mistake for art: a golden-haired child praying by her bed; a waif with a tear in his eye proffering a posy of flowers to, presumably, his mother. Excrement, all of it. Vintage leather sofa and armchairs. Pocky Asian man seated in the armchair with its back to the window.

"Mr. Black," he said, standing up and shaking my hand," it is a pleasure to meet you."

"The pleasure is all yours," I said. "I am not usually forced to call on people as a result of threats being made against my wife and child."

"Sit down, please." He waved me to the other armchair. "Brian, leave us for the moment." The heavy left and closed the door quietly behind him. "My name is Bashir Ahmed," said my host. "I am alarmed to hear you speak of threats to your family. Nothing is as important in life as a man's family."

"Your driver – the man who brought me here, the one outside in the Skoda – showed me a photograph on his phone. My daughter this afternoon, my wife at the house door. It's what persuaded me to come here. Otherwise…" I shrugged.

"Of course. I will look into this. But, to the point. You are working for Mr. Douglas Mortimer, I think."

"I work for myself, Mr. Ahmed. Mr. Mortimer hired me to find something out. I did, and I have been paid. That job is over."

"I see. And yet, two days ago, you called at a shop in Calder Street that I own and told my sons that you had a 'bride' for me. You are aware that Mr. Mortimer paid me a sum of money to help rescue a girl from a false marriage? I was in a position to be able to help him, fortunately, since I knew the man who had arranged the business. I was happy to help."

"Ah yes, Mr. Mortimer mentioned something. I am glad you could do that for him – and more so for the girl, obviously."

"Of course. So I am wondering why you tell my sons you have a 'bride' for me, as if I am the man who arranges these things."

"Ah well, that's easy. I wanted to meet the man who was decent enough to help rescue the girl Bartoš. I found the shop but your younger son said you were in Pakistan at a family wedding."

"Indeed. I only returned yesterday evening."

"Then your older son asked why I wanted to speak to you. I said I had some business for you. I hoped that would be enough to interest you. It was he who used the term, 'bride'. Not me."

"Ah. Perhaps you misheard him. Perhaps he said 'bribe' rather than 'bride'. This is a term he uses - in a jocular way - for an opportunity to make money. You know, if we stocked a certain brand of liquor, that would be 'a good bribe', he would say."

"Aye, well, that would explain it, certainly. I wondered." I gave him a pinchbeck smile.

He beamed. "This is all. How easily mistakes are made."

"Very easily, Mr. Ahmed. But let me say that, despite the bullying way I which I was brought here, I am glad to have met you. It is an honour to meet such a philanthropic man."

He beamed again. "The pleasure is mutual. Now, what can you tell me about the incident in Bathgate yesterday? I believe a man was knocked down in the street? And I believe the driver was my son. This is a terrible accident. It is made worse, they are telling me, because one of my son's friends kidnapped you until you were clever enough to make your escape? My son tells me this. It is only as you approach the policeman that Jamil sees who you are. Because he has knocked the man down, he panics and drives away. I am most angry at his behaviour here. He has brought shame on the family name."

"Okay," I said. "I wonder, then, why Jamil was in Bathgate at all, with two henchmen?"

"He was to call upon Mr. Mortimer, is all. Mr. Mortimer was not at home, it transpires, and they were on their way back to Glasgow when the incident occurs."

"Ah," I said, jerking my head up as if to say how silly is the way things work out. "I wondered. I hope Jamil is not in too much trouble. You seem a very nice family."

"He is in much trouble, and rightly so, Mr. Black. Not only with the police but with his father. But there, that is family business. I only brought you here to explain these things to you."

"I am very glad you did, sir."

"And now, before you leave – I will have you driven back – I will speak to the driver about the photograph of your family.

"It's not at all necessary, Mr. Ahmed," I said, standing up. "Do it at your leisure, if you must. I have to get back to Bathgate to let my wife get to work. If you would be so kind."

He stood also. "But of course. I have enjoyed meeting you, Mr. Black."

"It's been my privilege," I said, with a Cheshire Cat grin.

"Brian!" The door opened immediately and the minder in the polo neck stepped into the room. "Mr. Black will return now."

Brian escorted me to the pavement. I climbed aboard and Uriah started up the motor and pulled away. We were back on the Great Western Road in jig time and zipping back east. The driver said, “I trust you had a satisfactory meeting?”

“Very good, yes,” I said.

“Excellent. Now, sit back and relax. We will have you back in Bathgate in no time.”

I sat back and looked out of the window. But I didn’t relax. I was fully aware of what had just happened. It had been a bull session, a series of manoeuvres, old Bashir and me telling each other monstrous porkies and pretending to believe them, all the time sussing each other out. Posturing; striking attitudes. Playing charades. Dancing around each other like scorpions. Phyl and the bairn had been photographed to intimidate me, all right. He knew that I had shopped Jamil and his two goons. I had just received a massive warning off, framed as a courtesy.

Well, fuck that, Bashir my boy; fuck that.

Humble Pie had just dropped me in King Street and headed off west again when my phone went. It was Emma. Jennifer Kemp had been found dead.

30

She had been found that morning, in a seat in the last section of an Edinburgh tram at the airport. When the passengers had all disembarked, the driver had stood up to check the vehicle and noticed a woman still seated with her back to him. He had called, "Terminus! You have to get off here. This is the airport." But she hadn't moved. When he stalked up the tram, he found out why. She was skewered to the seat by a gully about a foot long. There was a seeping pool of dark blood on her chest, and her eyes stared straight ahead. She was as dead as the Roman Empire. Her suitcase was at her feet, and she was, indeed, wearing a yellow summer jacket and a pair of jeans, like her neighbour, Old Father Time, had told me. The driver had been seriously freaked out. It had been a busy tram. Kemp had got on at Haymarket, with maybe twenty others. He said no-one had looked like they were carrying a blade that size – most were dressed in light clothes. No, he had heard nothing that would suggest a struggle, let alone a violent act like that. No, he could not remember who was standing or sitting in her vicinity. People had got on all along the line – Murrayfield, Balgreen, Saughton, Bankhead, Edinburgh Park, the Gyle, Edinburgh Gateway, Gogarburn and Ingliston – the tram was full of people. The popo had identified her from her papers. Among her possessions was a ticket for London Gatwick.

I sat in Emma's office in silence while she told me all this.

"Somebody must have seen whoever did this doing it," I said.

"Not necessarily. If she was sitting there, and the guy who was the last to disembark plunged her then just got off, nobody would see it. It's an even more likely scenario, if he was surrounded by two or three associates."

"On Ruzena's orders?" I said.

"It's a distinct possibility. You phone her about Geraldine Hunter and, within hours Hunter is dead. Now the only other person really close to her, apart from Mortimer, is dead too. Feels like she must be at the back of it. Somewhere at least."

"So we need to guard Mortimer as best we can. Don't forget," I said, "the night Gilmour died, it was meant to be Mortimer. He's the number one target for fucking up the profit margins of organised crime in Slovakia. Hunter was killed because she opened her mouth to me just a wee bit too wide."

"And Kemp in case she did the same," said Emma. "Yes, that's how I see it. Ruzena isn't actually killing these people, but she's ... "

"Aye, she's the one calling the hits in."

"Must be because she's linked to organised crime; must be," said Emma. "The way I see it? Uncle Tibor is a major player in the trafficking of girls to Scotland. False marriages, prostitution, anything else. Not just Scotland but, for our purposes, the one that counts."

"And the story about Auntie Lenka getting Ruzena into modelling? Your family sized crock. Uncle Tibor wangled it through his connections."

"Oh, good shout!"

"So, his model niece owes him big time. Once he realises that this Scottish guy, Mortimer, is the do-gooder behind rescuing half a dozen or so of his trafficked girls, he calls in a favour from his niece. 'If you end up Edinburgh way, see what you can uncover.'"

"You think he told her to marry Mortimer?"

"No. Not at first. In fact, I suspect that was Ruzena's idea, farther along the line. Get herself in line for some mega bucks at a later stage. Like people have thought all along. No, I think Novak wanted her just to insinuate herself with Douglas and find out if what he'd heard was true."

"We need to find her."

"We do. And we need to protect Mortimer. Get him to fuck out of things for a while."

"You think he'd go?"

"Not for a second. But it's worth a try. I like the old sod; I don't want to see him topped."

"Okay. Do we go up there and talk to him about it?"

"You can't tell him that we think it's his beloved Roozh that's behind all this. It would break his heart."

"So what do we do? We need to talk to him."

"Yeah. Do you guys do it officially? I mean, you and Jim, say, or Gerry Vaughan?"

"What makes you think it's not official if I do it with you? Or on my own? I think it's best if you're there anyway. He trusts you."

"And it's not hard to see why."

"Let's just go and do it, smartarse, will we?"

I called Mortimer, just to make sure he was at home. I didn't think he would be anywhere else, not the way he was feeling then, but I had to make sure. I said Emma and I were on our way; was that kosher? He said aye, whatever. Didn't sound too jazzed about it.

On the way over, Emma wondered where Jennifer Kemp had spent the two days between Friday and that morning, and whether it had any bearing on her murder.

"Why would it have? I suppose she was flying to Gatwick to meet Ruzena."

"She might have family down there. No, what I was wondering was, what was the two day stay away from home for."

"We've no proof the old boy was telling the truth," I said. "He has probably seen her in the yellow jacket before. I suspect she thought she *was* meeting Ruzena, had arranged that, in fact, and just lay low till this morning – maybe even told Colonel Mustard to spin that line of bollocks if anybody asked. However, little did she know," I said with ironic emphasis, "that Ruzena had already organised her murder."

"Could be that," said Emma. "Could be. We should know more when Edinburgh's done with the body."

When we got to Manderley, I had to buzz Mortimer from the gates. And when we pulled up at the house, we had to knock the door.

"This man strikes me as beginning the signs of depression," I said.

"Very possibly."

Mortimer took us into the living-room, said very little as he did so. Emma said, "Well, Mr. Mortimer, I'm sorry to say that we still haven't found your wife. And, I'm sure you will have learned of the death of Geraldine Hunter by now."

"Aye."

"Well, I am sorry to have to tell you that Jennifer Kemp was found murdered this morning, too."

He put his face in his hands. "Aw, my God," he said. "You think they're after Roozh tae, don't ye? You think they're tryin' ti get her tae."

Emma looked at me. I pouted and nodded, shrugged. She nodded decisively at me. I took a breath.

"The police can't rule it out, Douglas," I said. "And they can't rule out an attack on you too. Remember Alex was killed. We're sure the target that night was you."

He lifted his face out of his hands and snapped, "Me? Who the hell would want ti kill me?"

"Mobsters in Slovakia," I said. "People you've cost money by rescuing those girls. You said it yourself, there's a lot of profit in trafficking people."

"But why Roozh…? Ah, cos she's Slovakian."

"That's a possibility, Mr. Mortimer," said Emma. "Now, the police are still searching for your wife. Forces all over the UK have been issued with … er, details. I'm sure we'll find her before any harm comes to her. But Jack and I are concerned more immediately with you. We
think you need protection."

"Whit kind a protection? I'm no havin' polis steyin' in the hoose wi me."

"Would you consider staying somewhere else for a while, Douglas?" I said. "Somewhere you can be guarded closely. Needn't be a …"

"Naw! I'm gaun naewhere." He looked at us both, then softened his tone. "I'm sorry, Jack. I'm just no. This is where I live. This is where Roozh lives. An', when she comes back hame, I want ti be here."

Emma pulled a face. "This is an isolated house, Mr. Mortimer," she said. "There's already been one murder here."

"Ah well, if Ah'm ti be kilt, it'll be here tae. I'm gaun naewhere."

"So you must have a police presence in the house for your safety and security," said Emma.

"Naw. I tolt ye's."

Emma looked at me hopelessly.

"Would you let me stay?" I said. He looked at me doubtfully. "We're getting on to be friends, aren't we?" I went on.

"S'pose so."

"How about that, DI Wood?" I said. "How about if *I* keep Douglas company? Would that be acceptable?"

Emma spoke to Mortimer. "Would that be acceptable to you, Mr. Mortimer? You trust Jack, and he knows what he's about. If you won't have police officers in the house, will you have Jack?"

"As long as I have access to police at all times," I said.

Mortimer said, "Aye, all right. Jack can stey. But naeb'dy else."

"You okay with that, Jack?" said Emma.

"Sure," I said. "Phyllis might not be quite as gung-ho about it but that's *my* concern."

"I'll need ti cancel these lassies," said Mortimer.

"The cleaners? Good idea," I said. "Just in the short run."

"Aye. I'll pey them just the same."

I was right. Phyllis wasn't too stoked about it but I stressed that I would only be staying at night and only for as long, or hopefully as short, as it took, to nab Ruzena. I would spend my evenings with Juliet and her. They were still of paramount importance. As the philosopher, Bashir Ahmed said, nothing is as important in life as a man's family. And so that Sunday night was the first I spent in Manderley. I felt like Maxim de Winter's new bride.

31

Mortimer had given me a key of my own and a doofer so that I could just zap the gates when I approached, without having to buzz him. I felt quite rich myself, activating the gates at eight o'clock, driving through and having them shut smoothly behind me. I still knocked the door though. Manners; the way I was brought up. It was still Mortimer's pad and I was still a guest, one he liked but would rather have done without, I was sure. I was merely tolerated, given the circumstances. I would only use the key if he was elsewhere.

He brought me in and showed me the guest bedroom I was to use. He looked at the little grip I was toting. "Ye can pit yer stuff in any a the drawers."

"Ah," I said, dismissively, "it's just a change of underwear and some toiletries." "Sure, sure. Please yersel'. Jist make yersel at hame an' I'll away an' pit the kettle oan."

"Down in a jiffy."

I hadn't mentioned the gun, my Taurus M85, .38 Special Ultra-Lite revolver, all loaded and neatly packed under my smalls. I didn't think it was a good idea to tell him. But I was damned if anybody was going to shove a sharpening steel into Mortimer, or a foot-long gully, for that matter. Not on my watch, not without my trying to dissuade them. I slipped the Tauser under the pillow. (I don't know why I did that, called it a 'Tauser' when I wasn't concentrating. I just found myself thinking of it as that. Maybe on analogy with a Taser. I guessed I was just losing it. The old boy is getting on a bit, after all)

When I went down, Mortimer had a cafetiere of reasonably decent coffee on offer, so I sat in the cloud armchair in the drawing room and sipped contentedly at that.

"I don't want you ti feel you hufty stick around me aw night," he said. "Just make yersel at hame in the right sense. Treat it as your ain hoose. I ken I'm no the maist stimulatin' a company for a clever dick like you. So if ye wahnt ti sit in Roozh's wee room an' read, that's fine wi me. I'll just dae ma jigsaw or watch the telly. That okay?"

"Sure," I said. "I don't want to make you uncomfortable in any way. Just you do what you do, and I'll hang back as much as I can. Stay out your way."

He puffed an amused breath down his nose. "I'm glad it's you, Jack. I couldnae a been bothered wi some strange copper or other. Here, that reminds me. I owe you a fair bit a money."

"No, you don't," I said. "You paid me handsomely already. Over the rate. I don't need any more."

"Ah but I said I would give you a life changin' amount if you got Roozh back, and you did. So ye changed *mah* life. Fifty thousand seem fair to you?"

"Och, away to fuck, Douglas. What would I do with fifty K?"

"Whatever the hell ye want. You've earned it. You deserve it. Look, you're lookin' efter me the now. Spend it on yer wife an' wee lassie. I can afford it."

"I don't want it."

"That's nothin' a dae wi it."

"Stick it up yer arse." He guffawed. "Tell you what," I said. "You can think of paying me that amount when we get Ruzena back a second time. All right?"

He pursed his lips. "I'll see." He obviously thought for a bit and then said, quietly. "She's up ti somethin', int she? That's what aw this is aboot. She's up to somethin'. "

"I've no idea, Douglas," I lied. "That's all police stuff. Far as I know, they're eager to find her so that she doesn't come to any harm. Same reason I'm here for you."

"Why would anybody harm her?"

"Because, like I told you – or, to be accurate, like *you* told *me* – you're the guy that's stopped them making money out of these lassies. What's the best way to hurt you? Through the one you love most."

He said simply, "I love her that much, Jack. I'm daft about her. I never thought I would love anybody like I loved ma mother. Never thought romantic love an' sex an' marriage wis for me. But Roozh is diff'rent. She's ma world."

Jeez, I nearly teared up. There was no bullshit about it; this was a guy telling me how much his woman meant to him. And she was as false as hell; I knew it.

"Nothin' else means anythin' ti me. Only her."

"Well, let's see if we can get her back again," I said.

"Why the hell did she *go* again? Somethin's no right."

He talked like this for two hours and the time passed like a snake over broken glass. When he stopped, there was nothing to say. Mortimer was right. We had hardly anything in common. I'd grown to like the old coot, but we shared no interests. About ten, I said I might go and read something in Ruzena's room. He asked if I wanted anything to eat. I told him I might just raid the fridge in an hour. He said okay and went to do his jigsaw.

I didn't read right away. I called Phyllis and had a chat, told her I'd be there early in the morning. After that, I went to Ruzena's sitting room and flicked through her Art books. At midnight, having eaten a cold chicken leg and drunk a glass of full fat milk, feeling like a cat, I went to bed. The lights were still on downstairs. I set the alarm on my phone for 1 a.m. and made sure the gun was handy.

I got up at 1, padded to the window and lifted a slat of the Venetian blinds. The grounds were as quiet as Calton cemetery. Nobody at the gates. I persuaded the door open and padded over to another guest bedroom, one at the rear of the house. It was as still as a tomb and smelt as if it had never been occupied. The blinds here were up and the curtains open. Nought there was a stirring in the still, dark night. It was darker here, not even the odd streetlamp to cast a glint, but I was satisfied there was nothing out there that shouldn't have been.

I did that every hour on the hour. All was as it should be. But, I'll tell you, when I got home at 7 o'clock, I was as tired as twilight. After I drove the bairn to school, I had some breakfast and climbed into my pit for a decent kip.

32

Elvis Costello woke me up at just after one in the afternoon. You think you're alone until you realize you're in it. I jerked out of sleep, my face stuck to the pillow with dried drool and tried to switch off Phyllis's radio alarm till I realised where the music was coming from. I looked sleepily at the screen on my phone. Emma Wood.

"Jack, where are you?"

"In bed."

"At this time…? Never mind. I was expecting a report on last night."

"Well, maybe you should have told me that, Em. All right. Here is my report. All clear. Quiet night. I checked the house every hour from 1 a.m. and there was nothing. Nada. Nichevo. I intend to do the same tonight. Over."

"All right, here's my report. Things are gathering speed in Kosice. The guy, Gregor, died. That's the one who was tipping the wink to Mortimer about lassies being trafficked to Scotland…"

"Yeah."

"So his brother has decided to spill the beans about what he knows. He's fingered several important people in Kosice and Bratislava, including our Tibor Novak. But others too. So Roos de Jaager's unit has pulled them and is promising results. The Dolezals have been taken for questioning in Mestre."

"My God! Quite a rush all at once."

"Yeah. It's the guy … I forget his name … Gregor's brother … his testimony. This fellow is a law student and is quite highly thought of. It's significant, for sure. But, added to that, Special Branch in Glasgow have pulled Bashir Ahmed, Jamil Ahmed, um … and Majid Ahmed. His two sons, I take it. Strathclyde SB working with the de Jaager unit as well, I'm led to believe. They are also looking for somebody called John Crawford."

"Yeah?"

"Used to work for Ahmed. The Ahmeds have a couple of stores, not just the Calder Street one, as well as a Cash and Carry place in Cardonald. Apparently, Crawford was a delivery driver for them. Well, Special Branch are after him too."

"And I'll tell you why," I said. "He drove Radka Bartoš from Birmingham to Glasgow. She said the driver was a guy called 'Craw'. She thought it might be the Scottish pronunciation of 'Crowe'. I'll wager that John Crawford's nickname is 'Craw'."

"So the lassies are brought to Birmingham," said Emma, "and there's a minibus or something there that brings them on to Glasgow. So Ahmed is a definite part of the organisation."

"Yep. I'm pretty sure."

"I'll pass that on to Roos. This investigation has picked up speed."

"Okay. Thanks for that, Emma. I'll keep you posted on Mortimer."

"All right."

I got up and showered, ate, packed my little grip again and drove into Bathgate. I was absolutely convinced now that Ruzena was not only a player in the Mortimer thing, her name was above the title. And, as Douglas himself had said weeks before, the money these bastards made out of the hapless girls' misery was phenomenal, and they would tolerate nobody interfering. Where life has no value, death, sometimes, has its price. I smiled grimly. A quotation, or near quotation, highly appropriate for someone called Douglas Mortimer. It was Emma's remark about the investigation having picked up speed that had me thinking. Several senior figures arrested in Slovakia, none more germane to Mortimer than Tibor Novak. Ruzena's uncle. If Novak had her note for the career in modelling, there was no more likely time for him to call it in than now. Now was when he needed favours in return. Mortimer was still the big prize, I was sure. But I had a fair idea that Grigor's brother would be under police protection too. There was nothing I could do for him. But for Mortimer...? Yeah. I had to be with him 24/7 from there on in.

I opened up, checked mails of all kinds and drove over to Manderley. Did the hi-tech shit with the gates. Drove down to the circle in front of the house. Walked to the door and pressed the doorbell.

Nothing.

Pressed it again.

Nothing.

I snatched my keychain out of my pocket, fumbled to the spare Mortimer had given me and opened up. Stood in the doorway and listened to the sound of silence. Called out, "Douglas!" But my words echoed in the wells.

Leaving the door open, I put my grip down, took out the Taurus and moved just as silently through the hall. Eased open the drawing room door. Nothing and nobody. Silked open the living-room door. Nobody and nothing. How had they got from the drawing room so fast? Same routine with the dining-room, the cinema room, the smoking room, the library, the kitchen, tiptoeing from one to the next, holding the gun upright in my right hand, caressing the doors open with my left. Nobody. Nothing. It was the same with all the rooms upstairs. Mortimer wasn't there. I felt a stab of foreboding.

Where was he?

I went back outside and walked to the garages. Pressed 121192 on the keypad of the third. I was pleased I'd remembered it after seventeen days. Her birthday, I guessed. The Roller was gone.

Where was he? Had he left of his own volition and why hadn't he let me know? Same reason I hadn't reported to Emma. You need to stipulate these things; not too many folk too hot at the old psychic. I pressed 0 and the roller slid shut. As I turned, the pale blue Dawn came through the gates and smoothly down the drive to pull up by me. He got out.

"Wasnae expectin' ye till the night," he said.

"Mmm. I needed to be here earlier. Where have you been?"

"I went ti the supermairket ti get some stuff. The lassies arenae here the now, mind? I didnae need ti let ye ken where I wis, did I?"

"Very careless of you, old man."

He smiled. "Ye know, I wondert how long it wid take a smartarse like you ti come oot wi a quote fi that picture."

"You recognised it, eh?"

"Wi a name like Douglas Mortimer, I've had ti pit up wi shit like that since the 1960s. Here, gie's a hand wi the shoppin'."

I followed him to the boot and lifted three of the laden plastic bags.

"I used ti get folk askin' me if the train goes to Tucumcari. I've had them ask aboot a natural faimly resemblance between brother an' sister. An' I havenae even got a sister. Just the name does it. It's been a while, though. Trust you. Is there anythin' you dinnae ken?"

"I only know one thing," I said, "and that is that I know nothing."

He thumped the boot shut and we headed for the house with the message bags.

"Is that meant ti be clever?" he asked.

"I think so," I said. "It was Socrates who was supposed to have said it, and he's generally recognised as having been clever."

"He was a guid fitbaw player tae."

I helped him unpack the groceries and suggested I could make one of my chilli con carne meals for dinner – he had all the ingredients. He seemed amused at the notion of my being able to cook. I told him watching Phyllis in the kitchen had put the garnish on my culinary skills. I wasn't Heston Blumenthal but I had managed all right all the years I lived alone. Besides, it would pass the time for me. So that's what happened. I rustled up a chilli and we sat and ate it in the dining-room.

"D'you think you'll find Roozh alive?" he asked, through a mouthful.

"I'm confident she'll turn up alive and kicking," I said. "You really love her, don't you?"

He nodded and said, "Like I would never have believed. I told you I thought I could never love a woman the way I love her. It's the truth. She changed me. She changed ma life. She *is* ma life. I ken I'm a successful business man; I don't care a hang aboot that any mair. I just want ti spend time wi ma wife. I just love lovin' her. And the fact that she loves me back makes me as happy as a king. That's what life should be for everybody. Love an' happiness."

I said, "As the greatest writer who ever lived put it:

Now, for the love of Love, and her soft hours,
Let's not confound the time with conference harsh;
There's not a minute of our lives should stretch
Without some pleasure now."

He said, "That's poetry. See, I cannae make that stuff go at aw. I just don't get it."

"It's Shakespeare," I said. "From *Antony & Cleopatra*."

"You comparin' me and Roozh ti Antony and Cleopatra?"

"Well, I wasn't but, since you mention it, here's a thought I've entertained from time to time: why shouldn't ordinary lovers be celebrated too? Just couples that spend their days in love with each other? Like *you* said, folk whose love changes their lives. Same goes for me and Phyllis too. It's just as profound a love as Antony and Cleopatra, or Romeo and Juliet. Better, really, because they were two sets of fuck-ups. Otherwise, there wouldn't have been any tragedy in the stories. That's what interested Shakey enough to write them."

"Did he no write happy stories aboot lovers?"

"Plenty. Those were just a couple of the tragedies I mentioned."

"Well, I hope me an' Roozh disnae turn oot ti be a tragedy."

Me too.

After dinner, we sat and sipped a rather forward little Pinot Noir – or, rather, I did the sipping, as he smoked and talked. He told me he wasn't really a drinker, but could take the odd glass of vino; it was really Roozh who liked wine and so he bought the best he could for her. Like everything else, he said. He bought whatever she liked, the best he could get her. She was worth it all because she had transformed his life. The money? The house? Didn't matter a Dundee damn now, because he had her in his life. And if she was to leave it, all the money in the world and the biggest house in it too wouldn't compensate for the loss.

"There's beggary in the love that can be reckoned," I said.

"Aye, whatever you say, Jack. That that Shakespeare again?"

I was forced to admit it was. And from *Antony & Cleopatra* again.

"What's the deal wi Shakespeare? What is it aboot him that gets ye sa worked up? I cannae make heid nor tail ae it."

I sat back in the armchair and puffed out a breath. "Well, Douglas," I said, "for me it's that the man knew humankind inside out. All the positive attributes, all the things that make men and women great – he not only knows them and can describe them better than anyone else, but he can describe them in language that nobody has ever matched, or ever will, in my opinion. The same goes for all the base aspects of human beings, the low, mean and criminal side of our natures. He's got that taped too. And his writing is just ... sublime. When he means it to be. It can bring a lump to my throat." I saw his quizzical look. "No, seriously. That's how good the guy was. Is."

"I'll tak' yer word for it, Jack. I'm just a dumplin', me. I was never any guid at school work. Sums I can just aboot dae. I can write a sentence, jist aboot. Ma spellin' isnae that great, though. Anythin' else? Na, forget it. I'm a dumplin'. An' dinnae bother bein' polite. You think sa tae."

"I try not to think of anybody as being a dumpling, Douglas. It's the old hippy in me. But I will say this. Your revelation about saving those girls has rocketed you in my estimation. I don't know any other human being who's done such a wonderful thing."

"Ah weel," he said, obviously unhappy with the talk, "how about watchin' a movie the night, eh? Jist ti pass the time? Ye havenae seen ma hame cinema in action."

"Good idea," I said. "You got a copy of *Rebecca*?"

"Have I got Rebecca? Tak' a wild guess!"

"Let's watch that, well."

He was about to answer when his phone rang. Well, droned. His ringtone was a pipe band playing *The Barren Rocks of Aden*. He looked and said, on a breath, "Christ in heaven! It's Roozh!"

I hissed, "On speaker, Douglas!"

He pressed the requisite button and said, "Roozh? Roozh? You okay, darlin'?"

I heard background sounds that indicated she was driving, or being driven. Then her voice said, "Douglas? It's Ruzena. Are you at home?"

"Aye, I'm here, darlin'. Where are you?"

"I am driving home. I will be home in a half hour. I want so much to see you."

"Me tae, hen. What happened? Where a ye *been*?"

"I will tell all when I see you. It is okay. I just want to make sure you are home. I do not have my remote for the gates."

"Nae problem. I'll be here. No worries."

"Ah, is brilliant, my darling. See you soon. One half hour."

"Cannae wait. Love you, darlin'."

"Yes, me too. Bye."

"Bye! Bye!"

He shut the phone. Then he looked at me. "Think this is a trap?" he said.

"It crossed my mind."

"That's what worries me. Why would she fuck aff fi Newcastle, no contact me for five days and then, oot the blue, phone me when she's half an 'oor fi the hoose? That's fishy, do ye no think?"

"I do," I said. "I'm glad you do too."

"What could it be? D'you think it's no her? I mean, I know that wis her, but d'you think it's no her that's comin' ti Manderley?"

"Possibly that," I said. "And possibly not *only* her. We have to get the police here. We have to ensure your safety – maybe hers too."

"Aye, that's what I was thinkin'. Maybe she's bein' forced ti dae this."

"Maybe she is. I'll phone Emma Wood."

"Haud up!" His expression suggested deep thought. "What if there's somethin' gaun oan? Say there's heavies wi her. What if the sight a police motors makes them hurt her?"

"They'll be here in less than half an hour. If I phone Emma now, they'll set off from Livingston right away. Blue light job."

"Cannae take the risk. We'll need ti dae it oorsels."

"What? I've only got one gun."

"You've goat a gun?"

"Aye, sorry Douglas. I just brought it for emergency use."

"That's brilliant! If there's heavies wi Roozh, we can blaw their fuckin' heids aff."

"Aye, right. Has it occurred to you that, if there are heavies with her, *they* might be armed too? Has that crossed your mind?"

"Ah, but we'll hae the element a surprise."

"Right, stop there, Douglas. Question – can you open the gates and leave them open? Jam them if you need to?"

"Aye," he said, baffled. "Easy as winkie. How?" He meant 'why'. It's a dialect usage that still confuses me sometimes, and I was born here.

"This is the plan. You open the gates right now and leave them open. I phone Emma Wood and get the police on the road – armed, if she can arrange it. In unmarked cars. If they get here before Ruzena, well and good. Cops in next room scenario. Cars behind the garage or something. If they arrive after Ruzena … well, we'll deal with that when it arises. Okay. Go and open the gates."

"Right. Will you hide if the polis arenae here when Roozh arrives?"

"I'll be right over the hall, in the cinema room. Just not watching *Rebecca*. Okay?"

"Okay. I'll dae it."

33

I don't know what Mortimer did to have the gates left open but he did it. Pressed a button on the gizmo in the living-room, I suppose. I looked out of the drawing-room window and saw the gates peel open and stay that way.

I called the gruntery in Livingston and got Shirley Honeyman. Emma was off duty but had given orders she was to be contacted the moment anything transpired in the Mortimer case. Why didn't I call her myself? Which I did, apprised her of the latest development and of the time scale involved. She said she would be at Manderley as soon as ever she could, and would bring some armed officers with her. I told her the gates would be open. Anything she needed to do, she should do, no hesitation.

Then I went up to the bedroom I'd been using and made sure the gun was loaded and ready to rip. Downstairs, Mortimer kept an eye on the front of the house from the window in the drawing-room – the 'lounge', in his terminology. No doubt, viewed from the gates, he was in silhouette against the low rose lighting, the curtains open. Very *Rebecca*. Meanwhile, I stood in the dark at the flouncy curtains in Ruzena's bedroom and kept a higher eye on the gates and the front of the house from through the opened blinds. I'd opened the transom. I was a little agitated. I had no way of knowing what the next half hour would bring.

It brought Ruzena.

I saw headlights on the Torphichen Road, maybe forty minutes after she called. They slowed down and turned into the drive. The Mazda. The back windows were tinted. Ruzena was driving. She pulled up in the gravel before the house and got out, a handbag over her arm. Mortimer was by her side at once; I watched him from above come striding out of the house and to her. I could hear their conversation through the open transom

"Roozh, darlin'! How are ye?"

"Douglas! I am well, I promise you."

He took her in his arms and kissed her, then spoke. His heart was full; I could hear it in his voice. "Why did ye go, darlin'? What wis wrong?"

"I'll tell you inside," she said. "I need a drink."

"Ha' ye got a bag?"

"Leave it," she said. "Come on, inside."

I crossed her bedroom in four strides and was down the stair and into the cinema room before they came in. I closed the door. My gun was on the little side table by the sofa, where I had left it. 'Be prepared': Jack Black's motto as well as that of the Boy Scouts and the London Rubber Company.

I heard them pass on towards the kitchen, talking. I took the door handle in my fist and eased it down soundlessly, slid the door open to hear them. "I heard, "Just a coffee, hen?" from Mortimer and "Oh yes, I'm dying for one," from Ruzena. Then I heard the front door click open again.

My heart bounded. I back-pedalled a step and lifted the gun, cocked the trigger. Moved to the room door again and closed it quietly to a crack, a crack through which I could see a slice of the lit hallway. Listened intently over the thump of my heart. Could hear the padded tread of one wearing soft soled shoes. Rubber soles, sneakers, whatever. Then a flick as his form crossed the lance of light in the crack of the door. I eased the door open and took a pace out, just as quiet as his.

There was the noise of a car engine outside, a shout I couldn't make out, another shout, and then the report of a gun fired. Up in the kitchen, the door open, Mortimer called in sudden alarm, "What wis that?"

I stepped fully into the hall as Mortimer, looking down the length of the passageway saw the intruder and yelled, "Who the fuck…?"

The intruder levelled a gun at him.

I said, "Drop it!"

The intruder spun round and smashed the gun into my cheek. I fell like a poleaxed stirk.

He turned back towards Mortimer and fired. The bullet smashed into something glass, I couldn't see what; I was dazed. I hoiked myself up on my elbow and put one in his calf, just as he fired again. He fell backwards. I guess I'd plugged him at the critical second. Up in the kitchen, Mortimer screamed as Ruzena's chest exploded in a burst of blood and she fell to the floor.

I got up and knelt on the gunman's back, put the nuzzle of my own gun to the back of his head, and said, "Slide the fucking gun across the floor! Do it *now,* you bastard!"

He did and I thumped the back of his skull with the butt of my gun. I stood up as two armed policemen burst through the front door. They levelled their semi automatic carbines down the hall and shouted, "Drop your weapons! Drop your weapons! Hands in the air!" I dropped my Tauser and put my hands up. In the kitchen, Mortimer was snivelling and cradling the dying Ruzena in his arms like some kind of latter-day, role-reversed Pietà.

Emma and Jim Bryce were there, behind the armed officers.

"Jack! You all right?" said Emma. "It' okay, he's with us."

"Aye," I said. "This bastard fired a couple of shots and one hit Ruzena by mistake."

"Cuff him."

I ran up to the kitchen.

Mortimer was crying. "Roozh, Roozh, dinnae go."

Ruzena, bleeding profusely, was saying, in a cracked voice, "Don't, Douglas. I am not worth your tears. Please."

"I love you, Ruzena, I love you. Dinnae die on me."

"I was not worthy your love. You are a good man and I am ..." She coughed, took a racking breath. "I am a two-faced liar. I never loved you. I was here only to hurt you..."

"Dinnae say it, dinnae say it. I don't care. *I* love *you*. It disnae matter what you've done. I've been happy these last three years for the first time in ma life. Actually happy, no jist makin' money. You're the one that done that."

She got her dying eyes on me. "And this is the man who will tell you how worthless a piece of shit your wife was," she whispered. "He knows. He is clever. He has worked it all out."

"Roozh, Roozh..." he snivelled. "Don't die. For God's sake, don't die..."

But she arched as he held her, coughed a sudden and appalling burst of blood on to her chin and sagged, dead. Mortimer leaned back, his dead wife in his arms, and howled his agony to the ceiling, more Lear than Antony. Why should a dog, a horse, a rat have life, and thou no breath at all?

Uniformed officers were carrying the intruder, slumped between them, out of the house. Emma and Jim were behind us, the armed guys waiting, weapons cocked, in the hall.

"Anybody else in the house?" barked Emma.

"No," I said.

Jim was on the blower, demanding an ambulance and paramedics at once. Douglas was bent over the corpse of his wife, blinded by tears.

34

If ever I felt sorry for a human being, I felt sorry for Douglas Mortimer. For all his success in life, for all the fortune he had amassed, only the previous three or so years of his life meant anything to him at all. And even those years were robbed of any meaning at the last. He found out his beautiful, modish young wife had never entertained the least affection or admiration for him. She had sought him out to wind him in, entice him, occupy him. Stop him from rescuing any more Roma girls from the clutches of the traffickers. All the details came out, over the course of the weeks following but, in the immediate aftermath of those events at Manderley, I was the one left to console him and condole with him.

The intruder and his associate, the one who had left the Mazda to warn him of the cops' arrival, the one who had fired a shot at Emma's car, and at whom the bacon had shouted, were carted off to the hoosegow.

For the rest of it - the paramedics examined Ruzena and pronounced life extinct at the scene. Once she was officially deceased then it was declared a crime scene. And, once again, the kitchen and hall were taped off. And, as before, Mortimer would not be allowed to stay in the building. I phoned the Dalmahoy for him and reserved a suite – the same one as he had before. Emma and Jim drove Mortimer to the Civic Centre too, to interview him. He asked if I could come with him. Emma said I would have to; I had to be interviewed too.

Once all that procedure had been gone through, Mortimer asked if I would accompany him to the Dalmahoy. I said, "Sure thing."

Jim said, "I'll drive you."

I sat in the back of the police car with Mortimer but he didn't say much on the drive out from Livingston to Dalmahoy. We were on the A71 at the back of East Calder before he said to me, "I don't know what I'm gonnae dae noo."

I said, "Don't concern yourself with that just now. You need to get some sleep tonight. Tomorrow is the time for thinking all the heavy stuff."

"Think I'll git any sleep the night?" he said.

"Take a sleeping draught."

"Sleepin' pills? I wid never use theym."

"I don't mean that," I said. "Break the habit of a lifetime and have a large whisky before going to bed. Should see you off just nicely."

Jim dropped us. I said I'd get a cab, but he said, no, Ma'am had told him to wait and drive me back home. Z-car taxis. I said, okay, I'd be as quick as I could decently be. Jim said to take all the time it needed.

Mortimer took the key for his suite from the bloke at reception, but didn't go there straightaway. He directed me towards the cocktail bar, a little room full of leather chairs and wood panelling, dimly lit and quiet at that time of night. I said I would have one and have a chat with him, but then I would need to get back to the family.

He walked there like he was doing it in his sleep. His mind was in its hammock and a thousand miles away. I told him to sit down and I'd ring for the drink. He sat. Said nothing, did nothing, just sat. I never felt as sorry for a man in my life. To wait till he was in his 60s for the love of his life to come along, and then in the space of a couple of weeks, to have all the happiness and security he had acquired over three years of marriage ripped from him. It wasn't just his wife's sexual attractiveness, though that would have been the major attraction at first. But it had grown, transformed into that combination of companionship, trust, loyalty and the desire for the loved one's health, welfare and happiness that, over time, blends the lover and the loved into two halves of the same being. Soulmates.

A flunkey came and took our order: one large whisky; one small one. We chatted about how the room was ideal for our situation, how attractive it was, and other meaningless gibberish till the guy brought the drinks on a tray. Douglas paid and waved the guy away. He lifted his glass of usquebaugh without looking at me. "It disnae maitter that she didnae love me, does it?" he said. Sipped.

I was seated opposite him. "Let me ask you one thing," I said.

"Go'n, then."

"After what Ruzena said to you tonight before she died, does that affect how you feel about her?"

"Naw. No a bit."

"Do you think it will affect the way you look back on your time together?"

"No in the slightest. I've been thinkin' aboot that aw the time. Lookin' back on the things we did thegither, you know?" He looked over, caught my eye and looked away. Then he looked back and held my gaze. "An' it disnae affect it. I think of it as the happiest three years ae ma life. No matter what she was actually daein', she made me happy at the time. The memory still makes me happy. An' I love… " He stopped, his throat catching, his lip trembling. Then he swallowed and said, "An' I love her for that. An' I always will."

"Then that's the answer to your question. No, it doesn't matter that she didn't love you."

"See, I don't believe she didnae love me. I ken noo that she didnae love me like she said she did, and she didnae love me like I loved her. But I cannae believe there was nothin' at aw there for her. I cannae. I know better."

"You're the one who knows what went on between you. You're the one that will know how she felt."

"What somebody says and what somebody does dinnae always match, eh no?"

"Absolutely not. You see it every day."

"You're a guid man, Jack Black. I'm hertbroken the now, but I ken this much. I've made friends wi a good man through aw this."

"I'm humbled that you think so."

"Dinnae be a stranger fi here on in, Jack."

"I won't. Now I need to get back. Take your time and sip your drink. It'll make you sleep. I'll bring a case of togs and shit for you tomorrow. Okay?"

"Okay. Thanks a million."

He was quieter, more contemplative when I left him.

I got in, kissed Phyl and told her what had happened. She was flabbergasted, of course. We jawed for a half hour and then she went to bed. I went to the study and slid my old paperback copy of the *Tao Te Ching* from the shelves. Long time since I'd read it. I'd done a course on Chinese literature in translation at university. Weird, maybe, but I'd enjoyed it. I wanted to check on something.

I was feeling humbled. Humbled by many things: by seeing the essential nobility of Douglas Mortimer, and his blinding love for his wife; by his good opinion of me, but most of all by my astonishing luck in having found the woman I loved so much and who loved me back just as much, maybe even more, undeserving as I was. A touch of the selfish in my thoughts, certainly, but no smugness. What DM had thought he was getting, was what I had, without even trying. Devotion, selflessness, loyalty. A soulmate. The other half of the sky. I thought of the Yin/Yang symbol, the Taijitu, how it depicted the complementary and interdependent halves of the world. Night and day. Light and shade. Male and female. I span the fidget spinner on my thumb, and watched the little red fan whirl itself into stillness, as I tried to remember what I had learnt of Yin and Yang. Not static. Their nature flows and changes with time. And I tried to remember how the phrasing that I so liked went in the second chapter of the *Tao*. Eventually, I just read it.

> *Thus being and non-being give birth to each other.*
> *Difficult and easy complement each other.*
> *Long and short form each other.*
> *High and low incline towards each other.*
> *Sound and tone harmonize each other.*
> *Before and after follow each other.*

Yeah, that was it. Yin and Yang. Female and male. Phyllis and Jack. That's what we had. That's what Mortimer thought he had with Ruzena. Some folk just get lucky; others don't.

35

Well, what I can tell you now took a long time to come out in the wash – and folk were doing the laundry in Kosice, in Mestre, in Glasgow and in Den Haag. But, still with no element of smugness, I can say that Emma and I got most of it right. But, more than that, my beloved had got it on the boko right at the very start, the first night I came back from Manderley and spoke to her about Mortimer hiring me to sniff after Ruzena and see if she was being unfaithful. She had wondered if there was 'something else going on.' Just a sixth sense she had had. Well, there hadn't been just *something* else going on – *everything* else was going on. And she had wondered if Ruzena was 'pretending to be something she isn't.' Was she ever.

It wasn't Auntie Lenka who got Ruzena into modelling; it was Uncle Tibor, as we'd thought. Tibor Novak, shyster lawyer of the parish and a man with many shady connections. Sure, Lenka had complimented Ruzena for years and said she should be a model, but it was Tibor, on Ruzena's pleading, who had greased a few palms and swung her the 'in'. And, if she had just stayed in central Europe, posing and pouting with all the skeletal junkies and other categories of fuck-up who strutted the runways, maybe she'd have had a reasonably lucrative career and been reasonably happy. Maybe even lived to middle age, at least.

But then, one Douglas Mortimer decided to act like a human being and rescue the cousin of one of his drivers from human traffickers. Radka Bartoš had been terrified of Mortimer at the start, he told the cops, and understandably so. Most male strangers in her life had tried to abuse and exploit her; why shouldn't this old Scot? He didn't, of course. He spoke to her and put her mind at ease, said he could employ her as a domestic if she liked – only till she got something better. Found her a place to stay. Told her, if anyone asked, to say that she had answered an ad in the local rag for a job. She was devoted to him, as a consequence. Working for him, a reasonably well-paid job with few hassles, was a dream come true.

As we knew, Mortimer being Mortimer, he didn't just leave it there. He tried his best to help other Roma kids get out of the shit life these bastards had planned for them. Just his way of paying tribute to the mother who had died too young, after bringing him up the best she could. He sprang four more of them, and it's my belief that he would have sprung a few more, only things intervened. In the shape of Ruzena Dolezal, model.

It had been mentioned to Tibor Novak that, on five occasions, a Scottish businessman had interfered in the traffic of Roma girls to Glasgow. He had demanded a name. It wouldn't be too long before he found out it was Douglas Mortimer, of Mortimer Logistics. His trucks rolled along the major routes of most European countries. He was a millionaire.

What did Uncle Tibor do? Called in the favour from his niece. Arranged that she be taken on by the Brio agency in Edinburgh. Asked her to do some field work, find out what she could about this interfering Jock. Most of the rest you know: how she met Douglas at the *Scotsman* do, how she winkled from him the information that he was, indeed, the dude who saved the girls. She strung him along, got him to propose eventually. *Ka-ching*! 'We're in the money, We're in the money, We got a lot of what it takes to get along'. Gold Diggers of 2014. And she kept Mortimer's mind on matters other than desperate Roma girls. Which suited her Uncle Tibor for a while. Maybe till someone further up the pecking order told him that Mortimer deserved to be punished. He had, after all, deprived the organisation of many thousands of Euros of income from the misery of five young women.

I'm navigating with no chart here, but I am fairly sure – Emma agrees – that Ruzena played the long game, concentrated on occupying all of DM's spare time, getting him to marry her, etcetera. Gave herself a chance to learn as much as she could. And *earn* as much as she could. She had to play it long in order to make to seem unlikely that she was involved, come the pay-off. Anything she learned was handed over to Novak and the gang. The Dolezal family would be involved too, holidaying chez Mortimer twice a year, hosting the happy couple in Italy, finding things out that way too. And then the call came. Exterminate! Exterminate!

Glasgow was involved – Ahmed's knowledge of Mortimer helped here, I suppose. The planning, design and backdrop was all left to Ruzena. She was, indeed, a clever woman. She knew the best MO would be for someone to tango him down in

Manderley when she was away from home. It's a remote house, ideal for deeds of darkness. The call came a couple of months before the night Alex Gilmour was smoked. Ruzena had to work out what to do exactly. Hence, her being 'different' to Mortimer, and him hiring me to find out if she was getting her sausage from another butcher. It was just that her mind was much taken up with devising his death. No biggie, after all.

So, she came up with the notion of texted threats against her husband from some amorphous group of traffickers. She even went as far as having some bozo text to her own phone what she herself suggested. But she was too smart for her own good, there. All the scriptural references. I didn't see it right away, but only she could have done that, a woman with a deeply religious upbringing, who read the Bible every night.

The plan was that she would skedaddle from Manderley on the Thursday night and somebody would be there on the Friday to welcome Mortimer home to his death. She was the one who switched off the CCTV, all right, no matter how convincingly she denied it. I guess, since the killer footered around with the window as he did, that Ruzena had told him to do it, and the plan was to summon Gilmour to the house and sneak in while he was there. It's a big house. While Gilmour was in Mortimer's office upstairs, switching off the alarm, the plan would be for the intruder to secrete himself in a room on the lower floor till AG went away again. Had to be that. There was no way Ruzena could risk anyone extraneous having a key while she was away. Suspicion would fall on her immediately. But something went wrong. Gilmour obviously discovered the guy and the fatal conflict ensued.

That was when Ruzena had to think even harder. She would have been contacted and informed of the kink in the plan. So she drove back to Manderley and left the book on Mortimer's desk, and 'Paris' written on the chalkboard before driving off again. Give the cops something to think about. Sharp stuff. She was, however, extremely fortunate that Mortimer, poor doting Mortimer, driving home to surprise his loving wife, didn't actually surprise her as she was leaving the corpse of their handyman on the kitchen floor.

She controlled what happened among the gang after that. When I showed up in Mestre, she was the one her father phoned immediately. She told Paolo to get a mate and give me a doing. Dissuade me from any further interest in the matter. Unfortunately, Enrico was a dimwitted loudmouth. He knew something of the Glasgow connection to the trafficking, the only connection he could make to Scotland. Hence, 'Glasgow boy'.

She had gone to Paris. I'm guessing she had intended waiting there for the 'dreadful' news that her husband had been rubbed out and she was the sole heiress to a big mattress full of old banknotes with big numbers. When things went skew-wiff, she had to fine tune things. It made no difference that I went over there to escort her; she had her back covered all the way. The peach gorilla and his team weren't there to threaten her; they were there to keep an eye on her. They acted on her orders. Big lovey-dovey reunion with Mortimer, murder date adjusted accordingly.

Easton had fucked up. He couldn't be used again. So, when the wipe-out of Geraldine Hunter became imperative, another hit man was used. A better one. One who managed to do it with no untidy edges. Maybe the same one killed Jennifer Kemp, maybe not. Doesn't matter. Underlines the heartlessness of Ruzena Dolezal. I've said before that she had to be a consummate actress. She was. Academy Award stuff. The second she felt threatened, when I mentioned what Geraldine had said, poor old Gerry had to go. And Jenny too, just in case. She had told the two women the lie that she thought there was nobody like Mortimer for his philanthropy. She had told Geraldine some of her backstory, including how she got into modelling, most likely. Geraldine - the girl she had shared a flat with. Made no difference. When Gerry had to go, go she did. The two gunmen from the night Ruzena died in Manderley are awaiting trial for that crime. Looks like they're in the frame for Hunter and Kemp too.

The Strathclyde cops huckled Ahmed and his cabal of relatives and heavies, including John Crawford, 'Brian' and Uriah Heep. That seems to have opened several big tins of animals with long, tube-like bodies and no limbs. Bashir the Bashful is involved in many other criminal activities, it appears. The case for the prosecution is a ponderous one. Trials start soon.

A filthy, messy business. One that has broken Mortimer's heart. It was broken even further by the discovery that some of the Roma girls brought from Lunik IX to the U.K. were brought in Mortimer Logistics trucks. Yep, Tony Appleby and Vaclav Strnad. Never more than half a dozen at a time, and only every so often. But they were involved. They're awaiting trial too.

36

Poor Mortimer. Given happiness in the form of Ruzena Dolezal, he had it snatched from him in the most brutal fashion three years or so later. And then to find that two of his own team had been involved in the very abuse he had striven to save five lassies from …? It was almost too much for him.

As he had requested, I didn't make myself a stranger. I spoke to him a great deal in the weeks after the horror events at Manderley. He told me he was considering selling off Mortimer Logistics. Wasn't interested enough any more.

"Don't do that, Douglas," I said. We were sitting on a bench in the afternoon sun at Manderley. "You have to keep doing it. It's your life's work."

"I hate that they bastards were drivin' lassies fi Slovakia, though," he said. "Me savin' five a them, and they bastards helpin' the animals that was dealin' in them. Why wid they *dae* that?"

"Money," I said. "It all comes down to money - lining your pocket and fuck anybody else. The Tory philosophy. It wasn't your fault they did it, and they've been nabbed for it. Mortimer Logistics is still a big success, and you're still a good businessman."

"Ah, it's guid a ye ti say that, Jack. Mibby I will keep it. But I've made ma mind up aboot one thing."

"What's that?"

"I'm havin' Manderley demolished. Naw, dinnae start in. It's fu' a memories that breck ma hert. Oh, I ken what we said. An' I ken what *I* said. I still love her, Jack. I'll never stoap. But I don't want the hoose any mair. An' I'm no havin' anybody else ownin' it an' livin' in it, walkin' aboot an' laughin' an' jokin' where Roozh wance did. I'll have it demolished but I'll hae a wee'er yin built where it was. Still be a connection ti the auld hoose and Ruzena. But it'll be better suitit ti *me*. However long I've got left. An' I don't think that's gonnae be long, somehow. Nothin' much left to live for."

And that's what he's doing. I drove past the other day and stopped to watch the demolition at work. Dozers and dumpers puttered around, whilst long-reach excavators, like vast insects, were ripping the house down to rubble and dust. I stood and watched them for ten minutes. It seemed apt to me, then. Mortimer was demolishing the last remnant of a life that had been almost totally demolished a few months previously.

He came to the office a week or so after things and handed me fifty thousand pounds in a huge brown envelope. Said he was a man of his word, and it gave him pleasure to give me it.

"I can't take that," I said. "It's ridiculous."

"Well, I'm no takin' it back," he said. "So it can lie on the desk there."

"I don't want it. It'll just lie there."

"So let it. Fling it on the fireback, if ye want. I jist ken I had ti give ye it. You did what ye said ye would. Well, noo I have tae. Enjoy it. You an' yer wife an' the wean."

"I would feel terrible taking it."

"Fuck off," he sneered. "Pit it in the bank for yer wee lassie gaun through college or somethin'. It's a present. Ye cannae refuse it."

He was, as they say round here, some man. A man I had initially scorned for his parochialism and his lack of education had turned out to be one of the finest people I've ever met. That was a rebuke for me, and I was well rebuked. You should never underestimate your fellow man. Shakey would have written a cracking play about Douglas Mortimer. Successful and rich, but undone by love. By the lure of a glamorous woman. And if, as Douglas had suggested, he hadn't long to go, the glover's son had the perfect closing line for his tragedy; the tragedy of a man brought low by love. From *Antony & Cleopatra* again.

Unarm, Eros, the long day's task is done.

Printed in Great Britain
by Amazon